Praise f[illegible]dbye

'Horace Winter is a character who will linger long after you've finished this highly original, moving, funny and elegant book'
Irish Independent

'A journey that is both tender and sad, but a joy to witness. A moving and truly absorbing read'
Image

'A quirky, tender and compulsive read. Horace Winter will win your heart'
Irish Examiner

'Horace is someone we all know'
Irish Times

'A bittersweet and redemptive novel . . . Horace is a tenderhearted, quirky man readers will come to cherish'
Publishers Weekly

'A melancholy yet gently optimistic novel built around a subtly ironic reconciliation of existentialism with the butterfly effect'
Kirkus Reviews

Conor Bowman was born on a Thursday in the west of Ireland. He is left-handed and hates coriander. In 1986, he stood up Samuel Beckett and has always regretted it. Incredibly, he was once offered a place to study in Cambridge University and that year changed his life.

His favourite writers are Graham Greene and A.M. Homes. Conor also writes songs. He has no mobile phone. He is not afraid of umbrellas and has an average sugar reading of 7.8. His hero is Elvis Presley. His favourite film is *The 39 Steps*.

Conor works as a senior counsel and lives in Meath. He is married with four children.

Also by Conor Bowman

Novels

Wasting by Degrees

The Last Estate

The Redemption of George Baxter

Henry

Horace Winter Says Goodbye

Short Story Collections

Life and Death (And in between)

No Shortage of Long Grass

CONOR BOWMAN

Hughie Mittman's Fear of Lawnmowers

HACHETTE
BOOKS
IRELAND

First published in Ireland in 2019 by
HACHETTE BOOKS IRELAND

1

Cataloguing in Publication Data is available from the British Library

ISBN 978 1 4736 4183 9

Typeset in Century Old Style by redrattledesign.com

Printed and bound in Great Britain by Clays Ltd, Elcograf, S. p. A.

Hachette Books Ireland policy is to use papers that are natural, renewable and recyclable products and made from wood grown in sustainable forests. The logging and manufacturing processes are expected to conform to the environmental regulations of the country of origin.

Hachette Books Ireland
8 Castlecourt Centre
Castleknock
Dublin 15, Ireland

A division of Hachette UK Ltd
Carmelite House, 50 Victoria Embankment, EC4Y 0DZ

www.hachettebooksireland.ie

For Moo,
My Love You.

Chapter 1

If starting at the very beginning is good enough for Julie Andrews, then it must certainly be good enough for me . . . Sometime in 1965, February, I arrive on the planet. Was it raining? Was it cold? Who can say, now, all these years later? I suppose it doesn't really matter, in a way, because babies are just born, aren't they, regardless of the weather? Nothing cloudy gets in the way of birth, no rain dampens the heat of the moment, even sunshine hardly matters at the hour of arrival, does it?

I imagine a room full of lights and people, a lot of pushing and pulling, then blankets and towels and hot water, like in the movies (I'm thinking *101 Dalmatians*). A little like with luggage carousels in airports, as I'm sure that, for those in attendance, there is a degree of trepidation and surprise while it's all going on. Then, eventually, the newborn is held aloft, like the Sam Maguire Cup, and the adventure begins.

I wonder about midwives: about the feelings they must have day in, day out – in the middle of the night, perhaps on trains or at 20,000 feet, when waters break that weren't meant to in ladies who were advised not to fly. How do these people, the gatekeepers of this world, feel about what they do? Is it a mix of excitement and concern, with a dash of upset thrown in from time to time? I don't know the name of the person who welcomed me into the world back then, so long ago, but I was helped into the light and someone cleaned me up and laid me down and heard the first sound I made.

Beyond that small room, away from everything I could hear, there was a vast world filled with Beatles songs and hydro-electric dams and mini-skirts and instant mash and tractors and the Rose of Tralee, and all the rest of it. Others arrived on the same day, taking the same train, but stepping down at other platforms all over the place. Is there an anteroom to here, where everyone waits and waits together until their time arrives? How insane would it be if a room full of about-to-be-born babies existed somewhere, like a glider full of troops approaching a drop-zone, waiting for the signal to release themselves, one by one, towards this earth, with nothing but a parachute of hope to keep them from falling too fast and/or drowning in the marshes? Perhaps we're all meant to rendezvous, at least those who land safely, and go on together to take a town or hold a bridge until reinforcements arrive. Who knows?

Anyway, I landed.

This is the point at which I should probably say, 'Let me show you the *real* Galway.' Then you and I would embark on a day trip through that wonderful city, and from time to time, I'd point out places and people and say, 'That was where I went to school,' or 'See that house? The family who lived there had a dog called Fever Lee,' or 'There's Lydon House – a woman called Joan worked there and patrolled the café every Saturday to see if teenagers were nursing empty coffee cups.' But what is the point of that, of taking you in a car and pointing at places and just saying things that I remember about the places I point at? You wouldn't know the people I mention, or even whether or not what I said about them was true. In the same way as you could drive me around *your* town, point and comment, and I would be none the wiser, either about who you really are or about what really matters. I don't drive!

I'm not really sure what is important anymore. All I know is that there have been things that occurred which I cannot fully understand. Which pieces of life are real? Which are imaginary? Is there a difference between illusion and imagination? What I want to do is to ask you to bear with me while I sort out various parts of my own life, then to make up your own mind about what you are shown.

So, you know there was a beginning: I landed. That much at least is not in dispute. Yes, there is a '*real* Galway' for me, but I cannot make it real for others simply because it's real for me. We are all the victims of our own memory; perhaps that is all we can say about that. The places are window-dressing. It's what makes us *feel* that matters.

If it's good enough for Julie Andrews then, yes, of course, it's more than good enough for me. A place to start: perhaps that's all we need. The rest, surely, is a mix of what we remember and what we are unable to forget.

I grew up in Galway or, at least, I was raised there. I'm not sure whether or not boys ever grow up. We live on Taylor's Hill, which is the Fifth Avenue of Galway City. It's a steep-ish climb, from the traffic lights at Nile Lodge up to the highest point of the road, where it begins to flatten out and leads west to Knocknacarra and Barna. At the spot where the flattening-out begins, if you look to your left you can see all the way down the slope of Threadneedle Road to the sea. It's a magical view. Out away at the mouth of Galway Bay lie the three sentries of the Aran Islands. Go down the hill and turn left along the seafront and you're in Salthill, the Las Vegas of Connacht, filled with hotels and slot machines and the bandstand remnants of better, or at any rate simpler, times.

The thing about Galway is that the sea is everywhere. When it rains, you can taste the salt and smell the ocean. There are lots of different bits to the city but no matter where you are, you can nearly always see or smell the sea. I don't mean in a bad way – not like the way you get to know the canals in Dublin, or the estuary in Shannon – no, I mean in a good, comforting way, like you can rely on the key being under the flowerpot or the credit unions being there when you need them, that kind of way. Galway is always heaving with people: in the summer it's the tourists; in the winter it's the third-level students from the university and the other colleges. There is a small good-natured country-town feel about the city, like it's always Christmas Eve somehow. The best bit about the whole place, though, is really the very centre of the city: the chunk that runs from Prospect Hill through Eyre Square, meanders down Shop Street and veers off to the left past the knitwear shop, Kenny's Bookshop. Tigh Neachtain's and The Quays pubs, then down to the Spanish Arch. That's the bit of the place a cardiovascular surgeon would be concerned about if Galway were a person instead of a place and had high cholesterol instead of a high season. Sometimes I'll think of one of those landmark places in the heart of Galway, and the next week when the *Connacht Tribune* newspaper comes out, there's a photograph of that very place on the front of the paper. Just coincidence, I suppose.

Our house is one of those to the right on Taylor's Hill, about halfway up, just before the girls' secondary school, also, rather unimaginatively, called Taylor's Hill. These houses were built in the 1930s and do not match. We have a gravel drive and a decent front lawn, and rose bushes, and hedges, and a monkey puzzle tree, which grows right in the middle of the lawn and has always overshadowed our lives and our home.

The house itself is two-storey with ivy climbing rather grandly up the front, so that in the height of summer the tendrils clutch at the sills or tap on the windows of the bedrooms. In the long back garden we have a huge greenhouse in which my mother successfully plants tomatoes, and a square vegetable patch, where carrots and cabbage and onions somewhat mysteriously grow only every second year or so. In the 'other' years they either don't appear at all or else are decimated by rabbits. I never did figure out why that happens every second year, but when they *do* flourish, it's like we're back during the war or something and producing enough to feed the whole neighbourhood.

Our family didn't always live on Taylor's Hill: at one stage we lived in Tipperary, when my father was working at Nenagh Hospital as a general surgeon. I was only five when we moved to Galway and had just completed my first year at Terryglass National School. It was a two-room school where Mrs Cleary taught junior infants to second class in one room, and Mr Cleary taught third to sixth class in the other. They were an odd pair – striking-looking, and huge. She wore a series of two-piece outfits, with a jacket and skirt, and sometimes when she bent over to fix the fire, the zip at the back of the skirt would open and we could see slightly more than we'd bargained for. The outfits were always of the brightest and most vibrant colours: pink tweed with green stripes is one I particularly recall.

Mrs Cleary's room always smelt of perfume and Plasticine ('marla', we called it). The large strips of new coloured corrugated Plasticine were unwrapped every now and then, and inevitably all merged into a uniform, dull brown poo colour, and would sit in rolled-up balls along the windowsill of the classroom waiting to be called into action on rainy days when playing outside was not an option. Mrs Cleary played a strange musical instrument, a long green and white thing with a thin mouthpiece and note buttons or keys along its sides. It looked for all the world like a small alligator. I don't remember the tunes, or whether we sang along or just listened as she played, or even whether she played in tune or if we liked it. The instrument lived in a box, a long one with a satin-lined drawer, which slid out to reveal the apparatus lying like a person in a comfortable coffin.

Mr Cleary was also very frightening. He spoke in a loud voice, which was constantly punctuated by coughs. He smoked a pipe, and would stand on the steps of the little school, at break and lunchtime, cutting pieces of tobacco from a dark block, then forcing them into the bowl of the pipe with another part of his penknife, which opened out like a butterfly wing. When the pipe was being lit, Mr Cleary would suck and puff, and light and extinguish a succession of Maguire & Paterson matches with a series of flicks of his thumb and wrist. The place reeked of tobacco. The other thing that comes to mind when I think of him is the almighty sound of his blackthorn stick on the desks, from the other room. This noise of terror came at us through the wall, like a preview of Hell, as he'd roar and shout his way through Irish poems nobody wanted to learn by heart.

One day a magician came to our tiny school in Tipperary and performed in front of the whole lot of us. We younger ones crammed into Mr Cleary's room, jamming ourselves in beside the older children. The only things I remember are that the conjuror wore a top hat and a cape, and one of his tricks was to put Joan Davoren into a big box where her head stuck out of one end and her feet the other. When the lid was closed, the man took out a series of swords and began to push them through the box in various places. Joan Davoren was in sixth class, and used to look after mine whenever Mrs Cleary had to step out for something. At the time, all I could think, as the blades made their way in one side and out the other, was who would mind us now?

I was only four and a bit years old when I was in that school, and I stayed for one year. I don't know how many people were in my class, or even in total in Mrs Cleary's room, but I know that at break there were only three boys on our side of the playground: Vernon Crosby, Michael Meagher and myself. Two of us would hold hands and be the horses and the other would grab our jumpers from behind and be the driver. I don't remember anything much about Michael Meagher, but Vernon Crosby had warts on his hands. Sometimes he tried to take them off, using a penknife behind the boys' toilets at the bottom of the playground.

One day when my mother was walking me home from that school, and there were whitethorn flowers on the hedges, we heard music up ahead, coming from a farm we had to pass by to get to our house. We kept walking and the music seemed to get fainter, even though we thought we were drawing closer to it. When we rounded the bend, we saw a man, who was bare from the waist up, carrying a portable record-player across a farmyard. The music was interrupted by a series of scratches and scrapes as the needle jumped with his movements. A long white flex trailed behind him and led all the way across to a window in the house. On the other side of the yard a number of cows had gathered inside a gate and were looking out at the man as he carried the music towards them. When he was three or four feet away from the cattle, he placed the record-player on top of a milk churn that I would easily have fitted inside.

My mother and I stood on the road and watched as the man turned up the sound and the cows continued to listen. As if sensing that he was being watched, he suddenly turned around and waved at us while, in the background, the cows seemed to sway ever so slightly in time with the words of the song, something about tears and a shed. I thought the song was about a cowshed. The man turned back to his herd and I asked my mother as we continued our walk home, 'Who was that, Mammy?'

'It was Elvis, love. Elvis Presley.'

I was an only child when we moved to Galway and into the house on Taylor's Hill called The Moorings, and that was how it remained. My father's name is Simon Mittman, and although his name sounds American, or even Jewish, he is Irish through and through. His great-grandfather had come from Norway in the nineteenth century and ended up in the wilds of County Limerick somewhere as an engineer on railway bridges. My mother's family were Dalys from County Meath and my parents met in college at UCD in the 1950s, when everyone wore ties and print dresses and attended dances at a place off Stephen's Green called the Irrawaddi Ballroom.

I longed for a brother or a sister, but none arrived, so we settled into our new life on Taylor's Hill where trees separated us from our closest neighbours – on one side, we had the Flynns with four daughters and an Alsatian dog (Leah); and on the other, a sculptor called Mr Rennick who lived in Galway most of the time, but in the summer when the weather gets better, went off to Australia where it is winter.

Although I was on my own a lot, I was certainly never lonely. The garden went back for what seemed to me to be miles. Far away, past all of the vegetable patches and the greenhouse, there was a wild untouched stretch where an old orchard had been forgotten. There was a small turn like the beginning of something else, and around the turn, until the garden ended, an area that was completely out of view of the house. At the extremity of the entire plot a brick wall was painted white. This was of unbelievably high construction so that even if I climbed one of the old apple trees I could barely look over it. Behind our garden lay the unexplored and vast fields that would eventually become Maunsell's Park housing estate.

For Christmas, when I was six, I got a cowboy outfit and a pair of white-handled Old West pistols, which were heavier than they looked. They took a roll of caps each, and when you fired, the smell of the caps was like burning. If you fired quickly enough, the guns would give off smoke from the opening where the hammer hit the cap. The noise the guns made was not really loud, more of a snap than a bang, but it was enough to scare off crows and Apache Indians and, at six, that was effective enough for me.

One of the bigger outposts in the cowboy world I inhabited was the garage that adjoined the house but only had room for a car if you cleared out everything else. We never did. As a result my father would park his car on the gravel outside the front door near the monkey puzzle tree, while the garage became a dumping ground for everything we'd ever owned but had not got around to throwing out. For me this was Heaven: the space took on the aspect of a goldmine, with its tunnels and passages into, around and through old tables, settees, paint cans and all the other paraphernalia and detritus of family life as it moved on. It included a cot and a stand-alone hairdryer unit that had once caught fire in the kitchen while my mother was sitting under it reading a magazine. Also housed there was the lawnmower: an ancient and faintly red Iverson petrol-powered Rotary Sickle Mower manufactured by the Rotary Mower Company of Omaha, Nebraska. On the side, a silver tag was secured by two small screws and bore the patent number: US 2165551 1938. This lawnmower had been ours when we lived in Terryglass, and I can still remember the distinctive, proud roar and cough of its motor when you started it by pulling the handle and moving the control to the 'Power On' position.

Once we'd moved to Taylor's Hill, a gardener, Mr Cody, came once a week to cut the grass and to clip around the flowerbeds in the front. When I was seven, in the summer of 1972, Mr Cody went away for two weeks to visit his daughter who lived in Donegal and I decided to take over his duties for him in his absence. The lawnmower was heavy as I pushed it out of the garage door and onto the patio behind the kitchen window. Inside, I could see my mother carrying a pile of ironed clothes across the kitchen and heading for the stairs. I remember thinking that I would mow the lawn and have it finished before she came downstairs. I wondered if cowboys ever mowed their lawns or whether their horses kept the grass short.

The starting handle was very difficult to pull. Each time

I failed to start it, the lawnmower simply retreated back at me, so that nothing happened: no noise, no engine roar or cough, nothing – just the clacking of the wheels as the thing rolled back towards me. I knew that I would have to find a way to keep the mower steady as I pulled the handle. In a flash of genius I remembered that the side passage leading around the garage to the front was just about wide enough for the lawnmower to be wheeled through.

I manoeuvred the Iverson Rotary Sickle Mower into the side passage and parked it sideways so that it was jammed between the garage and the wall that separated us from Mr Rennick's house and garden. When I'd secured it as well as I could, I placed one foot on top of the mower and pulled the handle with both hands. After two attempts, the engine burst into life. I remember its vibrations shuddering through my blue runners and up my leg. I began to jiggle the handle, trying to turn the mower so that I could push it down the passageway and out into the front garden.

I remember hearing my mother shouting behind me and I turned. The combined effect of her voice startling me, and the narrowness of the space caused me to stumble and lose control altogether of the mower. I fell backwards into the passageway. The newly freed Iverson Rotary Sickle Mower had somehow dislodged itself from between the two walls and, instead of now facing the front garden, was beginning to advance in the opposite direction, towards me, as I lay on my back.

As my mother rushed along the passageway, to try

to shut off the machine before it devoured me, I turned onto my side to get to my feet. There was an awful grating sound, which interrupted the smooth operation of US Patent 2165551 1938 – and then the engine stopped. I felt the most extraordinary pain in my right foot and saw chewed-up bits of my runner, sock and foot flying past me before I lost consciousness.

Chapter 2

'You'll be able to walk,' my father said, when he came into the children's ward with five student interns following him and hanging on every word he uttered. I watched one of them, a male student, mouth the words, 'He'll be able to walk,' as he wrote some notes. When I'd woken up from the surgery I had thought I was at home in my own room and was just dreaming about being in a hospital ward. I remember saying to myself, 'This is only a dream, don't worry. Wake up and you'll be fine.' But it wasn't a dream at all.

'Your father saved your foot,' Mammy said, when she came to visit me later on that day. I had visions of my foot being placed on the mantelpiece in the sitting room at home. What she meant, of course, was that he'd saved it from having to be sawn off the end of my leg. I couldn't remember being brought to the Regional, or being changed out of my cowboy outfit into my pyjamas. Nothing seemed to have happened between my falling on my back in the side passageway, seeing bits of my runner flying past, and now being in a bed in a ward – but, of course, so much *had* happened: oxygen, intubation, anaesthetic, me being wheeled down corridors to theatre, cutting, sewing, being wheeled back to the huge lift. And now my pyjamas – my favourite set, with the Indian tepee and the piebald horses – had a slit cut at the bottom of the right trouser leg.

My right foot now had only three toes, although it continued to feel to me as if I had retained all five. Through the swaddle of bandages I felt I could wiggle all of my toes, and even my nerve-endings believed they were all still there. So I didn't really think any damage had been done to my foot, not right away at least. Although I'd seen pieces of it fly past me in the passageway, I suppose I didn't believe in the damage until I *had* to. I'm almost certain that no one actually told me I'd lost two toes for quite a while. I was comforted with a lot of phrases, such as 'You were very lucky,' and 'It's incredible what they can do nowadays,' and 'Sure you'll be hopping around the place in no time.' I suppose bad news is always better told in dribs and drabs rather than being thrown at you in one go.

The bed was comfortable, I remember that, and for the first week or ten days I wasn't allowed to leave it. I ate, slept, peed and pooed all in the one place, because I was not allowed to put any weight on my damaged foot.

Around me in the ward other children were suffering

from a variety of ailments and conditions. Some had had their appendix or tonsils out. Others were thin and had problems with their blood. One boy, who was younger than me, had fallen off the roof of a car and hit his head on a stone. His name was Dominic and he spoke in a very high-pitched voice sometimes, but in a more normal voice when he talked in his sleep. One boy was in a wheelchair and had had his head completely shaved so he looked really cool. I don't know why, but I remember that boy's name was Michael and he wore a cardigan that was the same colour as the Galway football jersey – maroon.

My bed was at the end of the ward, near the window, and out of it I could see the vast bulk of the cathedral and, away to the left, the university. The grounds of the hospital lay below us three floors down, and in the car park people came and went, like ants in Dinky cars. The nurses were very kind and came around all the time and played board games with us, like Ludo and Snakes and Ladders; they read books to the younger ones and cuddled them when they cried after mammies and daddies and siblings had left, once visiting time was over. It was the first time I had ever been away from home. I think I liked being there, but I'm not sure I did. At some point during my stay, I became aware that everything beneath the bandage would not be as it was before, and I remember refusing to talk with one lady who brought me a set of crutches. The crutches were eventually put into the bedside wardrobe by one of the nurses, and each time they were mentioned, I ignored the issue. From the snippets of talk I allowed myself to overhear, and the general advice I only pretended to ignore, I came to realise that I had indeed been very lucky. Two nurses on night duty came round to check we were all asleep, but I wasn't. I listened with my eyes closed as they chatted in whispers at the end of my bed.

'Apparently Mr Dobbin wanted to amputate the whole foot. Something in the rust on the lawnmower blade had got into the bloodstream.'

'I heard from Ciara Wogan, who was in the theatre, that they weren't able to find Mr Mittman, and that when they did, there was absolute war. Apparently he stormed in and took over, shouting something about *him* being the only one who was allowed to decide whether his son lost the whole foot or not.'

'Jaysus!'

'Of course, himself and Dobbin don't get on at all since—'

'Oh, that was ages ago. It's someone else now, apparently.'

'Who? Give us the gossip!'

They began to move down the ward and I couldn't hear the rest. My father seemed like a real hero, though, riding to the rescue like the cavalry. I drifted back to sleep, wondering how long it would take me to grow new toes to replace however many I'd lost.

During my time on St Anthony's Ward, other patients came and went like holiday-makers in a campsite for diseased kids. I didn't get to know everyone's name, but I knew most of them: Barry Garvey, who'd had his tonsils out; Rachel Healy, who was there for a week with red blotches all over her arms and legs; Malachy Something, who was a 'hippofillerback'. That meant he wasn't allowed to get cuts anywhere on his body, or even nosebleeds, or else all of his blood would spill out and he'd die, unless he got an immediate refill. There was one girl called Paula or Pauline who had both of her legs in a cast because she'd jumped off the diving board at the end of the prom in Salthill when the tide was out.

Once there was a fight in the ward between two lads who wanted the same set of Lego at exactly the same time. There was a really strict nurse called Sister Angela, who was in charge of all the other nurses, and she arrived on the scene as the fight spilled into the aisle between the two rows of beds in the ward.

'Stop it immediately!' she roared. Despite her command, the two scrappers kept at it, so she walked briskly up to them and separated them by grabbing each boy by one of his ears and spreading her arms. The two lads were shocked by her actions. She held them apart and looked from one to the other, then back again.

'He started it,' both boys said together. Everyone in the ward waited to see what Sister Angela would do. The moment stretched itself out a little more, then Sister began to walk down the aisle with the boys' ears still firmly grasped. She marched them as far as the window and forced them to look out at the city.

'There are children out there who are sick and some of them don't even know it yet. And two of them, who could be in here getting better, aren't able to because you two clowns are occupying the beds they should be in. Do you want me to phone down to Casualty and ask them to send me two children who deserve to be made well, so that you two can get out right now?'

The antagonists looked at each other, then shook their heads silently and muttered, 'No, Sister.'

'Fine,' she said, and began to walk them back up the ward, still holding them by their ears. As they reached the mess of Lego they'd been fighting about moments earlier, she let go of them and told them to shake hands and 'let bygones be bygones'. One of them put out his hand, but the other, Dino, refused.

'Get dressed. Now!' Sister Angela snapped at Dino. She stood and watched, along with all of the rest of us, as Dino stripped off his pyjamas, then put on his normal clothes from the locker beside his bed. When he was fully dressed, shoes and all, he had to sit on his bed until his parents came to collect him later that afternoon. After that I never saw another fight in the ward.

One morning when I woke up, I saw that the curtain was drawn all around the bed opposite me in the ward. The last occupant had been a boy called Gabriel Mongan, and he'd been allowed home two days earlier because his appendix stitches had healed well enough. All of that day and the next the curtains remained closed, and every half-hour, or even less, nurses came and disappeared through the drapes, then emerged moments later, sometimes noting things on a chart, then going back in to leave the chart back. No sounds emanated from the bed. Nothing by way of cries or words escaped up and out over the rails to give us a clue as to who or what was being so carefully guarded by the green cloth curtain and its white curtain hooks. In the faint glow of the dim night light in the ward, the hooks looked like so many teeth in the mouth of an expandable monster. When one of the doctors arrived to visit that bed, there was even more activity and yet, for all of the comings and goings, none of us was the tiniest bit closer to finding out the identity of our new neighbour.

'Who's in there?' I asked Emily, one of the day nurses.

'Someone who needs a lot of quiet,' she replied.

As a boy who was used to exploring the garden at home on Taylor's Hill, and who was fearless in the face of either Apaches or Sioux raiding parties, I found the situation increasingly frustrating. I was not allowed out of bed, yet everybody could see me quite clearly and knew my name, who my father was and how my foot had been saved from the mantelpiece. But less than ten feet away from the end of my bed, a mystery was unfolding, unchallenged by anyone. Was it a spy who had been wounded in a secret mission or something like that? Maybe it was a dangerous prisoner from some war in Africa, who was locked in a soundproof cage but had some rare disease that only a children's doctor could treat – like extremely rare tropical

tonsillitis. Who could say? I longed to find out, yet I was confined to barracks and was not due to be allowed out of my bed for at least another week.

On one of my mother's twice-daily visits, I approached the issue from a different angle. 'I hope it's not contagious, whatever it is,' I said, with concern in my voice.

'What's not contagious?' Mammy asked absent-mindedly, as she rearranged the bananas and apples in the plastic bowl on top of my bedside locker. I flicked my head and indicated with my eyes in the direction of the sealed curtain across the narrow ward from us.

'I said I hope, whatever it is, it's not . . .'

'Not what?'

'Contagious, Mammy. We might all be breathing in toxic nerve germs right now. They can travel through curtains, even double ones!'

'What on earth are you on about, Hughie?' my mother asked.

I explained my concerns about spies and prisoners and toxic germs. 'Couldn't you ask Daddy?' I said.

My mother looked at me, then combed my hair back with her fingers. 'Would you like me to bring you in some more books tomorrow?' I knew she didn't want me to continue with that line of enquiry so I asked for my *Hotspur Annual* from the previous Christmas and left it at that.

My mother spent more time with me than my father did, but I knew he was busy fixing people in the surgery theatre on the floor below and, of course, saving people had to come first, most of the time anyway. Sometimes I had the feeling that my father didn't like me, but I suppose everyone feels that about their father at some stage. Although he was really generous with everything, like food and bicycles and school books, I wished he would play with me sometimes. He never seemed to have the time to play. My mother did, though, and she was even pretty good at Indian stuff, like making headbands with elastic in them so you could stick feathers up at the back and be in a different tribe, depending on the colour of the feathers.

I remember one time my mother and I made a wigwam in the front garden near the monkey puzzle tree. We used strong bamboo canes, which we'd got from Madden's nurseries up the road to use for the raspberries. Instead of the heavy thick tent covering that the actual Red Indians use, we had a white sheet from the airing cupboard. Mammy had this great idea, to get out the paintbox and brushes and paint our hands different colours and make handprints on the sheet. It looked absolutely brilliant, the way the light shone through into the wigwam when it was coming into evening and the sun was still fairly warm. When we went back into the house we left the tent up, but it must have rained during the night: when I went out the next day, it looked even more like a real wigwam because the colours had run into each other. The whole sheet was a wonderful mishmash of patterns and designs. Mothers can make great Indians if you have the right conditions at home, including a garden and bamboos and no raspberries left to support.

I decided to find out for myself what or who was behind the curtain. The expedition required a little planning and I tested the ground, in a manner of speaking, trying for the first time since the accident with our lawnmower to put some weight on my right foot. For about three days running, I asked the nurses to pull the curtains around my bed in the afternoon so that I could try to have a read of my books without the sunlight disturbing me through the window from the outside world. During these short periods of about forty-five minutes, before tea was served by the ladies with the trolleys, I eased myself into a sitting position, then slowly swung my legs out of the bed so that my feet could touch the floor.

The first time my right foot made contact with the lino, I thought I would die with the pain. I eased one of the crutches out of the wardrobe as quietly as I could, then began the task of trying to stand up straight on my left leg and let the crutch and my uninjured foot take the strain. I tried to hop, keeping my bad foot off the ground altogether. Anytime I forgot myself and shifted any weight by accident to my right foot, it was absolute agony. Slowly at first, but building up gradually, I eventually managed, after the third day's session, to make some decent forward progress. However, as I lifted the crutch to hop another step, it slipped. It seemed like the combined weight of everyone from the Claddagh to Connemara was suddenly thrust onto what remained of my limb after my father had worked his magic on what the Iverson Rotary Sickle Motor lawnmower had left behind. I collapsed on the floor and my screams brought nurses running like an Olympic relay team, passing the syringe of happy juice between them like a hypodermic baton.

'What on earth were you thinking?' Sister Angela asked, in a voice that didn't really expect an answer.

'I was thinking about what it would be like if I couldn't ever walk again,' I answered candidly. That seemed to stop everybody in their tracks, even if I hadn't quite got started myself. I remember the throbbing pain in my foot, as the blood began to flow back into it, and the sensation I had that my leg ended in a flat dead end, like the road at the top of Highfield Park, where cars couldn't get out.

Back in the cupboard the crutch would have to stay, I thought. There was no way I could use it at night, whatever little success I'd had during daylight hours. The noise would wake everyone up and I'd definitely be caught by the night nurses and sent home. The voyage to the other side of the ward would have to be accomplished by some other means. I considered recruiting one of the other patients as an envoy of some sort, someone to undertake the mission while I directed operations by a series of hand signals, kept watch for night patrols, and waited for their eyewitness account when they returned. After a short period mulling this over, I abandoned the idea, as no suitable candidate was immediately apparent. As well as that, such a course of action would mean trusting the courage and judgement of someone else, which were more variables I couldn't be sure of. No, I'd just have to figure out another way of carrying out the trip myself, or wait until my foot healed.

And so, that Saturday night, in late August, when the ward was heavy with the sounds of others sleeping and muttering about dreams they didn't know they were having, I forced myself to stay awake and counted as best I could the intervals between the nurses' patrols of the ward. I fought off sleep by imagining that I was able to fly, and pictured myself soaring above Galway City, then swooping low through her streets past the shops, where my mother bought everything we ever needed. I steered a course in Eyre Square over the statue of the man with the little hat and a broken plaster nose. Around the back of the Great Southern Hotel I flew, then in through the railway station for a moment, before soaring up the other side of the square and rounding the corner into Shop Street. I continued, Moons on my right, with its thousands of ladies' coats, and on my left, the magical toy shop Glynn's had on its upper floor, above the fancy goods shop that sold crystal clocks and glass ashtrays. My imaginary journey ended as I landed softly on the footpath outside Glynn's, right beside where the old blind man played the accordion and people put money into the leather purse attached to it on a small pole. The old man's eyes rolled in his head . . . And then I was back in the hospital, and it was time to go. The night nurses had just made a round of the ward.

As quietly as I could, I lifted the bedclothes off my body. My left leg was doing all the work and the injured comrade followed in the path it left behind. When both legs were free, I sort of shuffled round on my backside so that I could sit up on the edge of the bed. I leaned my left arm and hand on the bedside locker, supporting myself as best I could so that I could stand on one foot. I managed to shuffle along towards the end of the bed and sit for a moment on the visitors' chair, which had its back to the window. This was a good bit lower than the bed, and from there I hoped to get myself onto the floor. There, I would do the panther crawl along the wall and make my way across the divide. Just before I began to slide down onto the cold green linoleum, I remembered that my bed would look unoccupied, even from a distance. I put the two pillows under the blankets in a straight-ish line and hoped for the best.

When at last I was on the floor, I realised that every single movement I made would inevitably involve my right leg, and therefore my bandaged foot. It dawned on me that at least some measure of pain was inevitable. It was too late to turn back. I lay on my tummy with the buttons of my pyjamas making the tiniest of clicking sounds as I inched along. There was a shout from some kid in their sleep about 'cowslips', then the usual creak as one of the other patients responded unconsciously to the disturbance by changing position in their own bed. I was afraid that the nurse at the night-station up the corridor might have heard the noise and come back sooner than planned. But no one did.

The curtains that enclosed the bed opposite were overhead before I realised it. At first I thought something had fallen down, but then I twigged. I was across the border and into alien territory now. However well I might have been able to explain to the night nurse my being down on the floor as some sleep-walking variation, there would be no escape from her wrath if I were discovered with my head and torso under the curtains of someone else's bed and my arse end out in the wilds of no-man's-land.

As I moved under the curtain, I heard the unmistakable sound of the ward door being opened. In my haste to disappear from view, I kicked one of the bedposts with my injured foot. I knew that if I screamed out in pain, I would certainly be caught, and in all likelihood sent home or at least have my other foot amputated. I stuffed a fist into my mouth to stifle any sound and switched back into flying mode in my head to distract myself from the almost-unendurable pain that was convulsing my body in shockwaves. I was in Dominick Street now, swerving to avoid a truck delivering something to the shop that sold paper and schoolbooks. Down past the Atlanta Hotel and over the bridge I flew, turning right at The Manhattan and into Henry Street past the chipper, then veering into the narrow laneway that led to Ivor's Motorcycles and the amusement arcade just beside the canal. I opened my eyes and heard the creak of the ward door closing again with a whine, like an aeroplane in the distance.

When I looked up and began to roll over onto my back, I could see something: a shape or feature of shadow that seemed to point up at the ceiling. The floor was really cold now and I noticed it more acutely as I slid backwards into the bedside locker and began the difficult task of getting into a sitting position. I could see a body in the bed, under the clothes mostly, but up near the pillow there was an enormous head with a long pointy bit at the top. At least that's what it looked like to me. As I sat up, with my back against the locker, my movements caused a clinking sound behind my head. A jug and a glass, I later learned. The body in the bed began to move, and the vast head I'd seen before only in silhouette leaned out over the blankets and rose upwards.

I had no idea what kind of creature I had disturbed with my Panther Crawl and my glass-clinking manoeuvres. I was terrified. I closed my eyes and waited for the inevitable mauling or devouring, which I now clearly deserved for having disturbed the beast in its lair. I could feel the barbarian's breath on my hair and then, inexorably, the first touch on my face. The contact was not harsh. In fact, its gentleness was beyond unexpected. I waited and waited and waited some more, believing that at any moment now the tearing of me limb from limb must surely begin. I wondered whether there would be any of me left – anything recognisable. *Just leave enough for my mother to say goodbye to*, I thought.

Again the lightest of touches on my cheek, and I began to grow reckless in the presence of certain death. What was to be lost by looking carnage in the face? I remember thinking quite vividly, I wonder if the Green Wiper really does have a hooded hat and carries a scythe. I opened one eye, then the other, and looked up.

Above me sat a girl of about my own age. Her left arm was in a plaster cast, which was like a narrow table and stretched straight out in front of her, supporting the arm. There was very little light, except for a sort of gloomy column of moonlight. It came in over the blinds on the windows of the ward and leaked into the enclosed cubicle through a dip in the top of the curtain where two hooks were missing.

The girl's face was now becoming a little clearer as my eyes grew used to the darkness. She said nothing, but continued to look at me with big, kind eyes that reminded me of those of a cow I'd once seen on the edge of the golf course near the diving boards at Blackrock. Her expression was one of neither fear nor surprise. As she continued to look down at me, she moved slightly so that the scarce light caught her in its path. I saw scarring and scorching that began at her chin and disappeared down her front into a swathe of dressings, which were not unlike those that housed my right foot.

We stayed like that for a long time, and neither of us spoke or even whispered a word. Despite the absence of words, we did communicate, and I felt happier than I'd ever remembered being.

While we were busy not talking, our silence was disturbed by footsteps coming down the ward towards us. Simultaneously we opened our eyes wide in question, and each of us held our breath. The footsteps stopped directly outside the curtain and then, as I cursed the inadequacy of the pillows I'd left in my place across the aisle, there was the quick scratch of shoe soles turning, and the danger receded with the steps. The girl smiled at me and I smiled back, and I sighed and indicated with my eyes that it was time for me to begin the return journey. As I began to slide down the locker, so that I was on my back on the floor, the girl raised her good hand and opened and closed it slowly in a wave that might have looked like 'goodbye' but really meant 'hello'. And that was how I met Nyxi Kirwan for the very first time.

Chapter 3

The Town Hall Cinema was around the corner from the library and the courthouse. A man with one glass eye took your ticket on the way in and tore it in two. At least once a month, Nyxi and I went to the pictures together. Either her mother or mine dropped us down, and collected us from the wooden bench in Wood Quay, which overlooked the River Corrib as it rushed towards the Salmon Weir Bridge. Sometimes the water was low and you could see the bottom, with its rushes and spaghetti reeds, like someone with long spindly fingers playing the piano underwater. If it was raining when the film ended, Nyxi and I would take shelter in the doorway of the Lion's Tower pub on Eglinton Street and wait for the mother taxi to pull up in traffic with the drizzle dancing in its headlights as the indicator teased on and off against the night.

'How's the arm?' I'd always ask, as we waited for our lift home.

'Mighty,' she'd reply, 'and how's the foot?' Then we'd wait as long as we could before trying to say, at exactly the same time, what Mrs Walsh, in the sweetshop beside 'the Jes', had said once to us as we agonised over whether to buy Taytos or a Curly Wurly between us: 'Sure haven't ye three good arms and three good feet between ye?'

Nyxi had pulled a kettle full of boiling water down on herself about eighteen months earlier and had been in the Regional for sixteen weeks as a result. Skin grafts, surgery, pieces of her leg stripped off to be glued to her chest: she had gone through a terrible time as a result of her accident. The burns were mostly on her arm and chest, though, and when she was wearing her school uniform, only a little bit of the damage was visible – under her chin, in a splotch that was shaped very like Africa. She was a month younger than me but I always felt that *she* was actually the older of the two of us. She was tough and kind and brave and certain, and knew about things that were happening all over the world, miles from Galway and the life we filled with trips to the shopping centre on the Headford Road, visits to the Town Hall Cinema and taking part in school plays where neither of us got to do anything much besides carry props and understudy for people who never got sick.

She sang 'Tie a Yellow Ribbon Round the Old Oak Tree'

relentlessly that year, any time we were near a tree, or saw anyone with a ribbon, regardless of its colour. Nyxi had twin brothers, Micheál and Jarlath, and they were way older than her – maybe seven or eight years – and were in secondary school in Enda's on Threadneedle Road. One of them played underage football for Galway, minors maybe, and was on the subs bench in an All-Ireland final. But that was years later. Back then, when I'd known her for almost a year and a half, Nyxi spoke about singers and bands I'd never heard of, like David Bowie and Pink Floyd, as if they were actually friends of her brothers, rather than just the bands on records they owned. I was always careful to avoid saying anything that might give me away as someone who knew absolutely nothing about any music, except for the *Elvis Presley: 40 Greatest Hits* double LP my mother had bought for me, and which had greeted me in bright blue wrapping paper on my return from hospital.

Nyxi and her family lived in Renmore, in a house that was almost exactly halfway between Galwegians Rugby Club in Glenina and the Regional Technical College just before the Corrib Great Southern on the Dublin Road. Her father was in the army, and it was only a couple of minutes from their house to Renmore Barracks, which was right on the sea and could be seen clearly from trains as they left or entered the city. One December, before I'd ever met Nyxi, my parents brought me to Dublin to the Gaiety Theatre to see Maureen Potter in the pantomime. I always remember that as we passed by the barracks on the train my father said, 'What chance would those eejits have if they were sent up to the Shankill Road?' I didn't know then what he meant, but I do now.

Sometimes I'd go to visit Nyxi in her house. One time near Christmas her granny, who could only speak Irish, was visiting from Connemara. I thought everyone spoke English but that taught me different. Her granny was a huge big old lady with the same eyes as Nyxi, and a red and black cape that she seemed to wear all of the time, even when the radiators were on.

'You look just like your granny,' I said to Nyxi one day, when we were watching *The Waltons* in her house. Her grandmother was asleep in an armchair on the other side of the room.

'Get lost, Hughie,' she said. 'I don't snore.' We both laughed at that, as her nan continued to snort in her sleep like a train.

'What about *your* grandparents?' Nyxi asked. 'Do you see them much?'

'Well, my mammy's dad died about seventy years ago, I think, and Granny Daly lives in Dublin with my uncle Seán. We visit sometimes and I always share a room with her.'

'Does she snore?' Nyxi asked, with a grin.

I ignored the question but the answer would have been 'yes'. 'My father's parents have a chemist's shop in Waterford in a town called Lismore.'

'What are they like?'

'I'm not really sure. We don't see them much. But we did go there last Christmas for a visit and the shop was great, full of those tins of sweets you get for car journeys.'

'Are they the ones with the sweet powder all over them that gets on your clothes?'

I nodded. Nyxi always knew exactly the type of sweets you were talking about. Even if she didn't know the actual name, she was always able to tell you something really accurate about them that you already knew but would never have managed to say yourself. I loved that about her. I remember one time when we were in McDonagh's fish shop with Mammy, a little kid dropped a paper bag of sweets on the floor and his mother wouldn't let him pick them up. They were small cubes, like dice, with a rough, sugary surface. After the woman had left, and the boy was still pulling away from her hand and trying to come back for his sweets, it crossed my mind to bend down and get them for myself and Nyxi. Her voice cut into my thoughts before I'd even begun to make a move.

'Don't bother, Hughie. Once they've been on the floor, they get all covered in hair and germs even if you haven't sucked them before you drop them.' I didn't take her advice but she was absolutely right – as soon as I'd picked one up and put it in my mouth, I could taste dust and dirty stuff.

Nyxi's parents always seemed to be happy whenever I saw them together. Sometimes her dad would throw a tea towel across the kitchen at her mum or they'd be in the hallway of the house, laughing and trying to work out which of the Christmas lights needed a new bulb. One day I remember, as her dad was about to drive me home, Nyxi's mother came to the door and said, in a funny voice, 'Where's my big kiss?' and I thought she meant me and I turned and began to walk towards her – but she'd meant him. He came back and kissed her, and then she blew me a kiss as well, as if she'd known I'd thought she'd meant me. It made me feel full up with some kind of happiness, but a little bit empty, too. I'm pretty sure I never once saw my parents kiss each other. Not on-the-mouth kissing anyway, even at Christmas . . . Kiss-miss.

I had to wear this funny-shaped shoe when I got out of hospital and had learned to walk without the crutches. After the accident, whenever I went to have a bath, my mother would knock on the door of the bathroom when the water was running and say, '*Both* feet, Hughie, okay?' This was because for a good while I would always leave my right sock on so that I wouldn't have to look at the damage. I'd even get into the bath wearing the sock and so, although my foot did get wet, it never got cleaned and, more importantly for me, I couldn't see it.

The shoe was specially made, by someone in Switzerland, I think, and it had an extra chunk on the bottom and an additional piece inside so that my foot balanced out a bit instead of unbalancing me every time I took a step. It was very hard at first not to think about the foot without *always* thinking about it, but after a while I got used to being able to wiggle two toes that were not there. I know that probably sounds stupid, but that's the best way I can find to describe it. The biggest change really was that I limped if I tried to run.

At school there was always absolute madness at break and lunchtime when we were all out in the playground. Before the lawnmower attacked me, I'd been able to take part in everything. Okay, so I wasn't Pelé or anything, but at least I was picked for the monster soccer games of thirty-a-side we played on the pitch at lunchtime. Or for the rounders games we played, with a hurley instead of a bat, in the handball alley if the older boys were using most of the pitch. As we progressed through the school, though, I took part less and less in any of this, and eventually stopped standing in the bunch of lads who gathered, once lunch was eaten, to be picked by Johnny Dooley or Gary Coyne, who always seemed to be the captains. To be fair to them, they were super players. For at least a year I thought that Gary actually played for Liverpool because he wore their shirt. I had no idea that it was so far away from Galway.

One teacher stood out for me while I was at primary school. Her name was Peggy Donoghue and she taught me for three years in a row. She had a book of famous paintings in her classroom, and first thing every Monday morning, she would turn a page and show us a new image. They were all by one of the great artists – Rembrandt,

Monet, Manet or Van Gogh – and we would discuss the picture. I remember two paintings in particular: *The Laughing Cavalier* by Frans Hals, and a huge picnic scene beside a lake where women with parasols walked a few small dogs on leads. I think that was by Monet or Manet.

When I injured my foot, Peggy Donoghue saw to it that I could climb the stairs, from the playground up to her classroom, by staying behind with me every day for two weeks and helping me learn to navigate them without the crutch I'd had to use for the first while when I was finally back at school. She made an enormous effort to help me and I have never forgotten that. She spent an awful lot of her free time with me, and what made all the difference was her determination to make sure I was just like everyone else. She and Nyxi and Mammy were the only people besides me who really understood the foot thing and what it meant in my life.

I'd always known somehow that the Germans and the Japanese were nations of people who were well organised and punctual, sticklers for detail and conformism. Still, for years I was puzzled as to why their fighter pilots always seemed to attack at exactly noon in every issue of the *Hotspur* or *Battle Weekly*, the comics I read every week for years.

'Bandits at twelve o'clock!' was the weekly cry from Johnny 'Red' Redburn over the fighter plane's radio – he flew a Hawker Hurricane (for the Russian Air Force, for some strange reason). Years later, when one of the older boys at school spoke about learning to drive a tractor, and how one hand should be at ten o'clock and the other at two, I still didn't understand that he was referring to positioning on a clock rather than the time.

Meanwhile, Lord Peter Flint embarked on countless perilous missions behind enemy lines, while at the same time maintaining an outwardly anti-war stance at home in 'Blighty'. I felt a bit like that sometimes – as if I had two different lives. In one, I went to school every day and did my homework and tidied my room and ate my dinner, but in the other, I was utterly miscast and couldn't fit in at all either at school *or* at home.

My father grew increasingly distant from my mother and me, spending more and more time at the hospital or 'away', as my mammy would say, with a sad expression on her face, when she'd put two dinners on the table and a third in the bottom oven to keep it warm. We both knew the dinner would still be there in the morning when I was going out to get my bike and freewheel down Taylor's Hill to Scoil Iognáid on Sea Road.

Around this time I remember having a few disturbing recurring dreams. In one, I was walking with a schoolbag on my back and suddenly became aware of howling and screaming somewhere behind me. When I'd manage to turn around, three boys would be standing around an old dog and mistreating him. They taunted him with sticks and hit him and he wasn't able to get away. Sometimes,

I'd wake from this nightmare with the smell of burning in my nose.

Nyxi went to school in the Mercy Primary School in Newtown-Smith near the courthouse. When it was warm enough to go to school without a coat, we would meet every fine day after school, for as long as we could, until she had to get the bus to Renmore from the stop outside Syron House in Eyre Square. We talked and talked and walked, as I wheeled my bike beside her. Sometimes my foot got tired and we had to slow our walking, but Nyxi never made anything of it on our countless tours and detours of the city we both loved. It was almost as if the city itself was a third friend, to add to the odd pair we made, me with my Swiss shoe, and Nyxi with her arm that was so disfigured she said suds gathered in the dents on it whenever she washed her hair.

In school, the lads sometimes teased me about Nyxi. 'How's your girlfriend?' Martin Burke used to say, with a sneer, until he eventually got tired of saying it and no longer sneered with any real flair.

'I hear she let you feel her up, Mittman,' a boy in the year ahead, called Challa Flaherty, said to me as I unlocked my bike in the bicycle shed near Brother Doyle's woodwork room. I pretended not to hear him and, as I turned to wheel my bike out towards the school entrance, I heard him cough and spit a 'greener' after me. I felt it land in my hair. I couldn't give him the satisfaction of seeing me putting my hand up to feel for it, or wiping it away. He was about twelve when I was nearly ten. In a way, I lived in a cocoon at that time, cushioned from isolation by having finally made a friend, someone I could talk to about anything.

'Do you *want* to feel me up?' Nyxi asked, when I told her later what the older boy had said.

'No, I *do not*,' I responded, almost choking on a bag of Chipsticks and a mouthful of Lilt (with the 'totally tropical taste').

'Well, if you ever do, just ask,' she said, with a smile. Neither of us knew what we were talking about, not really, but looking back I know that if I'd needed a heart transplant, Nyxi Kirwan would have given me hers without a second thought. And I'd have done the same for her. Without hesitation.

Sometimes we'd go down to the docks and watch the *Galway Bay*, with its black-painted hull, or the *Naomh Éanna* being loaded up with cargo. Other times, we'd ramble round to Donnelly's coal yard, then walk out past Lough Atalia, so that Nyxi could catch the bus outside Hickey's Boat Supplies on the Dublin Road, opposite the Holy Family swimming pool. This was where people with handicaps went to learn how to swim. Whenever we walked out that far, I would always wait with Nyxi until the bus came, and then she'd leg it to the back and wave out the window at me as it drove away.

'Meet me on Saturday, Hughie,' she would often say, during the week, and then I'd spend all of Friday night looking forward to the next morning, knowing we'd have the whole day together. When I was nine, Nyxi got a bike for Christmas, with a promise that when the weather improved after Easter, she'd finally be allowed to cycle to school. That year everybody was talking about a song called 'The Streak'. I was in fourth class, and one day Tommy Joyce announced at break that he'd seen the film called *The Texas Chain Saw Massacre*. For about two weeks we gathered around him in the playground and begged him to tell us all about it.

It was a hot summer, and I remember that some film was being made around the docks. There were signs up, to make it look like the harbour was actually in Norway or Sweden or somewhere. A man from a building company was shot dead in a robbery of the bank in Lynch's Castle off Shop Street, but the thing I remember most about that summer is the noise of the bell on Nyxi's bike, a bright red Raleigh Chopper with the three-speed lever between the handlebars and the saddle, like a gearstick on a racing car. It never crossed my mind to wonder why she'd chosen a boys' bike, but it seemed exactly the right one for the strong and fearless person that she was. We cycled everywhere all summer long and became more inseparable than ever.

I couldn't have cared less about what everyone else in my class was doing. I had no wish to be invited to birthday parties where boys lined up and togged out and made-believe that they were in Croke Park or Lansdowne Road and imagined that they were Liam Sammon or Mike Gibson, or even George Best. The only thing I wanted to do that summer was to be free. And you know what? I was. I no longer just dreamed of making my way around the city as I pleased. I was finally mobile and, instead of limping when I tried to run or wearing a sock in the bath, I had some wheels under me and a travelling companion who wanted to keep on exploring the boundaries of the world we knew until we reached – God, I don't know where.

'America, maybe,' she said, as we met one day outside St Nicholas's Church in the heat of August and watched some tourists take photographs of the spire. My father had been at home that morning when I'd come down for breakfast. There was a taut silence between my parents in the kitchen. I'd spilled some cornflakes on the tiled floor and crunched them underfoot while walking to the fridge to get the milk. To my father, the noise of the cereal snapping seemed to be the loudest sound in the world at that moment. He exploded.

'For fuck's sake, Hughie, do you have to make so much noise?' he roared at me, as he dropped the newspaper he was reading flat onto the kitchen table. I'd been aware from time to time of his incendiary propensity, but I was still shocked when it happened this time. My mother was loading the dishwasher. She turned, walked up to the table and stood facing him across it.

'"Please do not disturb with cornflakes" – that's the sign we should get made up in Naughton's Hardware someday, and you can hang it around your neck. Whenever you're *here* for breakfast, that is.'

I had never heard my mother talk to him like that before, and she had certainly never spoken to *me* in that way. Since the accident I'd felt that my father had become more distant from me than ever, but I'd never really thought about why that was. That's not entirely true – I *had* thought about it, and, to be honest, I'd come to the conclusion that, because there was less of me physically than there had been before, it was perhaps logical that my father needed to love me a little less as a consequence. I was now damaged goods, I guess, so he saw me as a patient rather than as a son. He'd saved my foot and I suppose he believed that he'd done more than enough for me. Who could blame him?

The atmosphere in the kitchen grew in silence and intensity as my mother stared my father down, daring him to respond. She gestured to me with a look to bring my breakfast into the sitting room. I took the bottle of milk with me, and fixed my own stare on the red and silver foil top as I carried the bowl and the bottle past my father in a scene that was almost like something from *Oliver!*.

As I ate, I could hear them talking in low, whispered tones. I'll always remember that it was the only time I've ever left an empty cereal bowl and a half-full bottle of milk behind me in a 'good' room. I went out the back door into the garage and got my bike. I wheeled it across to the greenhouse, where I knew I'd left the pump to dry a week or so earlier after I'd rescued it from the grass where it had lain un-needed for ages. I shut the door and began to pump up both tyres until they were rock hard. My bike was gold and yellow in colour and had no gears at all – well, only one gear, I suppose. I could hear my parents' voices through the open kitchen window.

When I was ready to go, I was reluctant to go back into the house in case I'd make things worse than they were. I needed to let Mammy know I was going out, so I wheeled the bike across the back garden, between the vegetable patch and the greenhouse, in the hope that she would see me. She did, and I pointed towards the passageway and raised my hand in a wave. She waved back. I was halfway along the passageway when I remembered the greenhouse door wasn't closed, so I left the bike and walked back to shut it. The last thing I wanted was rabbits getting in at the tomatoes.

I secured the door and went on my way. My mother had her back to the window as I passed, and I suppose my father's view was obstructed by her, so neither of them was aware that I'd gone back to the greenhouse. Their voices were raised and, from what little I could hear, I detected real upset in my mother's stance and tone. But as I walked past the open window, I heard my father's voice as clear as daylight.

'*You* were the one who insisted on adoption, Deirdre. Not me.'

*

'Not America, Nyxi,' I replied, 'somewhere a bit closer'.

'I know!' she said. 'One of the girls on my basketball

team says there's a quarry near her house. She lives somewhere out past the Rahoon Flats.'

She might as well have said 'the moon', for all I knew about what existed out beyond the Rahoon Flats. This was bandit territory of an altogether different kind. Rahoon was a sort of wasteland at the edge of the city, where street lighting ended and cows began. It also had the only large-scale flat complex in the city, consisting of dozens of blocks of white-speckled, pre-cast concrete. It was a place that was designed to keep as many poor people as possible away from the rest of the city, by building up instead of out. All along the Seamus Quirke Road were caravans and campfires, dogs and prams, barefoot children with runny noses and pink cardigans, and tarpaulin tents with stacks of turf along their edges, which kept the rain and the rats out and the tinkers in. The flats themselves were imposing solid towers, which hinted at a solution but actually screamed warnings about every possible ill and terror that might befall you if you went wrong in your own life. 'That's where you'll end up, Mittman, the Rahoon Flats,' a teacher called Mr McNulty said to me once. 'It's where *all* the bad boys go to grow old if they don't grow up.'

With Nyxi Kirwan and her Raleigh Chopper as my companion, no road trip was too dangerous. Not even to Rahoon and beyond. We could have gone down past my school and back up Taylor's Hill but, instead, Nyxi led the way through Nuns' Island and past the flour mill, then around by the cathedral. I knew she'd chosen this route because it meant that we'd have to cycle past the hospital. That was, of course, where we'd met so it always energised us to be near it.

We cycled up the pavement on Newcastle Road, then turned left and out towards the flats. You could see them from about fifty miles away as you approached. I'd only ever been past them in the car before, and so, as we got closer, they seemed to have grown and multiplied to cover all the available space on the horizon. Three tinker children stared at us from where they were gathered around a bicycle, which was upside down, resting on its handlebars and saddle. The back wheel was off and lay on the ground. *Oh, Jesus*, I thought, *that's what happens to people who are stupid enough to cycle out this far: their bikes are taken apart and presumably the owner is killed or kidnapped or something.*

Nyxi, as if reading my thoughts, said, 'Just keep cycling and look straight ahead as if you have somewhere else to be.'

'How much do you want for the Chopper, missus?' a boy of six or seven shouted across the road to us. Behind him, a man emerged from a tent carrying a roll of carpet over his shoulder. I just knew it had a body inside.

'Is that a twenty-six-inch or a twenty-eight-inch wheel?' the boy called after us, as we pedalled faster than we'd ever done and stuck out our right arms to turn up the hill past the flats. No one bothered us or attacked us as we went past, but I knew that we were being watched by bad people from behind every single net curtain in the place.

The hill loomed ahead of us, like a runway to the sky, and as Nyxi changed gears on her wonderful chrome and leather steed, I imagined myself at the end of a long cattle drive on a tired horse, but one that would carry me up the hill because it looked forward to cantering back down when we turned later and headed for home. I knew that the horse would transform itself eventually into a Hawker Hurricane and race past the flats at the speed of sound on the way back.

Later, after we'd had to walk the last and steepest bit, past a pink house with an enormous chestnut tree, we lay on the grass above the quarry and looked down into the vast valley of blasted-out rock, which housed a litter of crushing machines. The sun beat down on our necks and backs. I could feel the vibrations coming up at me through the ground whenever a lorry thundered past. Nyxi had brought us a packed lunch of ham sandwiches and a Bobby bar each. We'd forgotten to bring something to drink, so I knocked on the door of a farmhouse and asked the lady for some water.

'Have this, a stór,' she said, when she'd come back from the kitchen, handing me a Lucozade bottle filled with milk. 'Just leave the bottle outside the gate when ye're finished.'

It was the most wonderful time Nyxi and I had ever spent together, with just the two of us, nobody telling us what to do or where to go. We fell asleep for a while on the grass. I woke up first, but didn't know how long we'd been sleeping. Nyxi slept with her good hand holding her bad arm in close to her. I took off my socks and shoes and looked at my foot. By then I'd got used to it mostly and didn't mind it so much. Across the road from the quarry a man began to mow his lawn. The sound of the engine, when it started, terrified me so much that I put my socks and shoes back on and woke Nyxi.

'I think we should head back,' I said. 'I'd say it's getting late.'

'Don't be afraid of the lawnmowers, Hughie,' she said.

'I'm not – I'm not afraid. It's just that it's late, that's all,' I said, but we both knew that wasn't true.

'If Billie Jean King can beat Bobby Riggs,' Nyxi said, with a grin, 'you can overcome anything, even if you're only a boy.' The droning of the mower in the background didn't seem so catastrophic to me, now that Nyxi was awake.

'What's "adoption"?' I asked her, as we got on our bikes and prepared to freewheel back to our other lives.

'I think it's when people buy babies from the nuns,' Nyxi replied.

Chapter 4

My mother got sick. I'm not sure how or when exactly it happened but, over a period of weeks, or maybe months, I began to notice some small changes that told me something was not right. We'd gone on holidays, Mammy, Daddy and I, to Portugal that year. It was the year I finished primary school, and Nyxi's father first went to Lebanon: these were big things. In Portugal we stayed in a hotel in a seaside town, just a few miles down the coast from Lisbon. It was a huge place, with televisions in the lobby and hundreds of women in bathing costumes and also quite a lot of seafood, like prawns and shark and stuff like that, on the menu.

Mammy was okay for the first few days, but one morning while we were having breakfast in the hotel dining room, she suddenly stood up and announced in a loud voice to the assembled diners, 'Your flights have been delayed because of fog,' and then, 'Elvis Presley has become an undercover FBI agent. He is *not* dead.'

My father and I just looked at each other. I imagined that some unholy scene was about to take place, but it did not. Instead of following with more announcements, Mammy simply sat down and continued with her breakfast as if nothing out of the ordinary had occurred. A day or two later, on a trip to Lisbon for some souvenir shopping, she bought four different postcards, wrote exactly the same thing on each of them, then addressed them to both of her parents at their old address in Belgrave Square in Dublin, where she had lived as a child. 'Mr Peter Daly', her father, had been dead for years. Granny Daly now lived in Rochestown Avenue. But Mammy had insisted on buying stamps and had posted the cards.

Apart from those two incidents, I enjoyed our holiday. I knew that my parents were making an effort to get on a bit better together. They seemed a little happier than they'd been for a while. I remember my father buying cones for us in an ice-cream parlour near the seaside. When Mammy said to the lady that she wanted rum and raisin flavour, my father said he'd have the same. At that precise moment, I thought everything was going to be fine.

The weird thing about what Mammy had said about Elvis Presley was that when she'd said it, in July, in Portugal, he was still alive. About three weeks later, as the summer holidays drew to an end, it was on the news that Elvis Presley died in his home in Memphis. It was as if Mammy had known something the rest of the world hadn't. Sometimes I felt as if I knew things too, like when the phone rang and I knew before I picked it up that it was Granny Daly. The death of Elvis hit my mother very hard indeed. She would sit for hours on her own in the sitting room, just listening to song after song after song. 'Suspicious Minds' was her favourite. I had always thought he was saying, 'suspicious *mines*', and I remember saying to Nyxi once, 'Of course you couldn't build anything, a house or a castle, or even dreams, on suspicious mines. What if they blew up?'

Meanwhile it had been decided during my last year in primary school that I was not to pursue my secondary education in the liberal halls of Coláiste Iognáid – 'the Jes' – but on the other side of the country at a boarding school in Kildare. I didn't want to go and I told my parents so in fairly stark terms.

'I'm not going,' I'd said, when my father handed me the brochure for the school earlier that summer, with its photographs of some boys playing rugby and others standing on a diving board, ready to plunge into the Liffey.

'You'll do what you're told, my lad,' my father the surgeon said. 'I'm not going to have you hanging around with a pile of Deep Purple fans in some Smoke Room, while that clown of a headmaster waits for you to do your homework whenever *you* feel like it. I was told by Paddy Purcell in Ward's the other night that his son was told he didn't have to bring in any school books at all, but could read whatever he wanted and they'd discuss it in class. What kind of school is that?'

'A liberal education is no bad thing, my father used to say.' Mammy weighed in on my side.

'When people say "liberal", what they really mean is "Whatever you're having yourself", and all free at someone else's expense,' he countered.

'I thought you believed in "free love", Simon?' my mother said. 'Isn't that one of the courses they're teaching now in the hospital?'

My father picked up the Newbridge College prospectus and handed it to me. 'I've already paid the fees, so that's that, Hughie. It's an awful lot of money, but I don't mind paying for education. It's never wasted, even if it isn't always rewarded.'

This sermon from my father came over the wires to the telegram room in my head, as I wondered about running away with Nyxi to South America or Limerick – somewhere we would never be tracked down. Nyxi's father was on a training course in the Curragh Camp, and I wondered how far away that was. What I knew, too, though, was that my mother's heart would break if I ran away from home.

'You're going and that's that,' my father said, before leaving the room. Moments later we heard his car engine start and he was off again, to wherever it was he went when he wasn't at home or at the hospital.

My mother gently took the brochure from me and leafed through it. 'It doesn't look so bad, Hughie. Maybe it'll be grand.' She smiled a rueful and unpromising smile. 'You'll have to tell Nyxi.'

I would, but I didn't know how I was going to. I knew that her father's absence was proving very difficult for her, yet I was in the opposite boat: *I* was being sent to County Kildare, not for six weeks but for the next five bloody years! I'd bought Nyxi a Benfica football shirt as a gift from Portugal, with money my mother had given me. Somehow I knew she would actually wear it. It had a high round neck and long sleeves so none of her scarring would show. I met her a few days later.

'It's gorgeous, Hughie!' she'd exclaimed, as she'd ripped open the wrapping. We were sitting in the bandstand beside Leisureland, our bikes leaning against both sides of the steps up. Overhead, seagulls squawked and soared on air currents, and I wondered when the mackerel would next be in along the shore. Whenever that happened, dozens of people would line the short stretch of coastline near there and cast endlessly and effortlessly, hooking fish after fish after fish.

Salthill was less thronged than usual, but that was probably because of the rain. Out in the bay, two sailing boats were racing around Mutton Island. In the background, the cries of people on the outdoor slide, a couple of hundred yards away, were less and less of a distraction, and the noise of the rain on the bandstand roof was like nature drumming her fingers on my heart, waiting for me to say something I didn't think I'd ever have to.

'I'm going away, Nyxi.'

She looked at me, kicking her heels against the wall on which we sat. 'Another holiday? Sure you're only just back.'

I shook my head. 'No, not a holiday. I'm going to boarding school.' There it was. I'd told her, and at the same time I'd finally admitted it to myself. I'd mentioned it only in passing to her a few months earlier. But back then I hadn't wanted to take it seriously. I'd thought it was just an idea that wouldn't ever come to fruition, like everlasting gobstoppers or my toes growing back. Until now, I'd always believed that my mother or God would save me, or that Newbridge College would burn down and no longer need to print brochures to send around the country, like bait on a spinner, to catch people like me and reel us in. At home we'd gone round in circles in arguments and talks about what was 'best' for me, and how the other options in Galway weren't really options at all. According to my father, Enda's (where Nyxi's brothers went) was 'GAA Catholicism'; 'The Bish' was 'the same as the Jes really, but with a uniform'. Mary's was 'essentially a reformatory' and, although they had boarders, they didn't play rugby. His crowning criticism of all local schools was 'Sure they're only around the corner. How much growing up are you going to do, Hughie, if you only live around the corner for the rest of your life?'

There was nothing else west of the Shannon that matched my father's ambition or, as I read it, that was for him far enough away to separate me from my life with my mother, on the other side of his marriage. I'd increasingly come to feel that he resented any time I spent alone with her, in the kitchen or out in the garden when I wheeled the barrow for her as she tended her vegetable patch or pulled weeds from the flowerbeds at the front. If we were having a discussion about something in the kitchen in the evening after dinner, he would often come in and demand to know what we were talking about. Whatever it was – school, a project about Russia for class, the places Nyxi and I had been on our bikes, the news about a bombing in a hotel in Belfast – he would immediately belittle my contribution: 'Sure what could you *possibly* know about that?' Then he'd demand that my mother help him find a clean shirt, or listen to some story of his about what was going on in the hospital. 'I've been thinking a bit more about what we discussed, Deirdre,' was like a mantra with him, and my mother's face would almost invariably light up, with happiness or hope, and she'd follow him out into the living room or up the stairs to hear whatever it was he pretended to have been considering. At such times, she would leave me with a look that said, 'Sorry about this, Hughie, but maybe things are about to get better for all of us.' Yet they never seemed to.

'When are you going?' Nyxi asked.

'In September,' I said. 'They've got labels with my name on them made for my clothes.' In a funny way, that had marked the end of the speculation about my future. It seemed to me that, once the labels had been made, there could be no going back, no retreat from the inevitable. What use would the labels be if I didn't go to boarding school? The shop wouldn't take them back, and the clothes they were made for had already been purchased, and could never be returned to Ryan's Menswear, now that I'd tried them on and the trousers had been taken up. The black blazer, which bore the crest of the school, could, I suppose, have been given to someone it fitted, if they found him – but it was the name-tags that signalled for me the end of all hope. Like a parcel sent out into the big world, I would forever wear a return address or at least a linen dog-tag with red lettering on a white background.

Nyxi knew that it had been discussed in my family a while back, but *she* and *I* had not had to talk about it properly. Not until now. Not until it was too late. I looked out to sea. The rain seemed to gather momentum and, between us and the promenade, it fell more intensely. It was like a barrier all around the bandstand, separating Nyxi and me and our bicycles from the rest of the whole world.

We sat side by side and said nothing at all for ages. In my head I imagined that I could talk to Nyxi, almost as if we had an invisible wire connecting our brains and could communicate with each other without having to let the words travel from our mouths and into the air, where they could be misunderstood or never taken back. In my mind, I told her that I wished we could fly away from Galway and always be together, or cycle like mad and never be caught by anyone, even if they were in a supersonic jet.

'. . . or just sit here forever and never be disturbed,' I heard her say, and I looked at her – but she hadn't spoken at all. The only thing I suddenly knew was that I loved Nyxi Kirwan more than anyone else in the entire universe. Of course I wasn't going to say something like that out loud, but in that moment, there, in the rain, on the bandstand, that was the only universal truth. I thought about what it would mean if we were separated for the next five years. Who would I talk to? Who would I be able to go places with? Who would even begin to understand that a boy with eight toes can feel pain and loss and love every bit as much as someone with ten toes or even an extra one? What would I have to look forward to on Saturdays for the rest of my life? Rugby matches, diving boards, school choirs, 'woodwork', 'art rooms' and 'two full-size snooker tables for use by senior boys only'? What kind of life would that be?

I was absolutely lost for what might be the right thing to say or do, to try to explain myself or to make things better or different. I felt as if I was about to start crying, and then I remember thinking that if I did and Nyxi noticed, I could always lie and say it was the rain, not tears, streaming down my cheeks. I felt cold and frightened and afraid of saying or doing something that would make things worse than they already were.

The rain began to clear and we still had the rest of the

day ahead of us. Nyxi pulled on the Benfica jersey over her clothes and tucked it into her jeans. As she did, she looked away, towards the garda station, and I just stared out ahead of me at the sailing boats in the distance. I knew that everything was about to change in my life and I did not want *some* things to change. Not ever.

We just sat there until the rain had stopped, and neither of us spoke a single word. It was as if talking might break the thin sheet of glass or ice that insulated us from real life. A car sounded its horn impatiently somewhere on the seafront. The scent of chips blew back at us, up the slope of the grassy field between us and the roadway. Everyone came to Salthill for their holidays, but we *lived* in Galway and knew the place when it was deserted in winter, when the busloads of tourists had gone home and the only sounds were the sea and the creak of B&B signs in the breeze. I knew that I would miss the sea when I went away. I pictured waves crashing up onto the promenade, the way they had when my mother and I had once gone for a walk out to the diving boards after my father had not come home for three nights in a row.

Nyxi hopped down from the bandstand and picked up her Raleigh Chopper. I thought she was going to leave me, go home and never speak to me again. She began to walk slowly, wheeling the bike beside her and heading for the sea. I didn't know what to say. After a few seconds, she stopped and looked back at me. 'Well?' she said.

'Well what?' I answered, and as soon as I spoke, I was

crying uncontrollably and my shoulders were shaking and everything. I'd never ever cried as much as I did there and then on the bandstand.

'Do you want an ice-cream cone? My mam gave me money. We can go to Feeney's and see if yer wan with the red hair is working. If not, we'll get choc ices instead.' We walked, side by side with our bikes, until we got to the narrow gate out onto the footpath near the Hilltop Hotel. Nyxi let me go first, and I was afraid to say anything in case I'd just start bawling crying again.

'Here,' she said, as we stood on the footpath and were just about to get on the bikes. I turned and looked at her. She untucked the football shirt from her front, then put her fingers inside one bit of it and lifted it to my face and dried my cheeks. I just let her and, when she'd finished, I opened my mouth and was about to speak, but knew it would only set me off again. 'It's grand, Hughie,' she said. 'I know.' And in that moment, I knew that she really and truly and honestly and definitely did.

The lady with the red hair, the one who pulled bigger cones than anyone else, was not working in the newsagent's that day. Somehow, I'd known she wouldn't be. And so we had choc ices. After that, it was as if we both knew that nothing more needed to be said, so we just cycled and cycled and walked, then cycled again all over Galway, until the sun started to go down on that Saturday at the tail end of August. In Quay Street we stared in the window of the craft shop, as a lady with an enormous arse rearranged the Aran sweaters in the display with her back to us. We couldn't stop laughing.

Down past the Claddagh, on Nimmo's Pier, we saw two men painting tar on a currach; one had a splash of paint on his face that looked like a moustache. In the grounds of the university, we cycled in and out between the trees in the garden behind the Old Quadrangle, and took off when someone shouted out a window at us. We were wheeling our bikes along the path on the Zhivago Records side of Shop Street as the shops began to close. The song 'Jeans On' from the Levi's ad was playing as we went past. We cycled out along the stony path near the railway track to Renmore. Some soldiers were doing manoeuvres in the huge field behind the army barracks and were climbing on ropes through the windows of the shell of a house they'd had built for target practice. At one point I thought I heard a siren, like from a fire engine or something, but I couldn't see one anywhere.

When we got to Nyxi's house, her mother made me a roll with ham and Calvita cheese in it, so that I could eat it on the bike on my way home to Taylor's Hill. Before I left, Nyxi disappeared upstairs, then came back down. She walked me to the gate and put her hand into the front pocket of her jeans. When she took it out, her fist was closed around something. She put it into my hand. It was a hand-made leather cross with a tiny thin silver chain so you could wear it around your neck.

When I arrived home, it was almost eight-thirty and I

hoped my father wouldn't be home so I wouldn't get given out to. There was an ambulance parked in the garden, with its two front wheels on the lawn and its back end facing the house. A man in a white coat, a doctor I supposed, was closing the doors of the ambulance, as I left my bike on the gravel and ran up to the front steps of the house. As the ambulance doors were closing, I saw through the space.

My mother was strapped to one of those trolley beds that has collapsible wheels underneath, like in the movies. She was shaking her head from side to side and shouting something I couldn't understand. I tried to open the doors of the ambulance and shouted, 'Mammy, what's wrong? What's happened to you?'

At the sound of my voice, she began to scream out my name, 'Hughie, Hughie, help me, Hughie, they're trying to kill me! Ring the guards, Hughie.'

'Hang on, Mammy, I'm coming!' I screamed, as I gripped both door handles and reefed them open. I felt myself being grabbed around the waist from behind and, as I was pulled and dragged backwards, I saw that both of my mother's arms were bandaged heavily and that the blouse she was wearing wasn't red at all, but white and covered with blood. She must have fallen through glass, I thought.

'Hughie, for Christ's sake, what are you doing?' my father roared, as he wrestled me in through the front door and held me, while the ambulance driver and his assistant closed the doors again and the driver got into the cab and started the engine. The back wheels spun and piles of gravel stones spat up at me and my father as we watched the ambulance drive away. The siren began to bawl as they sped out onto the roadway and into the summer traffic.

'She's a very, very sick lady,' my father said, when he came into my bedroom later that night after I'd put on my pyjamas and had just started to read in bed to help me get to sleep.

'What's wrong with her?' I asked. He pulled out the chair from behind the door, carefully lifted my clothes from it and put them gently on the floor beside my shoes. He carried the chair up to the side of my bed, and it reminded me of the time he'd had a pile of students with him when he'd done his rounds after I'd had the accident with the lawnmower. Only this time he didn't have his white coat on and *I* wasn't sick – Mammy was.

My father looked down at the floor for a short while, then knitted his hands together and rested his arms on his knees. He leaned in towards me and looked up again, his eyes meeting mine. 'Mammy's been very unhappy for a while now, Hughie. She has lots of things going on in her head and they're all mixed up. You know the way people's stomachs get when they've eaten the wrong things, or too much of them, or if they eat something that's bad for them?'

'Yeah.'

'Well, if your head gets full of the wrong things, or too much of some things, then the balance of everything else gets upset. I suppose it's a bit like a car: if you put milk into it, instead of petrol, the engine won't work properly.'

'Can you fix her? Like you saved my foot?'

My father inhaled deeply and said nothing for a little while. 'I suppose some of the reason she's unhappy is because . . . well, because of the way things have been here in The Moorings for a little while now. I know you've seen Mammy and me getting cross with each other sometimes.' I nodded at this. 'Well, sometimes people who used to get on very well don't get on well anymore. I know Mammy has been worried about you going away to boarding school, and wondering if you'll be all right.'

'Yes, I know. But I *will* be all right, I think. I'll try to be good and help Mammy not to be worried.'

'We'll all have to try a bit harder, Hughie. All of us. In lots of different ways, okay?'

'Okay. Can I go and see her in the hospital tomorrow?'

'I don't know, Hughie. It depends on what the doctors think is best for her. We don't want to upset her now, do we?'

'No.' I shook my head.

'She's lost a lot of blood,' he said. 'She needs time and space to recover.'

'I could give her some of *my* blood,' I said. 'Then she'd get better even quicker.'

A sad look passed over my father's face, a bit like the way a cloud shadow runs down a mountain in documentaries on television. He stood up. 'Just get some sleep, Hughie.

Tomorrow I'll ask Mrs Flynn to come over and mind you while I'm at the hospital. We'll manage somehow while Mammy's away.'

'How long will that be?' I asked.

'I don't know. Not long, I hope,' he said, as he stood in the doorway. I thought about who would pay for Mammy's treatment and whether we would have enough money to make sure she got better. I hoped we wouldn't have to sell the house.

'I'm sorry I cost you so much money,' I said.

'Don't worry about money, Hughie. We're fine. Everything will work itself out. Get some sleep!'

'I just want my other mammy back,' I said, as I switched off the bedside lamp.

'The one who gave you up for adoption, is it? Who told you about her, Hughie?'

I'd meant the happy lady who loved Elvis Presley and had all of her own blood.

Chapter 5

Mammy was in hospital for most of the rest of that year. When I came back from Newbridge College for Halloween, I was allowed to visit her every day in the in-patient psychiatric unit. She seemed more like herself by that time, much more so than she'd been when I'd seen her just before my father had driven me up to Kildare for my first term. Then she'd been very strange, slow and careful in her speech and in the way she moved. She was in a room on her own and she sat in a chair by the window while I sat on the bed. The last time we'd been in a hospital, *I* had been the patient. There was a huge window and a door out onto a patio area, but the door was locked and the frame had been painted so that it looked like it hadn't been opened for years. Outside, some patients walked around slowly in a circuit of the patio, stopping sometimes to sit on one of the wooden benches. There was a flowerbed in the middle of the enclosed courtyard, but I didn't like any of the colours.

At Halloween, Mammy and I spoke about school and how I was getting on.

'Are you making lots of new friends? I bet you are,' she said, as we sat in a day room and she had a cup of tea while I drank a mug of milk. Between us was a plate with three Marietta biscuits on it. She kept nudging the plate closer to me, but I wasn't hungry. The marks on her arms had healed, and I hoped that they'd given her a full check-up to make sure that no more blood would leak out. In her room she had a small record-player on the bedside locker and a nurse sat with us while Elvis sang three songs. One was 'Crying In The Chapel'. Then the nurse who'd carried in the record-player carried it out again after unplugging it.

'Do you remember the man who had the record-player on a milk churn, Mammy?' I asked, as the nurse left us, the flex trailing behind her like a tail.

'I do, I do, love. You were only very small then, Hughie. How on earth can you remember back that far?' She smiled a kind of sad smile, but in it I saw part of her old self reappearing.

Nyxi's mother took us to a bonfire on a beach on Halloween night. It was out somewhere past the castle in Oranmore.

'A man who used to be the captain in a submarine lives in that castle,' Nyxi said, pointing out the window at it as we drove by. She had written to me every single day since I'd gone away to boarding school. I needed her letters more than I needed food or water or anything else. The junior dean, Father Mulcahy, distributed the letters every day at lunchtime in the refectory.

There was no post at the weekends, so instead we spoke on the phone. I will never forget pressing Button A and hearing the coins drop down into the black box on the wall beneath the receiver, before the operator said, 'Go ahead now, caller, you're through.' I told Nyxi everything that was happening, in the space of the fifteen minutes I had, and she just listened and barely said a word until just before I had to hang up.

I told her all about the geography teacher who had the hilarious name, Mr P. Freely, and about choir practice, and how everyone stampeded down the stairs between study sessions on Wednesdays and Saturdays when we always got chips for tea. There were fights in the handball alley, when someone had 'claimed' someone else over a perceived insult or transgression, and everyone gathered around. There were legendary figures in the senior classes way out ahead of us in the school, like the tough 'Sparky' Heffernan, who wore blue suede shoes and could beat anyone in the year above him in a scrap, and Ginger Phelan, who played on the wing for the Senior Cup team and who'd landed a drop goal from inside his own half in a match against Clongowes. The school staff provided material for gossip and stories – especially Ma O'Neill, who was in charge of the cleaning staff and who had apparently taken the captain's boots and left them in the church overnight to soak up a miracle the evening before the Senior Cup final in 1970, the year Newbridge had triumphed against Blackrock when absolutely no one had expected them to.

Nyxi wrote *her* news in her letters: 'Jarlath is thinking of doing engineering after the Leaving Cert, and Mammy says he won't get the points unless he "gets the lead out", and stops spending all of his spare time in Lydon House with the crowd from Shantalla, who will be going to jail instead of college when *they* finish school next summer . . .'; 'Two lads with punk hairstyles were expelled from The Bish', and so on.

Every time someone turned on a radio, 'Mull of Kintyre' seemed to be playing. We'd all rush down to the TV room in the basement of Junior House Square on Thursday nights to see *Top of the Pops* between first and second study. I'd never watched it before, and suddenly I was hearing music that was different from anything I'd ever heard in Galway. Punk rock was just starting, and photos in magazines and newspapers showed crowds of boys and girls in London, with safety-pin chains hanging from their noses, connecting with the zips on their leather jackets. People pierced their noses and their ears, and sometimes you'd see photographs of Sid Vicious, lying on his back on a stage clutching a microphone stand, while hundreds of fans were trying to climb up to get at him and the other Pistols through a security cordon of police. It was absolutely mad.

I *did* make some friends – Alan Beechinor, who slept in the bed next to my own in our dorm, which was known as St Albert's Dormitory; and Richard O'Sullivan, who was not a boarder but sat beside me in most classes. There was a huge mix of different personalities and characters among the boys and the staff but, although I managed not to stand out from the crowd, I never really felt that I fitted in.

There was a guy in Senior House called Holt Quinn, who was a couple of years ahead of us. He was American, from Nebraska, and he made a lot of money from other pupils with a card trick in which you had to try to guess which of the three cards was the Queen. He'd shuffle them around and lay them out on a table, or even on the ground, and if you wanted to play, you had to put down your money before you guessed. You could take as long as you liked over making your choice, and he'd let people win early on so they'd bet more and more, before he cleaned them out. I saw one boy from fourth year, called Pluggy Dwyer, lose five pounds once in a single guess. He was so sure he knew where the Queen was; he was absolutely one million percent certain of it. Holt would always let the person who was guessing turn over the card themselves, so you couldn't say he'd changed the card after you'd made your choice.

Dwyer pointed at the card on the left of the three and said, 'It's that one.'

Holt Quinn took a ten-pound note out of his pocket and said, 'I'll pay you double if you're right, and I'll still let you change your mind now if you want.'

Dwyer stuck to his choice and lost. He was absolutely livid with Quinn, but probably angrier with himself. He insisted on having another go, and this time lost ten pounds in an attempt to double up and recoup his losses. Dwyer had a name as a tough guy and could have taken his money back by force if he'd wanted to, but didn't. I wondered why he hadn't.

'It would destroy his reputation forever if he did that,' Nyxi said down the phone line to me from Renmore. As always, she was absolutely right.

One thing I remember very clearly from around that time was how, on my way home on the train to Galway for Halloween, I was sitting opposite an old lady. She was wearing a hat that looked a little like a squirrel. I saw her in my mind's eye running in a wood trying to catch a squirrel. Then I felt a sort of buzzing in my head and I looked back at her. I suddenly thought that I knew the old lady and that she should have been wearing glasses but wasn't. A moment later, as I glanced at her, I remember thinking, I bet she's going to take her glasses out of her handbag and clean them, and then put them back into the bag instead of wearing them. And she did just that – exactly as I'd imagined. It struck me as weird, but it was just another of those funny things that seemed to happen to me every now and again.

*

On my last visit to Mammy at the hospital, before I went back to Newbridge after Halloween, I longed to ask her about my being adopted. As we sat together in her room, the nurse poked her head around the door.

'Just another five minutes, Mrs Mittman. Tea will be served then, all right?' My mother nodded, and I began to make a move across the room to where my coat was drying on the radiator.

'I love you very much, Hughie,' Mammy said. 'No matter what it says anywhere on any file or piece of paper, I'm your mother and you're my son.'

'I know, Mammy,' I replied. She smiled at me as I put on my coat, and we both watched the steam still rising from it along the sleeves.

'Is there anything you'd like to ask me?' she said, as I pulled up the zipper. I considered all of the questions that had been eating away at me for more than two months . . . What was my real name? Where did they get me? Did I have brothers and sisters? How much had they had to pay the nuns for me? Did they know who my 'real' parents were? How old was I when I'd been adopted? Why couldn't they have children of their own? Those questions and a dozen more, which were all variations of the same central question: who the hell was I really?

'Will you be home for Christmas?' I asked, as I heard the footsteps of the nurse and the noise of the tea trolley in the corridor outside.

'Yes, Hughie, I will. Of course I will,' she answered,

with a look of relief and elation and love on her face. 'And once I get home, I'll never leave you again. I promise. And when we're both home at Christmas, we'll talk about everything and not have secrets anymore.'

That was the last time I saw her alive. On 14 November 1977, almost exactly a week before she was due to be allowed home, my mother hanged herself from the curtain rail in her room with the belt of a dressing-gown she'd asked my father to bring in from home. I was called out of religion class to be told of her death. Until that moment I pretty much believed in God. Twenty minutes later, I stopped believing in Him.

The funeral was held three days later. My grandmother and Uncle Seán came from Dublin on the train and stayed with us in The Moorings. My father's parents travelled up from Lismore and they stayed in the Ardilaun Hotel just up the road from us. Granny Daly had had a hip replacement and she was barely able to get up and down the stairs, so Mrs Flynn made up a bed for her in the sitting room. Granny Daly was a tall, dignified lady, and although she was old, she had young eyes that held a hint of mischief in them. She was not afraid of my father – to her he wasn't some hotshot surgeon, he was the man who had made her daughter unhappy. I remember when we were getting ready to go to the funeral, she helped me put on my tie. We stood in the hallway and she made a special knot for it, then wiggled it from left to right so it rested in the middle just over the top button of my shirt. My father came out of the kitchen, buttoning his long black winter coat. He spoke from behind us, so we could see him in the mirror as we faced it while Granny Daly checked my tie one last time.

'Did I mention already that yourself and Seán will be travelling with us in the first car, Mrs Daly?' My grandmother did not answer him right away, but instead stared hard at him using the mirror.

'No, Simon, you *didn't* mention it already. But then there's so much else you never mentioned to me, it hardly matters now, does it?'

The funeral mass was in St Joseph's Church, near the canal. Nyxi and her parents attended. Her father wore his captain's uniform, and they sat on the opposite side of the church to us. Very few people were there at the beginning, but after a while the place began to fill a little. The priest was called Father McGarry and he came down from the altar wearing a black suit and shook hands with each of us. I thought that the mass would be in the church attached to the Jes school on Sea Road, but I think the reason we went to St Joseph's was because my father felt bad that I'd attended their national school and had then gone away for secondary to Newbridge. For all of that concern on his part, I was angry inside that what he cared about most was his own reputation rather than Mammy's death.

I looked over my shoulder just before the mass began,

and the church was only half full. I recognised my old teacher, Peggy Donoghue. I saw Mr Cody and his wife, and the Flynns and Mr Rennick our neighbour, and other people who knew either Mammy or Daddy or both of them. I thought for sure that I would cry, but I didn't, not even when my father and I had sat in the front row of the church on the previous evening at the removal and dozens of people had filed past and shaken my hand saying, 'I'm sorry for your troubles.' Some people I would have expected to be there weren't.

Father McGarry spoke about Mammy, although he'd never met her, and he talked about sickness and of how Jesus is always around when we need Him most, and although He doesn't have a telephone, we can be assured that He's always listening.

I was only twelve and a half, but even *I* knew he was lying. There *was* no God, no big man in the clouds with a beard and apostles and fishing boats and bread and wine and nail marks in His hands and the sign of the cross, just waiting for us to ask for help so that He could come down and be among us. It was all lies, every last bit of it. What kind of a God would let Mammy hang herself from a curtain rail when she'd promised to be home for Christmas? I was there with my tie around my own neck, and she was in a wooden box, not ten feet away from me, with ligature marks from a dressing-gown belt. She was the woman who believed in me and loved me and told me that, once she came home, she would never ever leave me again. She'd promised that very thing just before I'd left her room.

I remembered that time with the nurse and the flex and plug trailing behind her. It hadn't struck me back then as strange that Mammy wasn't allowed to keep the record-player in her room. I had thought that it was because the music might disturb the other patients. Now I knew why the nurse had taken it away. I'd never get the chance to ask Mammy any of the questions I'd been storing up for when she got well again. I'd never know so much that only she could have told me – about where I'd come from and who I really was.

But more than that, and more than probably everything else in my whole life put together, she would never know how much I loved her because I'd never told her. She had done absolutely everything for me since I was born – made sandcastles for me, changed my nappies, packed my lunch, stood up for me against my father whenever she could, and spent as much time with me as she had.

Now she was gone, and I would never wheel the barrow around after her again, or hear her voice through the bathroom door saying, '*Both* feet, Hughie, okay?' I would never be able to come in through the kitchen door again, and smell the scones just out of the oven and be allowed pick raisins from them while they sat steaming on the wire rack on the worktop beside the sink. Who would ever again suggest to me that we should dress up as cowboys and Indians, then follow me down past the greenhouse and crawl on their hands and knees after me into the wigwam, which wasn't big enough for the two of us, so that her feet stuck out under the side? When would I ever again build a house out of the cushions from the settees in the front room?

I knew, too, that she had never let anyone besides me make the cross on top of the soda bread with the knife before it went into the oven. In my head I saw the cross in the wood carved onto the top of her coffin, and I knew, just heartbreakingly, definitely knew, that all of her smiles and words and the things she thought, and her laughter, and the way she rubbed the tip of her nose with the tip of her right index finger, were now in that box with her and would go down into the ground forever and that I would never ever see her again. All of the songs she loved would never make her dance again in the hall while we decorated the Christmas tree. Why?

Father McGarry made a few references to a 'tragic accident', and he also used a word I'd never heard before – 'misadventure'. I didn't understand until much later that these were code-words for what had actually happened. Suicide, apparently, was a sin.

In the churchyard Nyxi came and stood beside me as the prayers were being said, and the small gathering seemed to have been blown together by the wind and the rain. Across the open-mouthed freshly dug grave, I saw Mr and Mrs Cleary from my old school in Terryglass. They still looked exactly the same as they always had.

Mrs Cleary was wearing an outrageously coloured red and purple outfit, which contrasted with the clothes of just about everyone else there.

As the two men with shovels began to fill the grave with clay, I remember thinking that there would have to be some left over after they finished. There were stones in the first shovelful, and as they struck the coffin in quick succession, I thought for one incredible moment that maybe Mammy was knocking to get our attention so that we would let her out. I was about to say something, to shout, 'Stop, stop, Mammy's still alive', but Nyxi took my hand in hers and said in a whisper to me, 'It's only stones, Hughie. Only stones.'

As we left the graveyard, I felt that some people were avoiding making eye contact with me. I also realised that the place where they'd dug Mammy's grave was on the other side of the graveyard wall, just through the gap, where there were only two other graves. I assumed that there wasn't enough room in the main cemetery and that this was the field they'd use next. It all seemed a little strange.

Granny Daly and Uncle Seán stayed for three nights and then, suddenly, the house was empty again, except for my father and me. Most evenings, one of the neighbours dropped in a casserole, or some cold meat slices wrapped in tinfoil. On the Saturday after the funeral, I met Nyxi outside Moons at three in the afternoon, about half an hour before the Christmas lights in Eyre Square and all down Shop Street were turned on by Bridie Flaherty, the mayor.

'I'm so sorry about your mum,' was the first thing Nyxi said.

'I know. So am I, Nyxi. I can't believe she's gone.' Nyxi and I held hands all that afternoon, not in a boyfriend/girlfriend way but because she was my best and, now, my only friend in the whole world. She was the only person I could talk to about what had happened. I had spent every single moment, since being called out of class on the Monday before, trying to find an answer to the only possible question that could be asked: why?

'Sometimes people just aren't thinking right, Hughie. That's what my dad said on our way home from the funeral.'

We were on the windowsill at the top floor of Kenny's bookshop in High Street. All the way up the stairs we'd been looked at disapprovingly by the dozens of writers in the photographs that lined each wall. I recognised only one of the people in them – a man called Michael Gorman, who wore a long, coloured scarf and sometimes visited Mr Rennick next door to us. One day he'd called with a parcel of books for Mr Rennick but he'd been out so he'd left them in our house. He had a kind face and twinkly eyes and huge curly hair. I wondered what kind of people wrote books and why they had all sent black-and-white photographs in identical frames to Mrs Kenny.

'She told me at Halloween that she loved me, and that no

matter what was written in any file or piece of paper anywhere, that *she* was my mother,' I said, looking out into the street to where the evening had started to rain down through the Christmas lights, which were just at our eye level.

'She *was* your mother, Hughie. Didn't she look after you, and buy you new shoes when you needed them, and let you paint your room whatever colour you wanted to?'

'I suppose so,' I replied.

'Well, then, she was definitely your mother.'

'But what about the adoption stuff?'

'What about it, Hughie? We talked all that out on the phone, didn't we?'

'A bit, yeah.'

'Well? None of that matters now. What matters is that she was your mother and she loved you and you loved her.'

'I never told her I loved her,' I said, and I could feel myself starting to cry.

'You don't have to tell grown-ups you love them, Hughie. They know everything. That's why they're allowed to tell us what to do with our lives, and we can't tell them what to do with theirs.'

'So they just hang themselves if they want to and that's it, is it, Nyxi?' I spoke now through a small trickle of salt tears, which seemed to take a detour off my cheek and landed on my lips, instead of just disappearing into the polo-neck of my jumper. I couldn't accept that what had happened had been my mother's choice.

'I'm not saying that, Hughie. What I mean is that even if you didn't say the *actual* words, "I love you, Mam", she still knew that you loved her.'

'My father must have spoken to her about telling me by mistake that I was adopted. *That*'s why she said the thing about "no matter what it says in any piece of paper".'

'Okay. But what does that prove?' Nyxi squeezed my hand, making me look at her.

'Well, it means she knows, or she *knew* that he'd told me I was adopted.'

'So what?'

'So, if she knew *that* and she meant what she said about not having any more secrets and that we'd talk about everything at Christmas, then dot, dot, dot.'

'Then dot, dot, dot what, Hughie?'

'Then she must have changed her mind about talking to me about everything at Christmas and instead she—'

'Oh, Hughie, that's crazy. She didn't change her mind about anything.'

'Except staying alive,' I said quietly. It suddenly struck me that now the only person left who understood the foot thing was Nyxi.

The next day, my father tried to engage me in conversation after Sunday lunch.

'We should talk about this, Hughie.'

'About what?'

'You know . . . about Mammy, and what's happened, and

what we're going to do next. I know you're going back to Newbridge on Tuesday. Father Mulcahy says he'll meet you off the train in Kildare.'

'Okay,' I said, sort of just agreeing rather than asking anything. I wanted *him* to fill in the gaps now in our lives, in our conversations, because I certainly wasn't able to.

'All of this is very difficult for everybody, but particularly for you because you're so young. We need to work out what we're going to do next, how we'll cope during the holidays when you're off and I'm working. Will we get someone to come in to help? All that . . .'

'Okay,' I repeated.

'Are you all right about everything, Hughie?' he asked finally.

I just wanted to scream and to tell him exactly how I felt, but what was the point? *You were the one who insisted on adoption, Deirdre. Not me.*

Chapter 6

I felt like my entire world had collapsed when I returned to Newbridge for the remainder of the term. The things I'd begun to take an interest in – such as the choir practice, and even some of the evenings drifting into the woodwork workshop, where Father Flanagan could be found sculpting religious statues – all that ended abruptly with Mammy's death. The leaves were now on the ground, shrivelling up and withering away, and that was how I felt my heart had ended up as well. The dormitory was smaller than I remembered it. In some strange fashion it was as if the walls had moved while I'd been away, and the whole place was closing in around us and moving inexorably towards a time when we would all be crushed.

I remember standing one day in the corridor outside the classrooms in Junior House and looking out the window to see the gardener lumbering across the courtyard towards a large potted plant, which had been knocked down or blown over. He was an old man, and a bit scary to us because he rarely spoke. I watched as he hunkered down, then used his strong hands to right the ceramic pot. No sooner had he exited the courtyard than the wind caught the plant and it fell over again, spilling more clay. The soil on the tarmac reminded me of the funeral, every detail of that day coming to my mind when least I suspected or wanted it. Things blowing over and being set right, then keeling over again, I thought, in the same way that no matter how much you wished someone wasn't dead, you couldn't change it.

Nyxi wrote with some of her news:

Some lads from the Tech on Father Griffin Road were caught with percussion caps they'd stolen from the IMI factory near the river. These are the bits that fit into the middle of shotgun cartridges and make the explosion. If you put one or two on the ground and drop a rock on them they make an almighty bang. They're everywhere now, everyone has them all over the town, and someone told my mother that a fella from Mary's had lost an eye when one splintered. I don't know if that's true, or maybe it's a story they're telling us to try and scare everyone off using them. I heard that if you bring unused ones into Eglinton Street garda station, they pay 5p for every hundred. I'd say that's a spoof or a trick to get people arrested. The *only other thing that's happened is I've entered the Galway Advertiser Christmas poster competition.*

Lots of love

Nyxi

I looked at the signature and the words written immediately above it. It was the first time she'd signed off in that way. I remembered holding hands with her and wondered if in fact, although we'd both been certain it was a 'just friends' hand-holding, it might indeed have been something else. I wondered if we'd have to get married. Of course we wouldn't – we'd never even kissed. One of the lads in the dorm, 'Clipper' Knox, told us he'd felt a girl up at Funderland on the roller-coaster. All of that stuff was interesting in one way but, in the real world of my own life, I had no time for roller-coasters or what might happen on them. I just wanted Mammy not to be dead. In a way, it doesn't matter what can happen to you or what you might get – or how many things, like feeling girls up, other people might get – when you can't have the one thing you want. I began to wonder if people only really want what they cannot have.

Miss Lawrence, our French teacher, was a small lady with a Northern accent, and nobody messed in her class. She was able to bring an entire class to silence with the merest of glances as she entered the room. I remember that when I returned after the funeral she asked me to stay behind after a lesson.

'Hughie, can I have a word with you, please?' she said, as we stood to leave her classroom. I was sure that she was going to rip me to shreds over my French essay. As the door closed behind the last of the other boys, I stood in front of her desk. I was afraid of what she might say, but at the same time I didn't really care.

'I'm sorry about the essay, Miss—' I began, but she shook her head.

'Don't worry about that, Hughie, we've plenty of time to fix that. Why don't you sit down?'

I sat into the front desk of the classroom and she sat on her chair behind hers.

'I was very, very sorry to hear about your mum, Hughie,' she said, in a voice that seemed different somehow from her normal one. I didn't know what to say in response. In my head I know that, for a moment, I felt angry that someone else was talking about my mother; almost as if my memory of her could become frayed around the edges if other people nibbled away at it by using her name. I didn't say anything at all. 'My own mother died when I was very young, Hughie. I know this is a very difficult time for you and for your father. I just wanted to say that if you need to talk about anything, anything at all, feel free to knock on my door at any time.'

'Thanks, Miss,' was all I could muster in response. We sat there awkwardly, for another short while. I wasn't sure if something else was expected of me. I just wanted to shout at her that I didn't care about *her* mother, so why on earth was she going on about *mine*? But I didn't. I just remained there and stared down at the desk. I don't even remember leaving her room, but of course I must have.

In my mind, most days were an endless series of hurdles to be climbed over. I saw my timetable as an obstacle course to be navigated in order to get to the bits of the day when I would be on my own. The three Fs of the Land War – Fair Rent, Free Sale and Fixity of Tenure – seemed somehow to be the subject matter of every single history lesson. If it wasn't that, maybe the Kitty O'Shea affair was what they were going on about. Geography was all about volcanoes and rainfall in the tundra and other vague, uninteresting things, which seemed so far removed from my own life as to be utterly irrelevant and unnecessary. I hated Irish poetry, and the notion of learning off lines of things I *clearly* didn't understand.

When I cast my mind back to my first term in the new school, before Halloween, before Mammy's death, I saw myself as a different boy altogether. Back then I was a living, breathing twelve-year-old, who wore a grey uniform and was starting to settle in, to adapt. Now I was still in the same uniform, the clothes with the labels Mammy had sewn on so carefully, but it was as if those labels were the only colourful things left, and everything outside me was grey and drab and dreary, and utterly detached from anything I might ever need.

It's hard to explain, but for some reason I began to think about my foot again. For years I'd almost forgotten it, but now it was a front-row item in my mind. I thought about the accident with the lawnmower, and of how my runner and sock, and part of my own skin and bone, had been chopped into little pieces by the blade of the Iverson mower. In my head, I saw myself lying in the narrow passageway at the side of the house, and my toes and sock and shredded canvas sneaker slowly flying back at me through the air. I relived the hospital stay, the pain of my bandaged foot striking the bedpost on the night I'd crawled across the floor of the ward and met Nyxi. But what I remembered most of all about my stay in hospital five years earlier was not the injury itself, but the words I'd gathered up from the air around me when I'd been flat on my back.

'Apparently Mr Dobbin wanted to amputate the whole foot. Of course, himself and Dobbin don't get on at all since . . . It's someone else now apparently'; 'Please do not disturb' . . . We all had to be quiet in the ward. Nyxi hadn't said a word for the first two weeks. I understood 'sssh' and nurses putting a finger to their lips and shushing the tiny children to sleep and reading stories to them, and comforting them when their visitors had gone because the kids were too small to understand why they'd had to leave. I heard again the voices of the boys who'd argued over the Lego set: 'He started it.' Somehow it seemed to me now as if the various snippets of conversation had all been part of some single event, all on the same day perhaps, and all leading to the same thing, or hinting at the direction in which I needed to look. My dreams were suffused with all of the same phrases and voices. I remembered again my father's words, 'You were the one who insisted on adoption, Deirdre. Not me.' I recalled, too, the anger in his face when I'd stepped on the cornflakes on the kitchen floor. 'For fuck's sake, Hughie, do you have to make so much noise?' 'Please do not disturb with cornflakes' – that was the sign my mother said we should get made up in Naughton's hardware shop for 'whenever you're here for breakfast', as she'd said. What had she meant by that? I wondered.

The thing about my foot was that I knew my toes were dead. I mean, they were dead because they'd been sliced off and were now, I don't know, in a bin somewhere in the hospital with all the other bits of people's bodies . . . Or had they perhaps never made it to the hospital but been thrown out in the rubbish bin at The Moorings and now lay in the dump on the Headford Road, being pecked at by thousands of seagulls? Who could say?

I remembered being with my mother once in Galway, shopping, and as we walked along Buttermilk Lane beside Anthony Ryan's menswear, a tinker lady had asked her for 'something for the babba'. It must have been sometime near Christmas, although I can't remember the lights or anything. Anyway, Mammy took some bread and a bottle of milk out of her bag and gave them to the lady. She'd just bought them, moments earlier, in McCambridge's in Shop Street. I'll always remember the lady's voice as she said, 'The blessings of God be on you, ma'am, and a verra hoppa Christmas to you.'

What I wondered about at the time, and since, was the value of words as a currency in human dealings. Were they completely meaningless and worthless, or was there a genuine benefit to my mother in the exchange of words in return for bread and milk? That milk would have been consumed under a tarpaulin tent on the Seamus Quirke Road, instead of being poured over cornflakes in our own house. 'Please do not disturb with cornflakes.' I wondered what it all meant, but I knew there had to be a connection somehow. The only things I had now in which Mammy lived were memories – those moving photographs in my head, where she could still talk and walk and do things, like let me cut the cross on the top of the soda bread before it went into the oven.

My head was filled with dozens of fragments of scenes and conversations – it was a little like being in a shop, when the contents of all of the shelves have been dumped onto the floor and mixed in a heap together, with someone now having the task of separating them all out so that they made sense again. I believed in my heart that there would be, somewhere in my own head, answers to all of the questions I had, if only I could bring myself to look for them in the right places.

There was a boy in the year above me whose name was Cathal 'Chips' Langton. He was well known throughout the school as a tough guy, who could fight with his fists and his feet, and who played rugby for 'the Inters'. We had all of our meals in the 'ref', the refectory, but mostly I remember him at tea-time when the food was something with chips. His tactic was to join the Junior House queue at the back, and then to skip the queue to be fed ahead of most other people, so that he could then line up again for seconds. His method for skipping the queue involved this elaborate game whereby he ducked behind people to conceal himself from the dean or whoever else was supervising at the time. This charade involved plenty of winks at other boys, and pulling at their jumpers, to use them to hide behind as he made his way along the inside of the line, between it and the wall. All the while, as he moved and manoeuvred, he would chuckle and smile and sometimes he'd say, 'Phew,' or wipe his brow with the back of his hand at you, as if to say, 'Weren't we lucky there? I was nearly spotted!'

The reality was that he was a bully, and if you didn't let him get ahead of you in the queue he'd hit you, or if he was caught near you and told to go to the back, he'd give you a look with a slashing motion across his throat as if to say, 'You're dead!' Everyone in Junior House was afraid of him. That included me, of course.

One time, not long before the end of that term, on a Wednesday evening in the refectory, Chips Langton was doing his usual trick of skipping the queue. I know it was a Wednesday because we only got chips on Wednesdays and Saturdays. It definitely wasn't a Saturday because of what happened the very next day.

Anyway, the queue was moving slowly enough, as usual, and I also remember that Father Tumilty was on duty. He was a decent sort and was the assistant junior dean. It began to rain outside, and the drops running down the window had caught my attention, meaning that I had my back to the rest of the room. I sensed a movement at my side but ignored it. Next I felt a sharp jab in my shoulder. When I looked round, Chips Langton had made a point with his knuckles and was drilling into my shoulder to get my attention.

'Hey, Milkman, move your arse. I'm trying to get past here,' he hissed, through his teeth.

'No,' I said, before I'd even realised it.

'What did you say, Milkman?'

I suddenly returned to my real life, from having been transfixed by the rain on the windowpane. I felt part of myself admonishing the other bit of me, which had responded without thinking. I started to correct my insubordination, by preparing to step aside and aid the creature in his pursuit of deep-fried potatoes, but then I stopped. There was something about the way he stood, sneering and expectant, that made me change my mind. I can clearly recall now how the moment seemed to drag on for ages and I was thinking, *He's going to hit you, Hughie*. But

I also remember a part of me, a different part altogether, deciding that I just didn't care. I know it probably sounds stupid now saying these things – as if a person isn't just one being but, rather, a series of clockwork motors all doing different tasks independently of each other, and you can open their chest, like a cupboard, and see the various mechanisms ticking away, all doing and deciding separate things.

'I said no – and my name isn't Milkman, it's Mittman,' I said calmly and defiantly. I sensed the boys around us becoming apprehensive for me as they witnessed this exchange. Chips drew back his right arm, which ended in a fist, and I waited for the blow. It didn't come.

'Langton, go to the end of the queue. Now!' Father Tumilty's voice sounded loud and clear, as he held the arm Chips had drawn back before it could strike me. Chips turned to face the priest and began to make his way back down the line of boys, which now stretched out the refectory doors and into the hall and, no doubt, contained some students who had already wolfed down a portion of chips and were hoping for more. I stood there, frozen, for a few moments, until the enormity of what had happened began to dawn on me. I had faced down a bully from the year above us, and I doubted the matter would end there.

My instincts were correct. Later on, during the same meal, I went up to leave my tray on one of the trolleys, which had small ledges where you stacked the trays of used dishes and cups. Langton came up behind me.

'Milkman, or whatever your name is, you're claimed! Tomorrow at five past eleven, behind the alley.'

I looked up from stacking my tray and I saw from the faces of the other boys that nearly everyone had heard the challenge. The word would have spread all the way through Junior House before the end of second study. I froze again. I looked across the vast dining hall and saw the figure of Father Tumilty with his back to us, talking to one of the kitchen staff. Of course I could approach him and let him know I'd been claimed, and he'd probably buy me some time, but I knew that a delay rather than a reprieve was all it would be. Sooner or later, Chips Langton would come and find me, and the longer I kept him waiting, the worse it would be.

That night in the dorm, after lights out, Alan Beechinor, in the bed beside mine, tackled the issue in a low voice. 'Are you afraid, Hughie?'

I knew there was no point in pretending to be asleep. 'A bit, yeah,' I answered.

'Are you going to turn up?'

I thought about that for a little while before I replied. 'I think so. It's not as if he won't come and find me if I don't.'

'Let him hit you once, then go down, Hughie. That'll be the end of it.'

That was the advice I went to sleep with. To be fair to Alan, it wasn't a bad strategy. He was a decent person and, although we hadn't spoken a lot since I'd come to the school, he was in some of my classes and we frequently shared toothpaste. I guess that counts as friendship in a boarding school.

I barely slept all night and it was the first thing I thought of when I had to get up the next morning. Perhaps that's how people in prison feel on the morning of their execution. The stripes on the towel seemed to move when I hung it on the radiator opposite my bed, and I delayed going down for breakfast as long as I could.

Someone had picked the lock on the recreation room downstairs, which was directly below St Albert's Dormitory, and just before I left to go to breakfast, the whole building seemed to shake from its foundations up to the booming reverberations of 'Whiskey In The Jar' by Thin Lizzy. It took Father Mulcahy most of the song before he found the keys and turned the record-player off. By then, however, people were already playing their air guitars on the stairways and corridors of Junior House, and for three or four minutes everyone was a rock star and all else was forgotten, even by me.

Double Irish. For the first time in my life, I wished the class would never end. When the bell rang, it seemed as if we'd been listening to Miss Duffy for just ten minutes, telling us all about a poet from the Aran Islands. Next up was English with Mr Egan, and I began to wonder if perhaps Hopkins wasn't a complete waste of time. All through the morning, though, my role in the looming tragedy behind the handball alley filled my thoughts and my heart. I wished that Nyxi was there. She'd almost certainly know what to do. But that was the point, really, wasn't it? There were few enough options in front of me. I could say that I probably thought of escaping altogether, out through the wrought-iron gates and into the town and away from it all, but even now I'm pretty certain Nyxi would never have considered that as a possible solution and so, consequently, neither did I.

The whole of Junior House seemed to have turned up to witness the fight. As I approached the crowd, having walked around by the prefabs, I felt the entire mob sense my approach and turn as one to look at me. A pathway opened in the throng and I looked down the space and saw Cathal 'Chips' Langton waiting for me, as I'd seen grooms awaiting their bride at the top of a church aisle in films. *What kind of wedding will this be?* I wondered.

'Milkman, you turned up anyway. I was sure you'd do a runner!' My opponent spoke loudly enough for everyone to hear his jeering remarks.

'It's Mittman,' I said 'M-I-T-T—'

Bang. I felt a surge of pain in the left side of my face. I staggered but did not fall.

'Your name is "Milkman", right? When I say it's Milkman, that's what it is. Spell it now.'

'M-I-T-T-M—' Bang. This time the pain was closer to the front of my face. I watched the fist withdraw and saw him shake it, and noticed there was blood on it. I wondered whether the blood was his or mine.

'Maybe you'd better just say it. Maybe your spelling isn't that good.' With this remark he sniggered, and I heard some others laugh with him.

'My name is Mittman,' I said, as defiantly as I could. There was a slight pause and then I was head-butted full force in the face. I felt the blood pumping from my nose and I looked down onto the ground to where a fairly large blob of it had landed on the side of a paper plane, which had been crushed underfoot for God knows how long. I remember thinking that my blood was far redder than I'd expected. Bright red, like paint, really, and not at all the shade I'd imagined it would be. The last time I'd seen my own blood, it had been mixed up with bits of my runner and part of my foot, so perhaps they had diluted its brightness. Who knows?

This time, however, I did fall. I remember wobbling on my feet for a moment, as the stain of my blood on the paper plane moved back and forth for a second or two, before I collapsed backwards onto the concrete floor of the handball alley. I remember being aware of a change now in the mood of the crowd. While at first they'd been thirsty for blood, it seemed to me that once it had arrived they'd instantly lost their taste for it. I remembered Alan's advice about staying down, but ignored it. I scrabbled around with my hands for a few instants, then began to get to my feet. My head felt as if a bunch of people were inside it, trying to kick their way out. As I finally managed to stand, I felt someone's hand steadying my arm as I teetered a little. Someone said, 'Leave him alone, Chips, he's had enough.' But Chips hadn't finished with me yet.

'I'm going to give you one more chance, Milkman.' I heard his voice but could not really see him, as my eyes were now streaming with bloody tears. 'Just say your name once – "Milkman" – that's all you have to say and this is over, okay?' I sensed fear or at least anxiety in his voice. That would be the end of it, a truce of sorts. If I showed him I knew my place in the animal kingdom, we'd be able to live in peace.

'My name is Mittman,' I slurred, through at least one broken tooth and a mouthful of blood. I waited for a punch that might kill me, but I didn't care.

'You're fucking crazy,' he said, before he turned and the crowd let him leave. It was the last time anyone ever called me 'Milkman'.

Chapter 7

Newbridge is an army town. I'm not really sure what that means, but it's the way it's often described. A short distance away lies the Curragh, its low, rolling plains covered with gorse bushes, the racecourse and a huge army camp, with a lookout tower and thousands of soldiers. There used to be a barracks in the town, too, right in the middle of Newbridge off the main street, but that's gone, long since demolished and replaced by a Gaelic football stadium where Kildare play their home games. I suppose Newbridge is full of army families. Maybe that's what they mean – where the main breadwinner is a soldier in the Curragh Camp, and where generations of fathers have been followed by sons who joined up. Though I couldn't imagine Nyxi or her brothers becoming soldiers. I'm sure they would never have been able, or wanted, to kill someone using a gun.

At the weekends there was study-hall on Saturday night, and also for an hour and a half on Sunday morning after church. Once the study-hall ended at 12.30 p.m., the rest of Sunday was free for the boarders. Some people had visits from their parents, who took them out to lunch in the Keadeen, or maybe off to Naas to smaller, more traditional hotels, where they caught up on all the news from home before being dropped back to school with a few extra pounds of pocket money. No one visited me and, to be honest, I didn't want any visitors. The only person who might have come to see me was my father, and I did not really want to see him. And so, on Sundays at least, my time was my own.

Between returning from the funeral and going home to Galway for Christmas, I had almost a full month back at Newbridge College. Apart from my beating at the hands of Chips Langton, people left me pretty much to my own devices and company. I felt that whatever small connections I'd made in September when I'd first come to the school, I was now drifting back out from some sort of shore, away from them again. I did not want the company of others because I knew that they would never be able to understand how I was feeling. In a few months' time I would be thirteen, and while, to an outside observer, my life was all ahead of me, I felt it to be pretty much over. Mammy was gone and was never coming back.

The sermon at Mass one Sunday was about resurrection. While some of the older boys sniggered at the back of the choir loft, I listened, and tried to believe that some of what I was hearing might be true.

'On the Last Day, when the world ends, we will all be raised up from where we have been buried. Our bodies will be reunited with our souls, and we will all go together to live forever in Heaven with Christ, who Himself was crucified as a man, died, was buried and rose again on the third day.'

I soaked in the words that Father O'Brien, the senior dean, was saying as they came at me through black speakers nailed to the walls along the sides of the church. He stood at the other end of the space, on the marble-stepped altar, speaking through the microphone like a pop singer on a stage. While the congregation below looked at their watches, or shushed children who were restless and eager to be off, I tried to visualise the Last Day. I imagined the grass coverings over the graves in Bushy Park churchyard, where Mammy was buried, rolling back like horizontal venetian blinds. Suddenly, all of the coffins would open and whatever was left of the dead people (skeletons, half-eaten corpses, decayed skulls and broken teeth) would rise up as one congregation, and hover over their former places of rest. As this macabre dance was taking place, the sky would be filled with all of the missing pieces of the various bodies from all over the world. Like a huge throng of people heading to Croke Park on All-Ireland final day, the bits and pieces necessary to reconstruct all the dead people in a particular cemetery or churchyard would take Exit 2, or Exit 9, and make their way to restore to their original forms the dancing, hovering, unfinished bodies. And then, when all the people were finally whole, a mist would descend over the scene and, as the mist divided, the souls would seep back into the corporeal entities they'd been separated from at death.

'Hughie! Hughie!' I felt a hand on my shoulder and opened my eyes. Miss Sheehan, the choirmistress, was standing beside me. We were alone in the choir loft, and the church below us was empty.

'Yes, Miss?' I said.

'You need to get up to the study-hall, Hughie. I think you must have nodded off.'

In the study-hall, I gazed at the rows and rows of schoolboys around me, all engaged in lives I felt had nothing to do with me. I opened a book on the desk and stared down at the type on the pages, my head supported by my two hands, elbows on the desk. The words seemed to move about, to merge and separate, then relax back into some formal order. A fly landed on the head of the boy sitting directly in front of me, Francis Gannon. I watched it for ages, as it explored his hair, then walked across the back of his grey-clad shoulders before jumping off the edge and flying away again up the middle of the room.

I was not able to concentrate on anything that morning, and I wondered if I ever would again. In my mind I kept seeing those dead people dancing, my mother among them. Then I wondered if another woman was out there somewhere, thinking about a child she'd given away, or sold, to the nuns twelve and a half years earlier. It was impossible to believe that everyone would meet up on the Final Day and be reunited with their souls. How could you swallow that story and call yourself a believer, when it was clearly all lies, only designed to make people feel better when their mothers died? There was no God because, if there was, He'd have made my father die instead of Mammy. He'd know I'd be better able to deal with that than I was with this. After all, apparently He knew everything.

In the afternoons, for three or four Sundays in a row, I set off after lunch, changing first into casual clothes, out of my uniform, and walked around exploring the town. Once through the huge school gates, I turned left, passed by the rugby pitches and made my way along the river. I turned up side streets, and wandered aimlessly for hours. From time to time, I had to stop and rest because my foot would begin to ache, but mostly I knew my limits and rested well before it moved from aching to hurting.

What makes one town different from any other? It's hard to say, although the people are probably part of it. I walked through College Park, and all around Roseberry, and even out the road as far as the greyhound track. Sometimes, I'd walk along by the river and throw stones into the water, and listen to the Liffey rushing by.

One Sunday, as I roamed around the town, I passed by a small narrow road I'd never noticed before, although I *had* walked in that area often enough. It was halfway up the town, and in to the right, past the premises of Kelly's Funeral Home. This was on the right-hand side of the main street as you walk up it and away from the bridge. The road was tiny, but at the far end I could see that it opened out into something more. It was about four o'clock in the afternoon and the street lights had already come on. Down behind me, all the way along Main Street, Christmas lights were strung across the town. I made my way along the passage, and found myself in a tiny courtyard with six or seven small cottages in a horseshoe around it. There were Christmas trees in two of the houses, and their lights were switched on.

For a time, I stood with my back to the laneway I'd come through and just looked at those houses. I allowed my gaze to follow them, along their line from left to right and back again, as though I was looking at a series of doll's houses in a toy shop and trying to take in the variety of contents belonging to each.

From one house, a man emerged with a huge dog on a lead, an Alsatian, I think, and he came out through the small garden gate of the house and walked right past me.

'Howya,' the man said, as our eyes met for an instant.

I nodded back in greeting and muttered, 'Hello,' under my breath, so quietly I could barely hear it myself.

After he'd gone past, I listened to the sound of his footsteps fading down the narrow lane behind me. Something inside me lurched, and I felt as though I was on a ship and it had pitched or rolled, and everything had been shunted over to one side. In my mind I heard again the sound of the stones in the first shovelful of clay as it landed on my mother's coffin: I'd thought she was knocking to be let out. I thought about the man with the dog, who had just gone by. He didn't know me, yet he'd greeted me. I thought back over the previous couple of weeks, and I couldn't remember the last time someone had spoken to me. Of course the teachers had addressed the class as a whole each day when we sat in their classrooms, but that was different: that was being taught. It was them doing their jobs and not a situation in which they were speaking directly to me and simply delivering a greeting.

Since the beating I'd endured a few weeks earlier, I was aware that I had gradually become cut off from the rest of the school. Part of it was by my own choice, of course: I didn't play rugby, nor did I want to. Sometimes, on Thursday nights when we crowded into the TV room in the basement to watch *Top of the Pops* between early and late study-hall, I'd watched the faces of my classmates as they sang along with the hits and I'd felt totally isolated from them. Alan Beechinor and Richard O'Sullivan were friendly towards me, but I'd found myself avoiding their company as soon as class was over. I suppose it's funny, or odd in some way, to look back and see how affected I was by that greeting from a stranger, when, by and large, the almost complete lack of human contact I had in my life at the time was mainly self-imposed.

But I *was* affected by his greeting. It was as though his word had been a knitting needle that had pierced the bubble in which I'd resided for some time now, exploding its membrane all around me. The afternoon air was chilling, and I felt it all of a sudden as it hemmed me in where I stood. It was the weirdest of feelings, like being too hot and too cold at the same time but not knowing what to do to make the temperature right. That man's one word – 'Howya' – came back to me like an echo, and I realised that sometimes you need the presence of other people to allow you to understand just how alone you are.

I missed my mother. I wanted some giant hand to swoop down and pick me up and throw me backwards through time into the previous summer, when she'd been alive. I knew that if I could somehow get back there, I'd be able to save her. Instead of seeing her being taken away by an ambulance parked under the monkey puzzle tree, I would distract her so that she'd be busy all the time, too busy to harm herself. Even if she wound up in hospital again after I'd gone back in time, I would stay with her, in her hospital room. I'd carry the record-player in and out from the nurses' station, and together we'd listen to Elvis singing his forty greatest hits over and over again through the speaker fabric on the lid of the device. We would be brought together through 'In The Ghetto', 'Don't Cry Daddy' and 'Guitar Man', and everything else Elvis wanted to sing, for as long as we had the strength to turn the record over and lift the needle onto the track we wanted to hear next. Above all, I would be there when my father arrived with her pink and yellow dressing-gown, and I'd discreetly steal the belt from it and give it to one of the nurses so that Mammy wouldn't be able to hang herself.

My eyes were sore and so was the rest of me, and I felt tired and cold and sad all at the same time, there on the street outside the doll's houses. Slowly, like a pressure cooker lets out its steam, I heard myself scream up at the sky.

It didn't sound like my normal voice, but the sound *did* come from inside me somewhere. I knew I was crying, but I didn't know if the tears were falling outside my body or inside. For all I could tell, they might have been cascading along the inside of my cheeks and spilling down into my heart. I began to shake, with the cold, I suppose, and then I felt myself fall forward onto the stippled tarmac of the public roadway. My legs refused to move, my arms were somehow glued to my sides, and nothing I could think or do seemed to make a blind bit of difference to what was happening to me. Somewhere above me I heard a voice, and I thought it might be Mammy, but I was fairly sure it could not be her. Like a boy frozen inside a cube of ice, I was cold and helpless, but then I knew that someone must have turned the ice tray over and run it under the warm tap, because I felt myself moving, being moved.

'You're fine, you're fine, Hughie,' a voice said. '*Tu es bien, tu es bien*,' was what I heard next. As I opened my eyes, I recognised Miss Lawrence, my French teacher. We were in a small sitting room with an open fireplace. The fire was low but alive, and beside the fireplace was a black basket full of turf. The settee on which I sat was creamy white and soft beneath me. I looked at my hands: they were bleeding a little on the palms, and dotted here and there with pieces of gravel, which had become embedded in them. I had never been in that house or that room before, but I had a feeling I knew where everything was. I somehow knew that between the settee on which I sat and the window behind me there was a doorstop in the shape of a squirrel and that it hadn't been used for years.

Miss Lawrence sat across from me, in an armchair made of the same material as the settee. She wore a red jumper with a yellow giraffe on the front. I could not remember getting from the front of the cottages to the settee: it was as though both events were from completely separate times, and wholly unconnected. I tried to speak, but no words came.

'You're all right now, Hughie,' she said. 'You just got a bit upset, that's all. I saw you from the upstairs window. You must have tripped or something.'

Although I heard every word she spoke, and heard it clearly, it seemed to me as if she was talking about someone else and talking *to* someone else. I tried to nod, to move my eyes to signal some sort of gratitude for my rescue, but nothing came of that intention.

'I heard about the fight,' she said, compassionately. I knew she was looking at my hand and my cuts. 'You've had a rough few weeks lately.' She smiled at me and suddenly she was no longer my French teacher – she was a stranger, another stranger who had reached into my cocoon and who wanted to help or to communicate with me.

All of the room was neatly decorated, tidy and ordered. I noticed a small wooden reindeer on the mantelpiece above the fire. Its antlers pointed up in a V-shape, like the stag on the crest of the school, with its Latin motto: '*Veritas, cur me persequeris?*' – 'Truth, why do you persecute me?' or, as Father O'Brien had once interpreted it for us in a civics class, 'Truth – get off my back.'

None of it made any sense to me – not God, not Mammy's death, not record-players with a speaker in the top, or men with dogs on leads, or flying corpses or cornflakes, or 'Please do not disturb' signs. None of it was what I wanted; nothing any of those things offered was capable of undoing the most awful thing that had ever happened to me.

'Is there anything you need, Hughie?' Miss Lawrence asked me gently. I knew what I needed, but I also knew that nobody could help me get it, because it no longer existed. I just needed my mother back, just that one simple thing. The world could punch me in the face as often as it wanted behind the handball alley; nothing would hurt me ever again, not nicknames, or hurricanes, or county council tarmac – not like this. I wanted to walk down to the end of the town, get into a taxi to Kildare railway station and take the train to Galway.

Once there, I wanted to walk down Shop Street, over O'Brien's Bridge, down Dominick Street past the Atlanta Hotel and round by The Manhattan and into Sea Road past the Small Crane. Then I would walk past Ernie's fruit and veg shop and Mrs Walsh's, and the ivy-clad Jes junior school, with its barbed-wire fence on which one of the Lallys had lost a finger while climbing over to retrieve a football. At the end of Sea Road I would saunter right, along Montpellier Terrace and the Crescent, where brass name-plates signalled the whereabouts of doctors and dentists. Finally I would make my way up through the traffic lights at Nile Lodge, with its pink paint, until I climbed Taylor's Hill to our own house and I would walk through the back door to find my mother baking bread. *That* was all I fucking needed. And I knew it was never going to happen. I'm sorry for using the F-word, but that was exactly how I felt.

And so when Miss Lawrence, my French teacher, in her giraffe jumper, in that lovely sitting room, asked me, in December 1977, whether there was anything I needed, I didn't tell her what I've just told you. What was the point? Instead, I asked if I could use the bathroom, then walked out the front door of her doll's house in that row of doll's houses and went back to the cocoon of my inner world, which, I was beginning to believe, was the only place where I would ever be able to survive.

*

The lights of Christmas were everywhere now. Almost every single house had a tree in its front room, and some people had put lights outside on trees in their gardens. At school, Christmas meant Christmas exams and the Christmas concert, or the 'Civic Concert', as it was known, in which each year was expected to put forward at least one act. I remember going to a meeting, where all of the first-year boarders sat around in the 'rec' room one night after study, trying to think of something to enter on behalf of our year. Eventually it was decided that a short piece, entitled 'The Ref' (as in the refectory), would be written by Patrick Bridey and Shane Costello. They would try to include as many parts as possible, so that anyone who wanted to could be in it. It seemed that the principal action in this piece of theatre would entail the mimicking of members of staff. I had absolutely no intention of getting involved, and nobody pressed me on the matter.

The exam week dragged, and I struggled to remain in the real world, as a succession of question-papers and answer-books were laid before us. Miss Lawrence had never mentioned the incident that had occurred a few weeks earlier, but I knew she was concerned about me, and also that she must have been decent enough not to mention it to anyone else. I wasn't supposed to be outside the school grounds, at any time, without the express permission of the junior dean, Father Mulcahy. I know that if he had found out about my excursions into the town, he would have been very angry.

As the week neared its end, I began to dread the trip home for the Christmas holidays. I was angry with the whole world, and I'm sure it came through in my tone down the telephone line to Nyxi, late on the Saturday night, as I sat on the floor of the phone booth in Junior House, just outside the door of the darkly silent staffroom.

'Don't you miss me even a little bit, Hughie?' she said, with a slightly nervous laugh.

'I suppose so,' I replied lamely, after a pause.

'Well, don't get *too* excited,' she said down the line from Renmore, 'or you'll give yourself a heart attack.' I didn't really know what to say to her but *I* had phoned *her*, so I had to say something.

'What's the atmosphere in town like?' I asked.

'Christmassy,' she replied curtly, to pay me back for the 'I suppose so' comment. I sat with the phone cradled between my ear and my shoulder. Without warning, I was crying. I knew she could hear me.

'Hughie?' she whispered. It was as if she was right there beside me.

'Yeah?' I said, through my tears.

'Everything is going to be fine,' she said. 'Don't you worry.'

But I knew she was wrong. Everything was not going to be fine, and I *was* worried.

On the night before we broke up for the Christmas holidays, the Civic Concert was held in the theatre in

Senior House. It was a grand space, with rows of hard seats that were welded together and could be stacked in piles against the walls when not in use. The whole school was there – teachers, pupils, kitchen staff and even the mysterious school gardener, who lived in a funny little cottage behind the tuck shop and on the edge of the Eller (first year team) pitches. I watched the first half of the show and even found some of it mildly entertaining. The second half was due to end with a performance by a rock band from sixth year called Street Trade. They boasted a savage drummer and a guitarist called Martin Flynn, who could reputedly play the instrument behind his back.

While people milled around the temporary shop at the interval, buying cans of Fanta and bags of Tayto, I left the auditorium and made my way out onto the diving board at the side of Senior House. Beneath me, the Liffey rushed past, in its winter hurry towards the weir beside Junior House where sometimes you'd see huge logs jammed in the rocks for days at a time when there was a flood up.

Christmas concerts are designed to bring people together. For what? To celebrate? To enjoy each other's company? I did not feel part of anything anymore: no grand seating plan waited up there for me, with a chair that had my name written on it. The notion of someone living in the sky, who watched over us all the time and cared about the life of even the tiniest ant, struck me as utterly implausible. Born in a stable in Bethlehem? How did we know if any of that stuff was even true? Even if there *was* someone called Jesus, who had been born in a stable, at least his parents hadn't put him up for adoption to a lady who would go on to hang herself in a psychiatric unit. That much I was sure of.

As I wandered in the darkness across the quadrangle, I could hear the bass guitar notes shaking the windows of the old theatre, as hundreds of schoolboys sang along to a song by Horslips. The night was not cold, but the sky was clear, and now and again I thought I saw a falling star, but it could have been an aeroplane. The story of three men on camels travelling from the east came into my mind, but I wanted to tell them to turn back. I wanted to let them know that there was no God, and that babies in stables aren't much different from babies born anywhere else. There were no miracles, nothing magical to hope for, and there was certainly no great Civic Concert in the sky, where all of the disintegrated concert-goers from down here on earth would be miraculously restored to wholeness on the Last Day.

When I walked behind the back wall of the church, I saw a stained-glass window depicting the Resurrection of Christ. I picked up a rock and flung it through the middle of the scene.

Chapter 8

The lights of Galway came into view in the distance, and the train rocked and rattled its way past a water tower. On my left was the start of the shoreline, with Oranmore Castle standing guard over the small inlet that marks the beginning of Galway Bay. The carriage in which I sat was fairly full of other people going home for Christmas. Opposite me, two old ladies chatted away in Irish. From the bits and pieces I could work out through the heavy Connemara accents, I gathered that they had been shopping in Dublin and had also gone to see someone who had just had a baby. I wondered if they might be from the Aran Islands – the three wedges of rock and sand and criss-cross fields that stand guard at the entrance to the bay and represent the last place to buy milk before America.

Further down the carriage a large family, a mother, father, and four children, would occasionally break into song and each time collapse back into their seats in convulsions of laughter. Perhaps they'd been to the Gaiety Theatre to see the panto starring Maureen Potter. Other people slept while we edged towards my home town, and the entire train seemed to be in the grip of something good and hopeful. Nobody seemed to mind if small children ran up and down the aisle. People had offered their seats to others who were older, and young men leaped to their feet to help even half-pretty young ladies with their luggage, lifting the bags effortlessly onto the overhead racks.

There had been war in Newbridge about the broken window in the church. That morning after the concert, the day we broke up for the holidays, we'd had only two classes after breakfast and then the term ended. The headmaster, Father Cogan, had visited every classroom. We were in the middle of Latin with Father Beirne when the principal arrived. We all stood up, but he waved us back down into our seats with the type of gesture the Romans might have been used to from the emperor on the occasion of a gladiatorial contest.

'Boys [he pronounced it 'buyse'], I am very sorry to have to interrupt your class, but a terrible crime has been committed, and I need everyone's help in solving it. Last night, or early this morning, a person or persons unknown engaged in an act of wanton vandalism and destroyed a stained-glass window in our church by throwing [I remember he said 'trowing'] a rock through it. Now, the gardaí are already involved, and they are investigating the matter, but I know that if Newbridge College boys are to blame they will own up and take full responsibility for their actions. I will be in my office later this morning from a quarter past eleven until twelve noon, and if anyone knows anything about this heinous crime, they can knock on my door and whatever they say will be treated in confidence.'

As the headmaster spoke, I did my very best to look straight ahead and avoided eye contact with anyone else. Father Beirne leaned against the deep windowsill of the classroom and folded his arms in support. It dawned on me that the scene I'd shattered depicted *their* employer. In a way, God was a sort of headmaster for priests, wasn't He? It pained me that I might have hurt Father Beirne's feelings in any way, or that I might have insulted him. He was a gentle man, who taught Latin to people who didn't really want to learn it. He was also responsible for the running of the wonderful school library we had, just beside the theatre. There was no book he wouldn't try to order in if you asked, and he clearly loved the library as if it was his own house. Father Cogan, the headmaster, was a different proposition altogether. The last thing I was going to do was to knock on his door and confess. I knew that I'd be expelled for certain. Now that the gardaí were involved, it would be even worse than that: instead of being sent home I'd probably end up in a prison camp somewhere, eating stale bread and drinking dirty water in a log hut with hundreds of other criminals, while armed guards with Alsatian dogs on leads kept watch outside. No, I could *not* give myself up. I wondered how long it would take for the stained glass to be fixed. As the headmaster left the room, and our last Latin class of the term recommenced, I had a sick feeling deep inside me, as if a big stone was stuck in my stomach.

That morning had passed so slowly that it was like the first reel had jammed in the projector for the Sunday-night picture show, and they couldn't find the next to make the film continue. Every noise, every voice, every footstep in the corridor held the possibility of capture for me, and I sweated coldly until I was safely on the train that evening and on my way across the country. There had been an air of frivolity in the school that day, as cars came and went in the quadrangle and boys were collected by parents and relatives and ferried away down the spaghetti network of roads to hundreds of homes all over Ireland. I hadn't seen my father since the time of the funeral, and we hadn't spoken on the phone or exchanged letters or anything. It felt strange to be going back to Galway, to our 'home', when it was no longer capable of being a real home because the very heart of it had been taken away in an ambulance, and was now buried in the extension to Bushy Park graveyard.

Behind me, down the railway line, lay the debris of my first term in my new school. That debris was contained not only in the coloured smashed glass on the altar of the church, but in lots of other places too – St Albert's

Dormitory, Riozzi's takeaway in the back street, the pavements of College Park, and the tarmac in front of Miss Lawrence's doll's house. It was also there within the confines of my desk in the study-hall, in the faltering decrepitude of my Christmas exam papers – in fact, it was absolutely everywhere that I had been over the weeks since Mammy's death. In a way, I couldn't have cared less if I were caught for my crime of shattering the Resurrection. Wasn't it all a trick anyway, that stuff about people rising from the dead and being put back together again?

The train began to slow down as we passed by Renmore army barracks, and I thought about Nyxi. At least it would be good to see her. Down on Lough Atalia the lights of the train were now mirrored in the water as we raced ourselves into Ceannt station. The noise and scent of Christmas were in the air, as a uniformed railway employee opened the carriage doors with a special key, and the crowd spilled out onto the black-and-white-tiled platform – among them master criminal and fugitive from justice Hughie Mittman.

My father was waiting outside the station in his car. He put my suitcase into the boot and set off on the short journey to Taylor's Hill.

'So. How was Newbridge?' he asked, as we turned left towards the docks after the Great Southern Hotel.

'The town?'

'No, the school. How did you get on? Was everything all right when you went back?'

'Yeah,' I answered, thinking about Chips Langton head-butting me in the face, and the Sunday afternoons I'd spent wandering around in a lonely daze. I sensed my father turning his head to look at me in the passenger seat, but I just stared straight ahead to a naval ship moored in the harbour with Christmas lights strung along its bow.

'Good, good. I knew everything would work out well. I'm glad you're settling in, Hughie.'

Settling in, I thought, as we drove on in silence around by the Spanish Arch and on towards Father Griffin Road. What does that even mean? Is it a process of spreading blankets and pillows on the ground somewhere, then making yourself a little nest in them so that you can sleep? Whatever else I was doing in Newbridge College, I doubted it was covered by the term 'settling in'. We drove up the steep slope of Taylor's Hill and I remembered back to the summer when Nyxi and I had raced each other down to Nile Lodge on our bikes. As if reading my thoughts and being annoyed by them, my father turned again towards me and spoke.

'And how are the lads, Hughie? You're probably part of a bunch of fellas now, who pal around together and share tuck boxes and all that stuff, huh?'

'Not really,' I said sharply, recognising that it was a swipe at Nyxi and my friendship with her.

'Oh, sure it's early days yet,' he said, with a forced chuckle. We swung right and in through the gates of The Moorings. There were no lights on in the house, and when we opened the door, the heat wasn't even on. I knew that if Mammy had been there, things would have been different. Everything would have been different.

Up in my room I unpacked, taking far longer than I needed to. The house felt so empty. It wasn't like Christmas at all, really. In the wardrobe, in the spare room off the back landing, lay an old black suitcase that housed the decorations for the tree. Mammy and I had always carried them down and dressed the tree together. But my father hadn't even bought a tree this year. I wondered whether he even lived here anymore, or if he was away when he could be or maybe slept at the hospital.

'Whenever you're here for breakfast, that is.' I heard again my mother's voice admonishing him all those months ago, and I wondered if it had meant more than just the sum of those words.

I remembered, too, my father's phrase on the night that she'd been taken away in the ambulance. 'Mammy's been very unhappy for a while.' Why had she been so unhappy? I wondered if it had been my fault. After I'd unpacked, and put my clean clothes away in my chest of drawers, and the dirty ones into the laundry basket on the landing, I suddenly wondered who would wash them now that she was gone.

You know how sometimes you start off in one place and end up in another, and you can't remember the journey in between, yet it must have happened? Well, that's what happened after I'd unpacked and thrown my clothes into the laundry basket. I have no recollection whatsoever of deciding to go somewhere else, or of the travel from the landing to there, but I found myself at the other end of the upstairs corridor and in my parents' bedroom. I was standing at the green wardrobe on my mother's side of the room, and I had opened the doors as wide as they could go. All her clothes were still there, her long dresses and her winter coat, and the plastic-covered white dress with pearls in which she'd been married. There, too, were the jumpers and cardigans she'd worn, folded neatly and embedded in the shelves that took up a third of the wardrobe.

I lifted a grey pullover from its place and buried my face in it. At first I thought I might just sneeze and there would be nothing, but I was wrong. Completely wrong. No sneeze came and, as I closed my eyes and let myself go, she was there, right there in my hands. Her scent had soaked into the fabric of the pullover and it reignited as soon as I made contact with it. It's hard to describe, but I'm not talking about perfume she used to wear, or make-up, or that soap she always bought that was purple and came wrapped in fancy design paper. What I mean, really mean, is that I was somehow able to smell *her* – to inhale the scent that was unique to my mother. I know that mothers can sometimes identify their own baby by their clothes alone, by their child's smell. In my case now, it was the same sort of thing – only in reverse. This was a child recognising his mother via a jumper she'd worn months earlier, when she'd been a living, breathing, loving person with all of her own body and blood and whatever it was that set her apart as a unique being. I breathed in as deeply as I could to store her inside me somehow, so that I could call upon her whenever I needed to in the future. I put down the jumper, then picked up the next and breathed and breathed and breathed until I was too tired and too sad to be with her anymore.

When we met on the Saturday, the day before Christmas Eve, Nyxi leaped into my arms, and threw her own around me. 'Oh, Hughie, it's *sooooo* good to see you,' she screamed into my ear in the car park of the cathedral, where I'd been waiting for her to arrive on her Raleigh Chopper. 'Did you miss me?'

'I suppose so,' I said. What I meant was 'Of course I did', but I just couldn't say that, not in that way, first-off after meeting her.

She stepped back from our hug and looked me in the face with a smirk and said, in a sarcastic voice, '"*Suppose* so?" That's not much of a greeting, is it?' I shook my head a little in agreement. 'I may as well go home if that's the best you can do, Hughie,' she said, with a grin.

'Okay, okay, I missed you,' I said, and I meant it and she knew it.

'That's better,' she said, linking my arm. 'Now let's lock the bikes and do a bit of Christmas shopping.'

And so we did. We wandered up and down the town,

exulting in the sights and sounds of Christmas in Galway City. The lights in Shop Street were magical, and there seemed to be no cross faces in the driving seats of the cars inching their way past Powell's at the Four Corners, and down towards Rafferty's music shop and the fishing tackle and shotgun shop, across the road from Colleran's butcher's. This was the butcher Mammy had always used, and I had loved to go into that shop at Christmas time and see the whole turkeys and geese, un-plucked, hanging on the back wall behind the counter, like a parade of feathers. Nyxi and I looked in the door of the shop and I saw sawdust on the floor beneath the feet of the ladies queuing to collect their Christmas-dinner centrepiece. The sight of the hanging birds, though, reminded me of something awful so we continued on our way.

In Kenny's bookshop, Mrs Kenny sat behind the desk on the left of the entrance. She knew absolutely everybody.

'Hello, Hughie, hello, Nyxi,' she said with a smile, and it made us feel all grown-up and important. We climbed the stairs and sat on one of the window ledges, looking down at the crowds of people who hurried by below us in High Street. I told Nyxi about Newbridge; about being 'claimed' by Chips Langton; about falling down crying on the road outside the doll's houses, and Miss Lawrence rescuing me, and about how I ran away instead of using the bathroom. Finally, I told her about the exams and the Civic Concert and shattering the Resurrection with a rock.

'Jesus Christ, Hughie! I can't believe you did that. What

in the world made you do it?' She stared at me with an expression of incredulity.

'I don't know, Nyxi,' I replied, and that was the truth, because I had no idea why I had suddenly taken it upon myself to do such a thing. It made no sense to want simply to damage or destroy something I didn't believe in anymore.

'You weren't drinking, were you, Hughie?' she asked earnestly.

'No, no, nothing like that.'

'Or . . .'

'Or what?' I said.

'Or taking drugs,' she said.

'What?' I was stunned by the suggestion.

'Well,' Nyxi continued, 'you're very close to Dublin up there in Kildare. I looked it up on the map.'

'So?'

'So there's bound to be drugs around if you're near Dublin,' she said. I thought about it a little before I answered. She was probably right – she usually was. But drugs or drink weren't things I'd ever, ever get involved in. I'd read enough about all that in the *Kairos Magazine* they gave out in civics class and religious knowledge. I remembered how every issue seemed to feature the lyrics of 'The Streets Of London' or 'Nowhere Man' to illustrate how easy it was to become a drug addict and to be always looking to *fix* something.

'I swear, Nyxi. I'd never get involved in any of that old rubbish,' I said.

'I'm glad to hear it,' she said. 'I'm not sure I could be your friend if you became a different person. That's what all that does to you, you know?'

'I know,' I said.

We sat there in silence for a little while, thinking about things, and not needing to say anything, and it was as if we were back in the time before – well, before everything had changed.

'They'll expel me if they find out,' I said.

'Then make sure they don't find out,' Nyxi said.

'And how do I do that?'

'Keep your head down, Hughie, and don't do anything else that's stupid.'

It wasn't guaranteed to work, but as a possible solution it was the best I had. Nyxi was the only person in the whole wide world that I knew wouldn't immediately call the gardaí if you told her something like that. Other people wouldn't wait a second before dialling 999 if you told them something of this kind, or about a war crime, or a robbery you'd been involved in, or anything like that.

'Let's go to Glynn's and visit Santa,' Nyxi suggested suddenly, as we sat there in the window of the bookshop. I was surprised at her proposition, because it had been years since either of us had visited Santa's grotto in Glynn's. We had felt ourselves to be too old for that some time back now. And yet the suggestion met with my instant agreement. Nyxi Kirwan is that kind of person: the type who always knows when the right time has come around to do something it might have been out of date to do at some earlier point in your life. I trusted her instinct.

We made our way to Glynn's, climbing the stairs from the gift shop below up to the floor where all of the toys were kept. It was a fantastic toy shop and I bet even someone who was sixteen or seventeen, boy *or* girl, would have been able to find something in there that would make them happy. Nyxi and I were too sophisticated to ask Santa for anything for Christmas, but we stood beside him, one on either side, and had our photo taken with him and his nodding reindeer. I thought it was a very grown-up thing to do.

Later in the afternoon we split up for half an hour to buy each other a present, and then we met up again outside Penneys in Eyre Square before making our way back to the bikes via the riverbank at Wood Quay. As we unlocked them, and prepared to go our separate ways, we exchanged gifts. I had bought Nyxi a chain with a little silver reindeer pendant. I knew she wouldn't wear open-necked stuff because of her scars but I was sure she'd be happy to wear the chain and reindeer under her top because *she*'d know it was there.

'Oh, Hughie!' she exclaimed. 'It's lovely, really lovely.' She handed me a small bag sealed with a piece of Sellotape. It bore the Roches Stores logo. She was giggling as she gave it to me, and I wondered what could be so funny. When I opened the gift, I got the joke. Inside was a Christmas tree decoration: a reindeer.

'Great minds think alike,' she said.

'Fools seldom differ,' I retorted, borrowing the line my maths teacher trotted out regularly when two or more people got the same wrong answer. We hugged again and promised to meet on New Year's Eve in Lydon's for coffee.

'Ring me if you need to talk,' she said, before she pedalled away on her Raleigh Chopper, over the Salmon Weir Bridge in the direction of Renmore.

We bought a tree at the very last minute. My father finally arrived home on Christmas Eve from the hospital, just in time to visit Madden's nurseries before they closed for the holidays. We set the tree up in the sitting room in the corner nearest the front window, and I went upstairs to the spare room and managed somehow to drag the suitcase full of decorations down the stairs.

'I'm not sure there's much point in decorating it, Hughie,' my father said, as he looked in on me to where I was standing on a chair and trying to put some tinsel on the higher branches. 'We'll only be here for a day or two.' On St Stephen's Day we were going to drive down to Lismore in County Waterford to spend a few days with my father's parents.

His voice startled me, not because I hadn't known he was there, but rather because it seemed so cold and empty of feeling. It was as if he was saying that nothing Mammy would have done at Christmas, including decorating the tree, was worth doing now. Later that day, Christmas Eve, the doorbell rang and I ran to answer it. A tall, slim black-haired lady stood there, holding an armful of presents wrapped in green and red paper.

'You must be Hughie,' she said. I just looked at her and tried to remember if I'd ever seen her before. I thought she seemed familiar, but I wasn't sure. Behind me, I heard footsteps as my father came out of the kitchen and joined me in the hall.

'Oh, I see you've already met,' he said, with a nervous laugh. He took some of the presents from the woman, then ushered her into the house and closed the front door behind them with a sort of flick of his foot. I'd never seen him do that before. We all stood in the hall for what seemed a long time, looking from one to the other in silence. My father and the lady exchanged looks, which incorporated little smiles and nods, as if they were speaking to each other but didn't need words – or couldn't find the right ones in front of me.

'Hughie, this is, I would like you to, em, meet Breege. Breege works with me at the hospital sometimes – she's a nurse – and she's going to stay with us here at The Moorings for a couple of nights. Is that okay?'

It was worse than being head-butted in the face by Chips Langton behind the handball alley. I was not able to speak at all, and I couldn't even get the words together *inside* me to say anything. Again, I saw the looks they exchanged, then had to witness the forced cheeriness and bonhomie of them deciding what to do next, whether to get her bag from the car or to light the fire – or could we even chance opening a present each?

'Hughie's done a fantastic job of decorating the tree, haven't you, Hughie?' I just looked at him. 'Why don't you show Breege the living room, Hughie? I'll get the, em, the luggage from the car.'

It struck me that perhaps this lady was one of the reasons that my father hadn't always been home in time for breakfast. Some pieces of the past began to slot together. An hour or two earlier he hadn't wanted me to put the decorations on the tree he hadn't wanted to buy in the first place. Now, he was showing it off to a woman who was going to stay for Christmas. I couldn't understand a thing, and yet in a way I suddenly understood everything. And why wouldn't I? I was almost thirteen years old, after all.

On Christmas Eve I woke up from a nightmare. In the dream, a helicopter was hovering a few feet above the quadrangle in Newbridge, and a storm blew up. The helicopter was pulling a huge plastic sign, which said, 'Elvis Presley: FBI Agent'. The sign was doing fine at first, trailing behind the helicopter as it hovered, and all the boys from Senior House were looking up at it in awe as they made their way across the tarmac for second study-hall. The next thing that happened was the helicopter being blown around by the storm, and the banner becoming tangled in its blades, so much so that they stopped turning. The aircraft flipped over and plummeted to the ground, upside down. Smoke and fire were coming from the engine and the pilot was trapped inside. Holt Quinn offered Pluggy Dwyer ten pounds to go and rescue the pilot, but he wouldn't accept the challenge. So everyone stood around, just waiting for the helicopter to explode. I began to run towards it and, when I did, I saw that Mammy was the pilot and that she was smiling, not trying to undo her safety harness at all. That was when I woke up. My alarm radio showed it was nearly one o'clock. It was Christmas morning; my first Christmas ever without Mammy.

I knew what I had to do – but of course I didn't want to disturb my father and his friend Breege. I crept downstairs, opened the back door, went out to the garage and turned on the light. After a few minutes I found the wigwam and pulled the bamboo poles from the slots they fitted into. As carefully as I could, I folded the tent into a bundle and tied it with three pieces of string to the crossbar of my bike. The lamp on the bike needed two new batteries so I got them from the radio in the kitchen and set off.

I cycled in around Shantalla, past the bakery and down the road to Cahill's Corner, then out past the hospital, the university, and the hockey pitch at Dangan. I saw the dim outline of Chestnut Lane to my right as I cycled past a thatched cottage. I knew that I was nearly there. Ahead of me, the church was painted white, and stood out like a lighthouse.

I parked my bike and carried the wigwam around into

the graveyard. I stepped through the gap in the wall to where the three graves were. I knew Mammy would be cold and so, just like when she used to get into bed with me and read me stories when I was very small, I lay on her grave and unrolled the wigwam so that it covered both of us. I knew that the colours on the tent had originally been put there in her handprints and mine, so it felt as if her hands were around me and my hands were around her, as we lay together that December night while I counted the stars, hoping that I would fall asleep or that she would wake up.

Chapter 9

'Hughie, where the hell have you been? We were worried sick about you!'

This was the greeting I received when I arrived home, tired, cold and wet, on Christmas morning. My father was standing in the middle of the kitchen. Breege's car was still parked at the front near the garage, but there was no sign of her – except, of course, in my father's use of the plural pronoun. There was a sweet smell in the air, like coffee with loads of sugar in it, and I saw from the clock on the wall that it was ten past ten. I stood inside the back door and just stared at him, in his creased corduroy trousers and his Farah-crested shirt, while I drip-dried onto the tiles, between sneezes.

'Well?' he said, waiting for an explanation. I could finally feel the damp on the inside of my jumper now as it seeped through into my top. I followed my father's gaze down the length of my own legs and realised I was still wearing my pyjamas. I had cycled there and back in them and never even noticed.

As my father drummed his fingers impatiently on the worktop, I finally spoke. 'I went to see Mammy.' It was a couple of seconds before it fully dawned on him what I meant. He opened his mouth to say something and then, instead, walked around me and opened the back door and looked out to where my bike was propped against the garage wall. The wigwam was tied to the crossbar with string. Under the frame of the bike, and between the wheels, a pool of water was beginning to gather on the ground.

My father came back around me and looked me up and down. 'You'd better have a warm shower and get some sleep. Breege and I will put on the dinner and wake you up in the afternoon when it's ready. I don't want you to catch pneumonia.'

His voice was neither kind nor angry, but more sort of matter-of-fact, as if he were giving directions to Salthill to a tourist who had stopped his car and rolled down the window to ask. I went upstairs, gathered some clean and dry pyjamas from my room and then went into the main bathroom to shower. I heard voices – my father's and Breege's arguing. I caught snippets of phrases – 'too soon', 'has to grow up', and finally, 'I think I'd better go.' This was followed by footsteps on the stairs in both directions for a few moments and then my father shouted her name beseechingly, in the same way a child who wants more ice-cream would say, 'Pleeease!'

My father woke me that afternoon at around half past two. Instead of having Christmas dinner we had reheated lasagne Mrs Flynn had made. We ate in the living room with our plates on our laps. The lights on the tree suddenly stopped blinking on and off after our lunch and I realised that my father had unplugged them.

'Pack enough clothes for three or four days,' he said, emerging from behind the tree with the plug in his hand. 'We're going to drive to Lismore today instead of waiting until tomorrow.'

We drove to Lismore in near silence. I travelled in the back of the car so that I could lie across the seat and get some more sleep, but also so I wouldn't have to make conversation with my father. I sensed that he was a mix of feelings about everything, and all I really wanted to do was to mark time until the end of the holidays. I woke up at least twice on the journey. Once was in a traffic jam in a town when another car, behind us maybe, repeatedly honked its horn. The second time was when my father called my name as we came into Lismore. I'd always loved that last piece of the trip, when you come round a bend and over a small bridge and, suddenly, there it is: a vast castle rising above the river and the trees, like a fairytale. It is a mix of high castellated walls and wonderful windows. I knew that somewhere inside those walls there must be a room where anyone would be safe. I wished that Nyxi was there with me to see the castle.

The last time I'd seen Granny Mittman was at Mammy's funeral. I didn't really know much about my father's family, or what it had been like for him growing up in Lismore. It is a tiny village, absolutely dominated by the castle, and almost everywhere you go in the village, you can still see it. I knew that famous people, movie stars and singers, would have stayed there – like Fred Astaire. My grandfather's chemist's shop was on the main street.

I remembered how once, some years earlier, we had all come down to Lismore to spend Christmas there. What I recalled from that visit was the sweet smell of mothballs in the room in which I'd slept. I remembered, too, the wonderful display in the window of my grandfather's shop, all red and white with fluffy cotton wool, which looked like snow, and a small green tree in the centre of the scene, hung with yellow snowflakes. In the shop itself, there had been displays of Old Spice sets, and lots of perfume. Behind the counter there were shelves full of old blue glass bottles and jars with the names of medicines written on them. They had heavy, thick glass stoppers that kept the medicine in. I remembered Mammy standing in the middle of the shop, and she had a bottle of perfume in her hand and she sprayed a little bit of it inside one of her wrists, then rubbed her wrists together and sniffed them in turn before offering one to me to smell.

'It's gorgeous, isn't it, Hughie? It smells like Christmas,' she'd said. And I think it did. I know that the perfume she liked most was called Charlie.

This time, however, it was just me and my father who were visiting, and there was a quiet in my grandparents' house that I think had always been there to some degree, but not as much as this time. It was a neat house, with covers on the arms of the armchairs in the front room and two doormats inside the back door in the scullery. They were the only people I'd ever met who had a scullery. Granny Mittman was very different from Granny Daly: she was a small, slight, quiet lady, who seemed to live in the back part of the house where food was prepared and eaten. My grandfather was a tall man with swept-back hair. He wore a long coat and a hat whenever he went outside, but then again, I suppose I only ever saw him during the winter. My father has a sister, but I've never met her and she was never really spoken about. I haven't found out why. I think her name is Margaret, but I'm not absolutely sure about that. Each time we stayed there, I remember how, before dinner, my grandfather would ask Granny Mittman, 'Will you have a sherry, Babs?' I guess that was his pet name for her. They were the only people I knew who drank sherry.

We stayed in Lismore for three nights. There wasn't much for me to do, so I just wandered around the sleepy little village and looked in at shop windows, or threw sticks into the river from the bridge, then rushed to the other side to see them reappear, while the vast, imposing castle looked on in the evening gloom. Nobody mentioned Mammy during all of the time we were there, although her funeral had been only about six weeks earlier. When I'd been asked how school was going, I always said, 'Not too bad,' and that almost always drew a response about 'settling in', 'new friends' and 'getting used to things'. I wondered if everyone spoke about me behind my back and had agreed on a certain number of standard phrases to use whenever the issue of my being in boarding school came up.

On my last morning in Lismore the sun came out, and suddenly it was not like winter at all. A huge patch of light shimmered on the surface of the river then seemed to race across the water and recede into the far bank, as though the earth on the other side of the river was hoovering up the sunlight. It was an extraordinary thing to see, and it made me feel better about everything. I went for a walk through the village. At one point I rounded a corner and found myself facing a stone memorial in a recessed alcove. On the stone were carved the names of local men who had died in the Great War. The names filled up one entire side of the monument. I wondered if there were more names on the other side and as I made my way around to see, the name 'Arthur' popped into my mind. When I got to the back of the monument there were three names written on it and two had the first name 'Arthur'.

*

Back in Galway, I met Nyxi on New Year's Eve and we cycled up to the quarry. It was completely different now: all the rocks were dark and damp, and even the pink house on the way up looked to have changed from the way it had been. It had an unfamiliar aspect to it and I couldn't pinpoint what it was. Nyxi, however, was much more perceptive.

'It's because all of the leaves are gone, Hughie.' And she was right. The vast chestnut tree was now a collection of naked branches, which clutched upwards at the sky, like fingers. As a result we could see the whole of the house for the first time ever. *That* was what the difference was. Before, we had always visited either during summer or in the autumn.

I treasured my time with Nyxi because I knew that, soon enough, the holidays would be over and I probably wouldn't see her until Easter. She had a corner of my heart and I believed it would always belong to her. There was so much I didn't know or understand about people, about myself, yet I wanted to try to find out. At the school I'd felt apart from everybody else, and I wondered how long that might last. Did it mean I'd be on the outside for the rest of my life? I didn't know. I thought about the broken window in the church. What if I was caught and brought to court? Or, worse still, suppose there actually *was* a God and I wasn't punished in this life but, instead, would be when I died? Would someone meet me at the gates of Heaven, and spill the broken pieces of stained glass into their hand, present them to me and point me in the direction of the basement stairs? I didn't know which would be worse, being punished in this world or in the next.

My exam results arrived on the morning of the day I was to return to Newbridge College for the new term. My father called me into the sitting room, and when I got there, he had the envelope in his hand. It had the school crest stamped on the front so we both knew what it was.

'Would you like to open it, Hughie?' he asked. I think he was offering me one of those 'growing-up moments', but I shook my head. He took out the results and scanned them, then handed them to me. I read down through a series of Ds and Es, with one B in English and a couple of scraped Cs in French and geography. The outstanding pillars of failure underpinning the lot were the NGs (No Grades) in religious knowledge and maths. As I read through the list of casualties, I could feel my father's anger growing and growing and growing. When I looked up, he was staring me in the face, waiting for some sort of response. I said absolutely nothing, and I could see that this was driving him bananas. Eventually he broke the silence.

'What the hell is going on, Hughie?' I wasn't sure whether or not an answer was required to this. What was 'going on' was that I was absolutely heartbroken about the death of my mother so I hadn't really bothered about how well or badly I did in the exams. I decided not to answer the question, and hoped that the silence might answer itself. 'Why am I spending all this money on your school fees, Hughie?' he continued. I now felt compelled to speak next or else things would go off the rails altogether.

'Because you wanted me to go to boarding school instead of going down to the Jes to listen to Deep Purple records.' I know I spoke the words, but I've no idea from what deep-down part of me they came. *Bang!* My father punched me on the left side of my face. I guess that was because he's right-handed.

The rest of that day was awful. He had to go to the hospital for a few hours to carry out an operation, after he'd been beeped to let him know that there had been a bad road-traffic accident on the coast road, out near Spiddal. Even with him gone, his anger, and the echo of it, lingered all over the house. It was the first time he had ever hit me, and I wondered if it was to become a regular feature of our relationship, now that Mammy was gone.

It seemed to me that people have many different parts to them – a bit like the postcard carousel in Feeney's shop in Salthill (the place where they gave out huge cones if you got served by the lady with the red hair). Depending on which way you turned the carousel, people got to see a different side of you. Who knows what prompted the carousel to turn? When I thought about people having different parts, I didn't just mean my father, I meant me as well. I had turned from being a normal child into a criminal deviant in a matter of weeks, and who knows where I was destined to end up if I kept going at this rate?

Packing was relatively easy, because Mrs Flynn from next door had come into the house while we'd been away, and had washed and ironed all of my clothes. Part of me wanted to stay on Taylor's Hill, because I feared what might lie in wait for me back at the school. Somehow I believed that indictment for the stained-glass crime was inevitable. What was I going to achieve back there, between potato scallops from Riozzi's takeaway and Latin classes with the gentle Father Beirne? The truth of it was that I had no friends, and no real purpose or aim for the rest of my life. I thought about Mammy reaching the depths of despair, and deciding to harm herself in her search to find a way out of being unhappy. What if it was hereditary, and I began to act or feel like that? I shivered at the thought.

When I'd finished packing, I remembered that I still hadn't put the suitcase of Christmas decorations back in the wardrobe in the spare room. A few days earlier I'd taken them all down, and my father had thrown the tree out into the back garden. He got rid of it in the way he'd always done, by pouring petrol on it from the canister for the lawnmower, then setting it alight. He ignited the tree with the flick of a lighted match with his wrist, in the same way as I remembered Mr Cleary, the teacher in my first school in Terryglass, doing years earlier when he was lighting his pipe.

My father and I had stood there, side by side, as the dry pine needles and branches blazed up into the night sky. The heat from the fire was overpowering for a few seconds, until the branches burned up rapidly and we were left with the smoking carcass of one of Madden's nurseries' 'finest Christmas trees'. As I put the petrol can back in the garage, I caught a glimpse of the lawnmower. I tried to stare it down, but was unable to resist blinking before it did. Even now, when it was asleep in the garage and weighed down by an old carpet, I was still terrified of it. I was aware of a tingling in my bad foot. I hurried out of the garage and bolted the door so that the lawnmower couldn't follow me.

When I was lugging the suitcase up the stairs, it didn't feel any heavier than it had been when I'd carried it down, although it now had the extra weight of the reindeer ornament Nyxi had given me. I wondered what it would be like to own a real reindeer. I'd never had a pet. My father hated cats, and Mammy was always afraid that if we got a dog it would be run over on the road, if it ever got out. Our neighbours on one side, the Flynns, had already lost at least two dogs like that. Maybe we should have got a reindeer.

It was more difficult to get the suitcase back up into the wardrobe than it had been to get it down. If it didn't slide fully along the top shelf, the doors wouldn't close. I tried getting a chair and standing on it, so as to push the suitcase all the way in, but that was no good either. In exasperation, I lifted it down and put it on the bed to see if maybe something had fallen out on one of the sides and was stopping its progress. When it was clear that nothing had been dislodged, I stood up once again on the chair and strained my neck to look into the wardrobe shelf. A plastic folder lay on the back left-hand section, and this had caused the blockage. I leaned forward and reached in as far as I could. With a good bit of difficulty I managed to get my fingertips under the folder and eventually caught a grip of it and extracted it from the far recesses of the wardrobe's upper shelf.

It was a plain black folder, with gold lettering on the front that read, 'Adoption Advice Pack'. Below that, in smaller letters, was written the name 'St Peter's Guild'. I climbed down from the chair, sat on the bed and opened the folder. Inside, there were two plastic pockets. In the left-hand one were two pieces of paper, on which were printed a series of short questions, then long answers of about a paragraph each. One was 'How do I know if my baby is happy?'; another 'When is the right time to tell my child he/she is adopted?' There were other details, about the law and getting birth certificates, and other official stuff. Most of it wasn't interesting at all. In the other pocket was a letter. It was dated 18 September 1966, and was addressed to my parents at our old house in Terryglass:

Dear Mr and Mrs Mittman,

I am pleased to be able to inform you that the Adoption Board of Ireland (Bord Uchtála na h-Éireann) has made a Final Order in the case of your application to adopt a baby through the auspices and offices of St Peter's Guild. You may collect your new baby boy at the Society's residential premises in Carysfort Road in Blackrock, County Dublin during business hours on 28 September 1966. Please telephone the above number and confirm the time of your visit at least forty-eight hours in advance of your arrival.

Yours in Christ,

Sister Concepta

This was extraordinary. Of course I'd known for a few months, ever since I'd overheard my parents through the kitchen window that day, and then my father's slip on the night when Mammy had been taken to hospital. Mammy had hinted at it, too, when we'd last spoken, but this was actual physical proof of the fact. I was holding it in my hands and could trace my fingers over the typed letters, and now I knew beyond all doubt that it was true. I know that may sound a little stupid, but say, for example, I'd questioned my father about it and he denied ever having said I was adopted, or contended that I'd misheard him, I'd never have been able to get beyond that denial and find out one way or the other for sure what the truth was. But this: this was real proof.

It was now absolutely clear in my own mind that I was someone else's child. What made it awful and even sadder was the sudden vexing realisation that the one person with whom I could ever have talked about all this was now dead. Mammy had said at Halloween that we'd all be home at Christmas, and that she'd never leave again, that we would talk about everything and not have any secrets. None of that had been true. Why had she promised me all that, then gone and killed herself? If I'd known that I was never going to see her again, there was so much more I'd have asked her, told her, and wanted her to know. But I'd never get the chance now. She had asked me if I had any questions, and I had wanted to ask her all about the adoption thing, but I didn't because I felt it would only upset her. And now she was gone and I was left with a suitcase full of decorations and a black folder with a few bits of paper that confirmed to me she hadn't even been my mother. None of it seemed right or fair. I thought I was going to cry, but then I didn't. Maybe I've run out of tears, I thought. I'd heard somewhere that the older you get, the less you cry. Maybe I was growing up.

As I prepared to put the folder back up onto the shelf, a small business card fell out. It had on it the name of the Adoption Society – St Peter's Guild – and an address on Fosters Road in Dublin. I put the card back into the folder then pushed it just a little way onto the shelf. I lifted up the suitcase and placed it on top of the folder, then shoved the whole lot back into place. Nobody else would ever know, or care, to go looking for it, but at least *I* would always know where to find it if I needed it.

My father drove me to the railway station. Down through the streets we moved wordlessly, the only sound the slapping of the windscreen wipers as they beat back the rain. In the air between us, inside the car, were the ghosts of so many questions that would never be asked, and of some things that could now never be unsaid. As we passed, there was a woman on the footpath on Sea Road who looked like my father's friend Breege, and might even have been her, but neither of us said anything about that either or the thoughts the sight of her prompted in each of us.

The city had long since forgotten Christmas, and only the very rare trace of it still remained – like the nodding Santa on the back counter of the railway ticket office. My father handed me the ticket and the change, which were passed out to him under the glass. He reached down to lift up my suitcase, but I was slightly quicker and his hand came up empty.

We walked out onto the platform and the train was already there, panting on the tracks with its doors open, like so many wings on a long insect. The noise filled the station and was thrown back at it by the walls and the roof. A railway porter went by, pushing a trolley filled with suitcases. I noticed how a piece of cloth – a scarf maybe – had come out of one of the cases, and was now trailing along behind the trolley, like a tail. I wondered if there had ever been a time when we would both have found that funny at the same time, and have laughed hilariously together, the way I imagined other fathers and sons might sometimes do. I wondered what we had in common now. Our surname maybe – yes, of course, there was always that. I wondered if somewhere down in Waterford, long ago, another boy had been called 'Milkman' by an older child, and had been punched in the face when he'd tried to stand up for himself. What I was sure of now was that I would never know.

We stood on the platform, sharing space and a surname, and not much more than that, I reckoned. My father had things to do and people to see. These were things and people I would never know about, except if they came to visit or to stay at Christmas some year. The only real thing we'd ever had in common was gone, dragged out of this world by a dressing-gown belt around her neck.

You were the one who insisted on adoption, Deirdre, not me.

If she wasn't my mother, then he most certainly wasn't my father.

Chapter 10

In the middle of January, it began to snow. We were making our way in from the Junior House TV room and back up to second study-hall when it began. Tiny flakes at first, barely visible against the night sky, and they floated down, instantly dissolving on our faces, in our hair, and as soon as they touched the ground. But it was a start. As we trudged up the stairs to the study-hall, I wondered if there was more snow to come. There certainly was. By the time we were getting ready for bed that night, there was already a thick mantle of white on the quadrangle, and the car belonging to the study-hall supervisor was almost indistinguishable from its surrounds.

The following morning, we couldn't wait to get out into it after breakfast and before classes began. It's not clear to me how it started, or who was responsible for it, but for about twenty minutes before the bell rang at 9 a.m., the entire quad was alive and bearing witness to probably the biggest snowball fight to have been seen anywhere, ever. It seemed that hundreds of boys were involved, and in essence it was a battle between Senior House and Junior House, with the church as a kind of demarcation point between the opposing sides. Although the seniors were obviously much bigger and stronger than we were, there were far more of us.

Even when Father Cogan arrived out into the middle of the battle, hostilities continued for another couple of minutes. I had joined in with the rest of the crew from Albert's Dormitory to protect the left flank, where mounds of fresh snow were available on the grassy slopes that bordered the river. The whole thing seemed to last for hours, but was probably no longer than about fifteen minutes from start to finish, yet within that short spell I felt for the first time that I was part of something larger. No one notices in a snowball fight whether you have a limp or not. It was a warm, comfortable feeling under the continuing snowfall.

When I'd first returned to Newbridge after Christmas, my dread had been that someone had come forward to the headmaster and named me as the culprit behind the window incident. I waited almost daily for the hand on my shoulder, or the entry into my class of a messenger from Father Cogan's office to say that I was wanted. When nothing of that nature occurred during the first week back, I began to relax a little.

There were other things going on in the school, though, which probably warranted more immediate attention by the authorities. Some boys began to complain about things of theirs going missing: books from desks in the study-hall, small amounts of money they might have had in their bedside lockers, tuck food they'd been keeping in their larger lockers, that sort of thing. It meant that people began to be suspicious of everyone else, and boys could be seen covering up their tuck boxes when others approached, or giving sideways glances of distrust to anyone who seemed more than usually interested in their business.

'Matthew Hegarty says that someone tried to break into the tuck shop,' Alan Beechinor whispered to me as we were brushing our teeth at adjoining sinks one night.

'When?' I asked. 'Do they know who it was?'

He shook his head. 'Could be townies,' he said, his mouth full of toothpasty water, before he spat it into the sink. 'Townies' was the collective term for anyone who didn't attend the school. It was a catch-all label, encompassing boys from the Patrician Secondary School in the centre of town, plus vaguely described sinister gangs of boys who seemed to live on street corners, waiting for the chance to attack anyone in a grey jumper and trousers who went to 'the College'. Apart from that, we heard underground stories about girls who 'had no respect for themselves', and who seemed similarly to lie in wait for innocent souls like ourselves to defile, with their short skirts and French kisses (whatever they were). Among the older boys, there was also talk sometimes of 'French letters', but I never got around to finding out what was written in them.

Apart from the series of thefts, and the massive snowball fight, in January things at Newbridge settled back to normal pretty quickly after Christmas. I didn't play rugby, because of my foot, but there was a lot of talk about the SCT and the JCT (Senior and Junior Cup teams) and their prospects in the upcoming Leinster Schools' Competition at both levels. About two weeks before the first game in the cup, the horrific tradition of 'cup song practice' began. This entailed all of the Junior House years (first, second and third) being hunted down, and driven in a herd, like cattle, into the theatre a couple of times a week by the older boys, in the period between study-hall sessions, to learn and practise the songs to be sung on the terraces at the upcoming cup games. One of the songs was sung to the melody of the chorus of the song, 'Jesus Christ Superstar', and went: '*Neeew-bridge, su-pe-ri-ior – best team in Leinster, we know we are.*'

The other songs weren't much better or worse than that, so the practice continued for half an hour at a time, with fifth- and sixth-year boys patrolling the school for draft-dodgers, then mingling with the mob in the theatre and thumping recalcitrant singers on the shoulder with their fists and thereby 'encouraging' everyone to join in. It was a little similar, I imagined, to the ancient art of press-ganging for the navy.

One evening, when we were all spilling out of the theatre after singing practice, I decided to visit the art room because it was bucketing rain outside. This was the place where arty students could work on projects in their spare time. As always, the scene was being supervised by Father Flanagan, the main art teacher in the school. He was an enormous man, with huge hands and a bald head, which resulted in the nickname 'Cootie'. Father Flanagan also conducted one of the two full choirs that Newbridge College boasted. When I went into the art room, there were only a couple of students there, working on the large woodwork table near the rear. Father Flanagan had his back to me when I entered the room, but he turned around as soon as I closed the door behind me.

'Ah,' he said. 'Mr Mittman. You've come to help me, I presume?' I wasn't sure how to respond to this, so I mumbled something quite incoherently, then began to walk across the room to see what he was doing.

As I approached, I saw that beside him was a large piece of paper, with what looked like a jigsaw outlined on it. Inside the pieces of the jigsaw some words were written, which I couldn't read at first. As I bent down, I saw that the words denoted various colours. 'Crimson', 'blue', 'holly green', 'deep black' were some of the ones I remember. It all seemed a bit strange.

'What do you think, Mr Mittman?' the old priest said.

'I don't know, really,' I replied. 'What's it all about?'

'Stained glass,' he said, whipping away the huge sheet

of paper. Underneath, on the work surface, lay a number of coloured pieces of glass. They were not in any apparent order, but seemed rather to be a scatter of different shapes and sizes. I knew instantly what they related to, and I wondered whether Father Flanagan was able to witness all of the blood draining from my face, as I felt it must surely be doing. I looked down and pretended to be concentrating on the glass, so that I wouldn't have to make eye contact with him. Part of me wanted to confess there and then, but most of me felt compelled to hold back that admission. Nothing was more certain: my expulsion from the school, and a probable criminal prosecution, would follow any such avowal on my part. I picked up one of the larger pieces and turned it this way and that, trying to breathe calmly and regain what little composure I'd been able to muster in the first place.

'Would you like to help me?' he asked.

'Yes, yes, of course,' I stammered.

Father Flanagan looked at his watch as the other occupants of the art room began to clear up their work in order to be on time for second study. 'Well, Mr Mittman, we can make a start on it tomorrow night, then. I'll see you here at seven thirty and I'll show you how to cut glass.'

I just nodded, and began to back away towards the door. It would be a gilt-edged excuse to miss cup song practice, but who knew what other perilous waters it might lead me into? Father Flanagan was shaking his head as he resumed his task, and he said to himself, to the room, to me and to the world, 'If I ever find the blighter who broke that window, I'll wring his bloody neck.'

As I stepped out into the rush-hour mob in the corridor, I involuntarily put a hand to my own neck and imagined the Coot's great hands around it, slowly squeezing the life out of me. Like a dressing-gown belt, I thought.

Back up the stairs we all pounded, until the study-hall was full. I watched the supervisor for a bit, as he watched us while we were supposed to be studying. What a lonely life, I thought, just pacing up and down the aisles between the desks, among schoolboys who didn't really want to be there. In sixth year the boarders had rooms instead of dormitories, and each room was shared between two. I suppose the theory was that they were almost adults, and could therefore be trusted to study by themselves for the Leaving Certificate exams in June.

I wondered whether Father Flanagan suspected me of being the culprit, but I reasoned it out and realised that of course he didn't. I had wandered into his workshop by chance, and he'd merely used my visit as an opportunity to get me to help him. Perhaps he knew about Mammy and all that, and was just trying to help me find my place in the greater scheme of school life. Who knows why he'd asked me to help.

For a change, I actually applied myself to doing my homework, and made great progress with an Irish essay about summer holidays. The thought occurred to me that time would pass much more quickly if I was engaged in trying to read and write and plan further work than if I simply watched the clock. The rest of study that night raced by, and so did the remainder of the week. Perhaps things were starting to look up at last.

My optimism was utterly misplaced. Two incidents occurred on the following Monday – the first Monday in February – which shook me to the absolute core of my being. After breakfast it was the routine for most boarders to go to the study-hall and collect whatever books would be needed for the first three classes. This meant that we, the boarders, didn't need to lug around heavy schoolbags with all of the books for the day in them. Sometimes as we came down, a few boys wouldn't have put on their school ties yet, so they'd dart into the dormitory for them before continuing down the stairs to class. I was putting on my tie, in front of the mirror over the sink, when there was a clamour near the door of the dorm, and the headmaster, the junior dean and the assistant junior dean all arrived into St Albert's.

'Is Neil Martin here?' the junior dean, Father Mulcahy, asked loudly.

'Here,' answered a voice from the opposite side of the dorm to mine. The three Dominican priests in their white robes proceeded around by the radiator at the end, and then I heard Father Cogan's voice.

'Is this your bed, Neil?'

'Yes, Father,' the boy answered.

'Can you open your bedside locker, please, and take

everything out?' This time the speaker was Father Mulcahy.

'Why, Father? What's wrong?' the boy asked.

'Just do it!' snapped the headmaster. As the couple of us on the other side of the dormitory lingered to see what it was all about, the junior dean came around to our side and motioned silently to us to go on down to class. In the distance, below us in the building, an electric bell was heralding the start of first period. We trekked to our classroom, all of us curious as to what could have prompted a raid on one of the boys' lockers by the 'White Dorm Troopers', as they came to be known. It wasn't long before we found out.

The entire ref was abuzz with the news at lunch.

'They found stolen stuff in his locker,' Harry O'Leary informed everyone at the table, as we ate what looked like pork chops accompanied by some sort of yellowy vegetable, which was mashed up and served in scoops.

'What kind of stuff?' Alan asked.

'Books, one or two bracelets . . .' O'Leary continued. I remembered the bracelets I'd seen some lads wearing, chunky silver chains with their own name or the name of their favourite soccer team engraved on the plate bit in the middle. I'd never worn jewellery. The only bracelet I'd ever liked was Mammy's charm bracelet, the one she wore when she and my father went out to a dinner dance sometimes and I had a babysitter.

'They're still looking for the rest of it,' O'Leary concluded.

'So what's happened to him?' another boy asked. I didn't know his name, but he was in the year ahead of us.

'He's been suspended, apparently,' said Harry. It was serious stuff.

The fate of Neil Martin consumed the dinner-, tea- and breakfast-table talk for the rest of the week, displacing the fervour that had begun to grip the school over the upcoming Senior Cup game against Terenure that Thursday in Dublin. There was an air of relief, too, about the place, at the capture of the thief who had been operating for the best part of a month. There is a certain calm and satisfaction that comes when others have been found out in their wrongdoing and we ourselves have not. That feeling floated along behind me, too, like a billowing cape for the rest of the day – but was abruptly terminated at the beginning of second study.

Each of us had an assigned seat in the study-hall, and mine was on the left, exactly four rows from the back of the hall and three desks in. I lifted the lid of the desk to get my geography book, intending to try to learn something about glaciers for the class the following day. There, on top of all of the books and copies, was a small white envelope with my name typed on it in lower-case letters: 'hughie mittman, first year'. I took the envelope in my hand, and glanced around to see if anyone else had noticed what I had found. The supervisor was just about to make his turn, halfway up the hall, so I stuffed the envelope into my trousers pocket and decided to try to time my opening of it for when he was right up at the top of the room.

Apart from Nyxi's, I'd received no letters while at school. There was no postmark or address on this envelope, so it had to have been hand-delivered. I'd heard rumours about secret midnight parties, and even of a trip into the town on weekends to visit coffee shops or pubs. Perhaps it was such an invitation that lay within the envelope in my pocket. The itch to find out burned in my mind for the next forty minutes, until I finally got the opportunity I'd been waiting for. The supervisor was talking to one of the Senior House boys up near the windows at the top of the hall, so I grasped the chance and opened the envelope. Inside was a single small folded piece of paper. I glanced up nervously, then unfolded it. I read and reread what was typed on it a couple of times, until my head began to hurt.

> I know what you did. Leave 5 pounds and this note in the envelope in your desk or I'll tell everybody. 24 hours.

The room began to spin and I looked up. I hurriedly stuffed the note into my pocket and tried to get on with my homework, but I couldn't concentrate on anything. This was the nightmare scenario I thought I had been lucky enough to avoid. It was more than six weeks since I'd broken the window and somehow I thought I'd managed to get away with it. I had begun to help Father Flanagan to make the pieces of stained glass that were needed to repair it. Wasn't that enough? Wasn't it at least a start?

Why had someone waited until now to send me this

note and to threaten to expose my wrongdoing? That was very difficult to explain. Or was it? Perhaps one of the boys who worked in the art room had seen me helping with the stained glass, and figured out that it had been me who'd broken the window. Or had the gardaí taken fingerprints from the rock, and then someone whose father was a garda had found out they were mine and decided to make me pay for my crime? But, if that was true, why hadn't the gardaí themselves just called around and arrested me? Could the note be from an adult? Had Cootie figured it out, and decided to get me to pay for the cost of the repairs as well as helping him in the workshop with the glass? Oh, God, I didn't know what on earth I was going to do.

For the rest of the study session, my mind galloped in lots of different directions. The room seemed to be warm, yet I felt cold, and from time to time I shivered, as if someone had suddenly opened a door to the outside and it had been snowing. I looked around at the faces of my classmates, some intently focused on their work and others fidgeting or clock-watching. I wondered if the person who had sent the letter was there right now in that room, watching me for my reaction when I'd read what they'd written. If they were, then they'd know I was worried to death about what to do next. If they told the headmaster about me now, I'd be expelled – wouldn't I? What if they had no proof, but only suspected I'd thrown the rock through the church window? How could I ever know that? The only way to find out would be to ignore their demand for money and see what happened next. That would be fine if nothing happened, but what if they told everyone about me and if they had proof? Suppose they'd seen me, actually witnessed me throwing the rock? What would I be able to do then? If I denied it, it would be their word against mine. Of course my denial could easily be refuted by dusting the rock for fingerprints, like they did in *Columbo*. Mine would be all over it. I should have worn gloves.

The rest of the study session passed me by altogether, and I was absolutely terrified as to what was about to happen next to me. Back in the dormitory I forgot to take my socks off before I went to bed, and that really wasn't like me at all. I looked at Alan, as he Sellotaped a newspaper cutting to the inside of his wardrobe door. It was the three girls from *Charlie's Angels*. Everybody in Albert's Dorm fancied Farrah Fawcett-Majors.

Could I talk to Alan about the note? I thought about that, but then I realised that the first question anyone would ask if I showed them the note would be 'So, what did you do?' Then I'd have to tell him about smashing the window of the church on the night of the Civic Concert, and was there any guarantee he wouldn't simply run to the junior dean and betray me? Perhaps it had even been him who had written the note in the first place.

That night I barely slept at all. I had a frightening dream, in which I was being led around a courtyard in

India, or somewhere foreign, by a chain. Someone was pulling me along, and the chain was attached to my wrists, which were manacled. The courtyard was full of children. They were way younger than me and had big brown eyes and very shiny black hair. Each time I moved, I shuffled on to face the next child who stood in a line around the perimeter of the yard. As I faced each one, my jailer, whom I couldn't see but who had Father Flanagan's voice, would say, 'Point out the wrongdoer', and each child in turn would raise one or other hand and point at me.

I decided to phone Nyxi. She would know what to do. I rang her home from the payphone in Junior House, instead of going to breakfast the next morning. I had to catch her before she left for school.

'I'm sorry, Hughie,' her mother said, when she heard my voice. 'Nyxi's gone to Sligo with the school hockey team for a couple of days. She's only a sub but at least she might get a game.'

'When will she be back, Mrs Kirwan?' I asked.

'Not till tomorrow, Hughie.'

'Oh,' I said, while my heart sank all the way down to my ankles. Tomorrow would be too late. The note had been absolutely clear about the time limit: '24 hours'. For all I knew, that might run out at the very instant the first study period ended, at half past seven that evening. I replaced the receiver, which felt so heavy now that it was like I was putting down a dumb-bell instead of a Bakelite handset. Nyxi had really been my last chance to find a solution.

The only other person in the whole world I could have spoken to, who would have known what to do, was Mammy. She would have had the answer to all of my questions, and whatever advice she would have given would have been exactly on the button. Mammy was the kind of person who didn't mind if you didn't have ten toes. She wouldn't think ill of you, or love you any less. I couldn't even contemplate ringing my father and asking his advice. I knew he'd be absolutely livid if I told him about the window. He'd lost the plot with me over the Christmas exam results, and he was very busy all the time anyway, saving other people's lives, and also probably trying to figure out what to say to Breege about everything. Anyway, there was no point in telephoning the hospital and asking him what to do: it might disturb him in the middle of an operation, and when he'd go to take the call, perhaps Mr Dobbin would come in to take over from him, and someone would lose their foot when my father could have saved it.

There was nothing else for it: I would just have to pay the money my blackmailer demanded.

Chapter 11

The following day was very difficult for me. I wished that Nyxi had been around to talk to, but this was something I had to face alone. At the eleven o'clock morning break I wandered up the stairs to the study-hall. I sat at my desk for a moment and looked around me at the other empty desks, the straitjackets waiting to be filled. I got up and walked to the top of the room, then stared out the large window at the river. As I gazed down, I saw two magpies alight on a large log that was stuck in the weir, wedged between wet rocks. What was it again? 'One for sorrow, two for joy'? Perhaps the universe was mocking me. Or maybe not, I thought. Maybe answers lay all around us, all of the time, and what we had to do was to look for them in the right places. I thought about the letter, demanding money, then instructing me to leave the note in the envelope so that my blackmailer could retain all of the evidence of his crime. He was cleverer than I was. That was for sure. Or was he?

The events of weeks earlier replayed themselves in my head like an old black-and-white movie. I saw myself behind the church on the night of the Civic Concert, a rock in my hand, then watched in slow motion as it weighed my arm down and swung up like a pendulum. I saw the action of letting go, watched myself watching the glass break and the rock disappearing into the church through the hole it had made. I wanted to hear in my head the splintering of the stained glass but, instead, heard the sharp thud of a stone on the wooden lid of a coffin, within which no one was knocking to be let out.

The bell for next class sounded, somewhere below me in the classroom corridor underneath St Dominic's Dormitory. I looked for the magpies again before I turned, and saw that they were still there. As I left the study-hall, I noticed for the first time ever a small door in an alcove at the top of the stairs. It lay between the supervisor's office and the opaque glass doors that led to the priests' residence.

Throughout the rest of the day, I churned all of the pieces of information I had in my mind. Yes, there was always the possibility that the letter was a hoax, a try-on, someone chancing their arm. But what if that was not the case? I knew that sometimes the fear of things was almost as great as the thing you were afraid of: the sound of lawnmowers in the distance was more than enough to scare me, even when there was no danger. But there was more to all of that than just fear: I knew that too.

The night I'd spent in the graveyard was something I carried with me now, like being able to tie special knots in the Sea Scouts before you'd even been at sea. If I'd stood back at Christmas and thought about what I'd been planning to do – cycling out to Bushy Park in the middle of the night in December, and lying on the ground wrapped in a wigwam – I think most parts of me would have said, 'You're mad, Hughie, wait until the summer.' But I *hadn't* waited. Instead I'd taken the batteries out of the radio and used them to power my lamp, then gone exactly where I wanted to go – to see Mammy and to be with her at Christmas, like I'd always been with her every other Christmas before.

The low hum of hundreds of other boys going about their day in Newbridge College acted like a soundtrack to my thoughts, a comforting drone of normality, as I decided how best to act. Mr Egan had spoken about the theme that ran through Hamlet, the play we were studying: procrastination, the inability of the main character to be decisive, to be the cause of things happening, rather than just waiting for them to occur, then hoping to be able to react appropriately. 'That we would do, we should do when we would.'

When I visited his room, after classes had finished that afternoon, Father Mulcahy was surprised to see me. 'What can I do for you, Hughie?' he asked.

'I know it's not a bank day, Father, but I need some money to buy a gift for my father's birthday.'

He looked up from his desk, and I saw in his face the questions he should have been asking, such as where was I going to buy the gift, and why hadn't I asked for permission to go into the town. But he didn't ask any of those questions. Instead, he seemed happy to find me engaging with the outside world after a long winter. He pulled out the 'Allowance' ledger from a drawer in the desk, and made the necessary entry, before getting out the cash box and opening it with a key. He thumbed through the money held by an elastic band, then pulled out a five-pound note.

'I hope you get something sensible for him,' he said with a smile, as he gave me the money. I put it into the same pocket where I carried the note.

That evening, as first study drew to a close, I raised my hand to ask for permission to leave early to get to the library. The supervisor seemed happy to allow me to do so, even though the practice was to use one's library-visit permission during the second period of study. It seemed to me that everyone was going out of their way to help me get back to some kind of normal balance in my life. At the beginning of the study session I'd put the money in the envelope, and placed it on top of the pile of books so that it would be clearly visible to anyone who opened the desk. As I did so, I remember thinking that perhaps my plan was madness itself. But at least I *had* a plan. That was the difference between the person who had found the note, and the person who had put the money in the envelope almost exactly twenty-four hours later.

Instead of going to the library, I closed the main door of the study-hall after me and stood, motionless, at the top of the Junior House stairs, just around the corner, so that I could not be seen by anyone who might glance through the scratchy glass window in the centre of the doors. After a minute or so had passed, I crouched on my hunkers, then crawled past the door of the study-hall and continued around the landing until I'd gone by the supervisor's office and had reached the alcove. Once there, I reached up and turned the handle as quietly as I could. The door gave a tiny squeak, but to me it sounded like a tree falling in a forest. I waited for the door of the study-hall to be flung open. Nothing happened. I nudged the narrow door open almost fully, then crawled around the base into the confined space at the foot of the stairs that led to the clock tower with its four faces, which told different times. 'The four-faced liar,' Mr Egan, our English teacher, had once called it.

I sat on the bottom stair, waited and listened. Some short time later the exodus from the study-hall began, and the first cohort of escapees clumped down the stairs to temporary freedom. I could hear, or at least thought I could, the progression of differing sounds as the room cleared, from the oldest down to the smallest boys in the school. Finally, the noise of the last group on the stairs receded. This was followed some moments later by the single footsteps of the supervisor who, as usual, went downstairs too, to have tea and biscuits in the refectory on his own and to read the newspaper from cover to cover during the one-hour break between study periods.

At last I was surrounded by total silence. I wondered if my blackmailer would show. I even considered, for a short while, that I was suffering from some kind of delusion and that there wasn't a danger or a threat, and that no envelope lay under the lid of my desk, or that if one did lie there, it was empty.

The stairwell was dark, and I was frightened, unnerved, when a noise seeped down the stairs to me, until I realised it was just the mechanical preliminaries of the clocks beginning to strike eight. They were not all synchronised so the chiming continued for quite some time. I peered out through the door, which was ajar, but was afraid to abandon my hiding place to escape the noise, in case I disturbed my quarry. There was only half an hour left within which he could strike before study resumed.

I had almost given up when I heard steps on the stairs coming up from the landing below outside St Dominic's Dormitory. I wondered if it might be the supervisor returning, but when I saw the grey-clad figure opening the study-hall door and slipping in, I knew that something greater was about to be revealed.

I waited until I heard the door click shut before I came out of the place where I had been for almost an hour. I walked quietly across the landing, and through the glass I saw a boy leaning over my desk. As I watched, I sensed that he was about to turn around and look back the way he'd come in. I stood to the side of the door, out of view in case he did look. A moment later, I looked again and saw the boy closing the lid of my desk with one hand, while the other held up the envelope triumphantly, like a ticket that might admit him to somewhere slightly better. I grabbed the handle of the door and opened it noisily. The boy turned instantly. It was Chips Langton. I remember being surprised to find it was him instead of anyone else. I suppose I don't know what or who I had expected from the situation.

'Mittman, what the fuck are you doing here?' he said defiantly.

'Waiting to meet my blackmailer,' I said.

'I don't know what you mean,' he said, in a voice which was a bit less confident. I walked a little way into the hall, and his hand let my desk lid drop into place. It sounded across the empty space like a pistol shot. I remembered the cowboy outfit I'd got as a present years ago. How I wished I had the comfort now of those heavy pistols. Chips began to walk down the centre aisle of the study-hall in a direct line towards me.

'Give me back my money,' I demanded, as he walked slowly in the space between us.

He held the envelope in his hand and waved it at me. 'This?' he said. 'Is this what you want?'

'Yes,' I said coldly, knowing I was in the driving seat now. I could see fear in his eyes, as he seemed to realise I had outwitted him. He opened the envelope, took out the note and the money, then crumpled up the fiver and threw it across the nearest series of desks.

'Then go and fetch it, you fucking lapdog,' he said, and made a run for the door. I stood in his way. He lowered his head and started to turn sideways to barge his way through, past or around me. I saw in that instant the sum of all that I was. I also sensed the echo of his fear. He was trapped. He'd been afraid to call me 'Milkman'. I was David and he was Goliath, and my broken tooth was no match for his brute force – yet I knew that if I allowed him to get away, I would be right back to where I'd started.

'You're not leaving,' I said. The words stopped him in his charge, and he stood with his face in mine. I could feel his hatred like an impediment between us. My mother was dead yet I was alive, and something about that contrast made me stand my ground.

'So you don't mind if I tell everyone?' he said calmly.

'Tell anyone you like,' I replied.

'They'll expel you,' he said, with a leer.

'No, they won't,' I said. '*You*'re the one who'll be expelled.'

'For what?' he asked.

'For blackmail,' I answered.

'This isn't blackmail,' he retorted. 'I'm selling my silence about it, that's all.'

'About the window? That's not silence, that's blackmail.'

I knew as soon as I'd let go of the words, even before his expression told me he hadn't known at all, that the balance of power in the struggle had now shifted fatally. What an eejit I'd been. Of course he hadn't known: he was just taking a flyer that I'd have something shameful I didn't want revealed. Something made me think of the incident earlier in the week with the White Dorm Troopers. 'How many other people have you done this to?' I asked. 'Apart from myself and Neil Martin.'

I saw from his reaction that I'd found a weak spot. I knew that if I could keep him there until the supervisor returned everything would be out in the open. Chips Langton seemed to understand that too, at precisely the same moment. He lunged for the door, but I threw myself at him and held onto him, like he was a mad cow that was trying to get away. I felt his punches rain down on my face and my body, but I just gripped his pullover and clung to him like he was a life-raft, which I suppose in a way he was.

Suddenly we were on the floor, and struggling in the dust. I felt my head being pushed back as he tried to break free. There was some movement in him now, and I tried to use it to my advantage. I managed somehow to wriggle round, and found myself behind him with my left arm underneath him, holding on, while my right fist grabbed onto the iron leg of one of the desks. I do not know where I got my strength from, but I'd say that a lot of it was pure fear. If he got away, it would be my word against his that anything had ever happened. At all costs I had to keep him in that room, until somebody else arrived from the outside world – someone who could see the truth, and protect me from the harm that this nutcase had wanted to visit upon me. I remembered the fight we'd had behind the alley, when crowds had gathered round us to watch my face being smashed up when I refused to agree that my name was 'Milkman'. I was thinking about my broken tooth, when I felt an excruciating pain in the back of my right hand. Langton had bitten me in an attempt to escape.

I tried to regain my grip but could not, as he turned and twisted with a new energy. I held onto his jumper for as long as I could, but he got to his feet and I was now prone on the floor, just looking up at him. I tried to get up, but only managed to achieve a sitting position. I saw in his eyes what was going to happen next, just a split-second before it actually did. He lifted his left foot to kick me full force in the face. I heard the door open.

'Langton, Mittman,' the headmaster's voice bellowed. 'My office. Now!'

We'd both had to turn out our pockets and we stood there, like a pair of Russian gulag workers caught stealing bread.

'Without the envelope, I can't tell which of you is lying about the blackmail thing,' Father Cogan said, waving the note around, at the end of our trial in his office. Chips claimed that he had found the note in *his* desk and had lain in wait to apprehend the person who'd sent it. I made my case about taking out the fiver from my allowance that same day but I had no way of proving that it was the same note. Chips said he'd left the envelope in his desk with the money in it, and had surprised *me* in the act of taking it out of *his* desk just before Father Cogan had discovered us fighting on the floor of the study-hall. 'One of you is as bad as the other,' the principal said. 'It's impossible to know who did what. Have either of you anything more to say?'

'No, Father,' I said. I wondered how Chips had got rid of the envelope between here and the study-hall. He must have dropped it somewhere. Perhaps I'd be able to find it if I went straight back the way we'd come, as soon as we got out of the office.

'Cathal?' the headmaster asked. I'd forgotten that 'Chips' was not his real name. 'You're a year senior to Hughie. I'd have expected more from you, to be honest. Have you anything to say before I decide what to do with the pair of ye?' Chips looked down at the carpet and shook his head. I didn't expect him to say anything, but then he spoke.

'I can't keep it to myself any more, Father.' I looked up at the headmaster and he gazed at my blackmailer.

'You can't keep what to yourself?' the headmaster asked. Cathal Langton shook his head from side to side silently, as if wrestling with inner demons who were in a battle with forces that were compelling him to do the right thing. 'What is it, Cathal? Out with it now or—' He didn't get to finish the sentence.

'We had a fight before Christmas, Father. Myself and Hughie, and you see—'

'Yes, yes,' said the headmaster, impatiently. 'I know all about that. I was told a few days later. But what has that got to do with all of *this*?' he raged, holding up the blackmail note in one hand and the now-straightened fiver in the other.

I saw over the headmaster's shoulder that, outside, a car had driven into the quadrangle and was now turning opposite the river. Its reversing lights came on and the vehicle began slowly to manoeuvre around to go back the way it had come. For a moment, the headlights penetrated the window behind Father Cogan, and made him look like a Christ figure surrounded by light. Cathal 'Chips' Langton continued.

'I know that I was to blame for the fight, Father and I tried to make it up with him afterwards, two or three times.' I glanced at him, but he continued to look down at the carpet. 'Then, just before we went home for Christmas, the day before the Civic, I'm nearly sure, I met him outside the recreation rooms and I offered to shake his hand. "Let bygones be bygones," I said to him, but he wouldn't.'

I couldn't believe this – the sheer brass neck of a liar! It was as if someone was playing a trick or something. I had to do something to stop it.

'That's not true,' I shouted. 'None of it is true!' The headmaster put up one hand like a traffic-duty garda.

'You'll get your chance in a moment if you've something to say.' He nodded his assent to Chips to continue.

'Well, well . . . the next thing after he refused to shake my hand, he said to me, right up close, "I'm going to do something cat-melodeon wrong and say you did it and everyone will believe me. Because you broke my tooth, I'm going to break something else and blame you for that as well." That's what he said, Father, God's honest truth. And somebody broke the window in the church. I knew that if I didn't pay the money, he'd say it was I done it.'

It was probably the longest speech that boy was ever going to make in his whole life, and he wasn't going to fall into the Shakespearian trap of not acting in time. I thought the Oscars people might burst into the room at any moment with his award. I knew that I would never have used the expression 'cat-melodeon', and hoped that this would show him up for sitting on the throne of untruth, for unleashing his legacy of lies. As I turned to open my defence to the white-robed arbiter of the dispute, Father Cogan spoke first.

'Hughie, *did* you break the window in the church?'

It was a simple request for information, now out there in the room like a spear through everything Chips had just said. It was a spear that was pointed straight at me, not at anyone else. I knew that this was the time to tell one simple lie and to move on to the real issues, which lay all around me. If I told this one fib, I would then be able to find the whole truth. My life would be saved. I knew that the right thing to do there and then was to do the wrong thing.

'Yes,' I answered, looking the headmaster square in the eye. He breathed in deeply and then passed sentence on both of us.

'Cathal, you're suspended for one week for fighting in the study-hall. Hughie, I'm expelling you from Newbridge College. I'll telephone your father tonight and ask him to collect you tomorrow.' He then handed *my* fiver to my blackmailer and put the note down on his desk. He sat down and opened a file in front of him, indicating that the meeting was over. My only thought was to retrace my steps now, and try to find the envelope. It was my final hope. As we left the office together, I turned right to make for the study-hall. Chips Langton turned left towards the exit into the quadrangle.

'Hey!' he said, as we separated. I turned round and he bared his teeth in an evil smile and pushed a white blob of chewed paper to the front of his mouth with his tongue. He closed his mouth and swallowed, then waved at me and was gone.

Chapter 12

I thought I would feel something different from what I actually felt. That sounds silly, perhaps, but when I opened the box containing the jigsaw pieces of the previous twenty-four hours or so, and put them all together, they made something quite different from what I'd been expecting. There was the life I used to have (the one with wigwams and soda bread in it) and the life I had now, and somehow they had got mixed up.

Alan and I had gone down to the toilets at the bottom of the dormitory after lights out, and we'd discussed everything that had happened.

'Langton's going to pay for all of this,' Alan said. 'I'll make sure of that. I'll get some of the other lads together, and we'll make him confess the truth, and you'll be allowed back.'

'No,' I said simply. 'Don't do anything.'

'Why?' he asked. 'He's the one who blackmailed *you*, and probably Neil, and who knows how many others. You didn't do anything wrong.'

'Apart from the window,' I said, with a grin.

'Okay, yeah, well, apart from that,' he agreed reluctantly. We stood there, looking out the window of the dormitory toilets, at the stars in the sky over the school, which was asleep.

Somewhere in the distance a goods train rattled past the town. And somehow I knew, at that exact moment, there was no point in talking about the envelope being eaten, or whether there was something to be done to try to undo what had happened. I felt a warm fuzz in my head, which wasn't in any way diluted by the cold winter night air. I wondered about other things, bigger things, and saw a falling star, and thought about a lady hanging in a room in a psychiatric hospital, and I heard the whirring of the pedals as Nyxi and I freewheeled down from the quarry on our bikes. I thought I'd be angry, or sad, but somehow I was neither of those things. Before I went to sleep, on my last night in Newbridge College, I thought about the river and the clock tower and the odd orange light of the streetlamps, and the kindness of my French teacher, and the suitcase of Christmas decorations, which just wouldn't go back into the wardrobe no matter how hard I tried.

The following morning, I packed all of my clothes and personal effects (a poster of Elvis Presley with a tear up the middle, and the leather cross on a chain Nyxi had given me the previous summer), and jammed everything into the suitcase Father Mulcahy had retrieved for me from the luggage room in the basement. I had gone with him to point it out, and had been astonished to enter the vast underground space filled with hundreds of suitcases and bags and boxes. It was like something I'd seen once in a black-and-white film about the war.

There was an odd silence in the school that morning, as if someone was sick and everyone else was tiptoeing around so as not to wake them up. Mr Egan passed us by in the corridor of Junior House on his way to class, as we came back up with the suitcase.

'Keep up the reading, Hughie,' he said, with a short salute. It was a goodbye that was couched in other words, but behind it I felt he was also saying he didn't think I was a bad person. I wondered if I *was* bad. What was the real measure of that?

Up in the study-hall, I cleared out my desk, and put all of the books and copies into two heavy plastic bags, which each bore different advertising insignia. One was for Gola football boots, the other from Moons in Galway. The bags had been given to me by one of the girls in the kitchens when I'd asked earlier that morning. And yet they seemed somehow to be a sign of something more than they were. I'd been wearing Gola runners when I lost my two toes, and Moons department store was where Mammy always bought her clothes. How had those two particular bags found their way to a school on the other side of the country? How had they been given randomly to me, when I needed bags to carry my books for my journey back to Galway? It was strange, yet so ordinary a thing that maybe I'd made too much of it, when there was nothing much *to* make of it.

Something made me think of the three-card trick that invited people to lose money on the turn of a card: 'Can you find the Queen?' I thought about three people, all the same height and dressed identically, laid out, face down, on the grassy bank that overlooked the river at the edge of the quadrangle. Supposing you had to choose one to turn over, and had to nominate in advance which you thought was a particular person. How would that be? They all looked the same when they were lying face down, the people and the playing cards.

I looked out the window of the empty study-hall and down into the quadrangle. Boys were walking in all directions on their way to their next class, and suddenly one of them stopped, looked up at me and met my gaze. It was Holt Quinn, the boy from Nebraska who did the card trick. We were connected for just a split second, and I looked away first. I thought it was another coincidence, then wondered what it was called when coincidences coincided.

When everything was packed, I carried my case down to the office in the reception part of the priory. All visitors to the school were directed to report there, according to the sign on the way into the car park. The girls in the reception room had the radio on and were having a tea break. I heard the melody and lines of a song by ELO called 'Mr Blue Sky'. It was a song full of feel-good animation, like a rollercoaster carrying people along on a path to something better than they already had. A part of me stood back from the suitcase and the bags on the tiled floor, and could not understand how most of me felt. Why wasn't I raging with upset, or crying about the injustice of it all and saying how life wasn't fair? I thought about Granny Daly and Uncle Seán. How were they coping with the loss of their daughter and sister respectively? That was something that had never even entered my head before then, in the few months since Mammy's death. I decided to leave my suitcase and belongings there, just inside the door of the priory, and to take one last walk around the school before my father arrived to collect me.

Outside it was chilly, but the sunshine was trying to break through. I was still dressed in my school uniform, although to all intents and purposes I was no longer obliged to wear it. I remembered the scene from *The Sound of Music* when the children are all lined up in the hall in uniforms and responding to different whistles. They lived in a film, but of course they were just actors. Outside the film they were other people entirely. I had heard somewhere that there was a real Von Trapp family, on whose lives the film story was based. They probably couldn't sing, which was why they'd been replaced by Julie Andrews and Christopher

Plummer, and everyone else, and the nuns in the convent who were supposed to be Austrian but who spoke and sang in English. I remembered the bit near the end, when the Von Trapps were all hiding in the graveyard in the grounds of the convent, and the Germans were looking for them.

Behind the handball alley, on a small island, was a garden where pupils of Newbridge College were not allowed to walk. I went onto the island over the concrete bridge and walked around to the other side where a small channel had been diverted from the Liffey to power a mill wheel. There, on the bank of that separate body of water, lay an ancient burial ground for priests from the Dominican community. Some of the headstones were no longer upright, but leaned down to the ground, like people doubled over with laughter.

I felt movement beneath my feet, as though I were standing on a railway bridge when a train was passing underneath on the tracks below. The shiver of the earth ceased abruptly, and I wondered if it had happened at all. I turned and began making my way back towards the science labs. They were housed in prefabs at the outer limit of the school grounds, just adjacent to the gardener's cottage and the exit that gave onto the back lane down to Murtagh's shop. I heard the sound of an old wooden sash window being opened, its frame shuddering in the act. When I looked up, I saw that the window that had been opened was the one in the toilets of Albert's Dormitory – the one that Alan Beechinor and I had looked out of the previous night. As I continued to look up, two heads appeared but I could not make out whose they were. I thought for a moment that the pair resembled myself and Alan, but that was impossible, of course. Probably the cleaners, I thought, as all of the lads were in class.

In a hedge beside the Eller pitches, a pink ribbon had become entangled. It blew out from time to time in the breeze and acted like a warning as it caught the eye. It flapped at me, as I chose my steps carefully to avoid a puddle on the rough track around the rugby field. It hadn't rained in days, so I wondered where the water had come from. I reached out a hand, caught the ribbon and pulled it taut. In faint blue lettering I saw the words, 'Happy Birthday'. As I let go of it, I remembered that my own birthday was only a couple of weeks away, out ahead of me, like a registered letter waiting to be collected. It would be my thirteenth birthday, and the first Mammy would miss. I didn't even know if there would be a cake this year. The puddle seemed for a moment to change colour from dirty brown to red, as I watched the ribbon fall back into place and wondered who had lost it and whether they'd ever used it to tie up their hair instead of to hold on their birthday. Perhaps it had once been tied around a cake.

I passed by the green galvanised shed where the gardener kept the tractor and the huge attachment that could cut the grass on the playing fields. The shed was locked with two padlocks, which I found a little strange. Maybe he was afraid that the tractor might try to escape.

I took the long way round the rugby pitches, and imagined the thousands of boys who had played games on that ground since the school had opened in the late 1800s. There would have been hundreds of games played, I reckoned – with losses, wins, draws, fights, injuries, laughter, cheers, and good and awful times of high drama, and low points where the hearts of an entire team had been broken when the other side scored in the last minute to win. If no one ever grew old, or if every pitch was a different floor, like in a hotel, and if time worked differently, then could someone, like me, walking by, see all of the hundreds of players at the same time, all reprising their own matches endlessly, like mountains of vinyl records on record-players, with all of their needles constantly returning to the beginning of the hundreds of different songs?

It was an amazing proposition, the idea that everyone just went on and on and on doing the same thing endlessly, exactly the same thing. Was there a room somewhere else where someone pretended to be Hughie Mittman, and was fated to remain twelve years old forever, peeping round the corner of the door that led to the clock tower, or remembering jamming an Iverson Rotary Sickle Mower, US Patent 2165551 1938 into the passageway at the side of a house?

As I continued my course back to the main part of the school, I heard a baby crying on the other side of the dense hedge. When I reached the traffic gate near the tennis courts some moments later, I fully expected to see a mother with a pram emerging from the footpath outside the school. People from the town could freely access that part of the grounds and walk through to the main entrance as a shortcut or, of course, to visit the church. When I got to the end of the path and looked, no one was there in either direction.

My last port of call on my farewell tour of the school was the church. I was drawn to revisit the scene of my crime, and I wondered whether or not that was a common impulse among my fellow criminals. I remembered that over Christmas I had been afraid that, if my act of destruction was ever connected to me, I might be interviewed by the gardaí or even end up in court and possibly in prison. All of those concerns seemed utterly childish and unrealistic to me now, yet I could not tell you exactly why that was. Was it because when I'd confessed, the night before, my punishment had been proportionate? Or was it that my own perception of my wrongdoing had been exaggerated?

At any rate, it did not seem to matter much now. I walked past the large brown board that had been tacked outside, over the disfigurement I had caused to the Resurrection scene. It would keep the elements out, or prevent the damage getting any worse. I thought I would feel some kind of remorse or shame, but instead I heard in my head the song from the office radio, and my step was light instead of heavy. I knew that in a short while my father would arrive, and that all of that other life I had (and, in being at Newbridge, had somehow run away from) would be around me once again.

I made my way into the church. No one else was there, not even the one or two older parishioners who, any time I'd been there before, seemed to be permanently present at one of the side altars, praying or lighting candles and putting coins in the brass boxes. A statue of St Dominic stood on a low plinth in a side altar and, as I passed by it, then drew level with the confessional boxes, I realised that I had neither made my confession nor taken communion since Mammy's funeral. I was a bit surprised to make that discovery there and then, as if I'd walked into a bookshop and suddenly remembered that I had stopped reading a long time ago. I stretched out my right hand and touched the corner of each pew as I passed by, as if I were blind and could only make my way by touch. As I walked I *did* close my eyes and continued like that, slowly and blindly by touch, until I reached the altar and there were no more pews. I opened my eyes.

The broken glass had, of course, all been swept up a day or so after I'd thrown the rock. I saw that although the board outside the window was pretty square or rectangular, the damage I'd caused was not square, or even, or symmetrical in any way. In fact it was difficult to see how a single blow to any other part of the scene with a rock could have caused any more destruction and ruination. At least eight separate panels of stained glass, and all of them different colours, had been either seriously impaired or totally obliterated. As I stared even more closely, I saw others now, which were further up and just ever so slightly cracked. They, too, would probably have to be replaced, and it was difficult to see how such work would or could leave other innocent panels completely unaffected. I saw now the full and catastrophic effect of my act: the destruction of colour and the shattering of a scene on which the artist had worked for months or years, visualising, interpreting, then bringing the Resurrection to life. Whatever I believed in, I had had no right to destroy that meticulous piece of workmanship, which had been made by an artist and shared with everyone who cared enough to look upon it.

I became aware of the slightest of breezes around me, as if someone had opened a door. I glanced around, but no one was there. As I directed my gaze back towards the altar, I saw that the remaining candles on the stand at the side altar were guttering to extinction. They all went out at the same time. I expected to see smoke rise from their corpses, but no smoke appeared. I was amazed by this.

Maybe they're special non-smoky candles, I thought. There was a noise now in the air, like ice cracking under children's feet, or the crunch of a powdery kind of snow, or maybe more akin to the crinkle of a cellophane wrapper on an Easter hamper. I turned as slowly as I could, and saw that the sound was coming from the stained-glass window. In the gaps of broken and absent portions of the Resurrection, small tendrils of liquid glass seeped out into the voids, as if each lead-surrounded portion was a baking cut-out being filled from a height with colour.

Instead of being surprised or frightened, I was curious. I stepped up onto the marble-floored altar and began to approach the steadily self-repairing glass, which I had desecrated on a night in December. I felt the heat of the molten glass now, radiating out of the wound, which was somehow mending itself, or being mended. The heat was too intense for me to be able to get any closer so I backed away incrementally until the discomfort was beyond me.

'Hughie?' a voice said gently behind me. I turned to see a woman wearing a headscarf and an overcoat. I had not heard her come in. Her head was bowed. I stumbled slightly as I stepped down awkwardly from the altar. I glanced back at the stained glass: all of the empty portions of the Resurrection were now filled in and complete once more. The remaining damage, all the way across the scene, had healed and was perfect again, including the slight cracks at the outer limits of the vast scene.

I turned back towards the stranger who had called my name, and as I did so, I saw that those two pieces of information did not fit together. The lady lifted her head and pushed back her headscarf so I could see her face. It was Mammy. I closed my eyes and blinked and then, when I opened them again, she was still there. This was some horrific trick being played on me, someone dressed up as my mother, made up to resemble her, to torture and terrify me. It couldn't be anything else. Or was I dead myself now, and was this what Hell was like – windows that mended themselves and dead people who walked among . . . among what?

I stared at the lady and then I became angry. I wanted to harm her, whoever she was. Or was that right? Maybe I was tired, and this person was just someone who knew my name, and I was merely pretending to myself that she was my mother, when all of the time she was actually someone else's. The lady was still there when I opened my eyes the second time. I glanced behind me at the stained glass and it *was* fixed, every single solitary last bit of it. I tried to tell myself that nothing was real if I didn't believe it to be, and then I confronted this strange, awful, yet familiar and beautiful woman.

'Who are you?' I asked, in a voice that seemed like someone else's. I watched as she took a step closer to me. She held out her arms towards me. My eye was caught by the sight of the candles, which had extinguished only moments earlier, spontaneously reigniting.

'It's me, Hughie,' she said. 'I've missed you *so* much. I've watched you falling apart and it's all my fault and I'm so, so sorry. I never wanted to hurt you. I just want things to go back to the way they were. I want you to be happy again, and to help me make soda bread and to decorate the Christmas tree.'

'It's not you. You're not my mammy,' I said, as I began to reach out and try to put my hand through this imposter, this ghost, this vindictive hologram, which had come to do me harm or destroy me, or even worse.

'It *is* me, Hughie,' she implored. 'How can I make you believe that?'

'You can't, because it's not true,' I said, raising my voice. She reached out and tried to touch my face but I wouldn't let her. I put up my hands to protect myself, as if she was a dangerous, crazed woman who was acting in a play I no longer wanted to keep watching. 'Get back from me, get away, you mad bitch. Why have you come here to frighten me? I never did anything to you. I don't even know you.' I closed my eyes tightly, but I could smell Charlie perfume in the air. I began to shake and to cry and to believe that hellfire and sadness were about to rip my heart out.

Her voice pierced through the haze of whatever was happening, like an announcement being made on a train, whether or not you wanted to hear it.

'It *is* me, Hughie, please believe me. How can I— Oh, God, what is there that I can do to show you? I've kept you in my heart every single minute since that awful day in the hospital. I know that you've been shattered by what I did. I know that you're broken and that I'm responsible for that. I know that Nyxi held your hand when you needed someone, and that she told you in the window of Kenny's bookshop that I loved you and that I know you love me, even if you didn't say the actual words. I know that it's been *so* hard for you with Daddy and his, his "friend", and how he hit you when you answered him back about the school fees and the Deep Purple records, and how none of it is your fault. When that teacher picked you up off the pavement and brought you into her home, I wanted that to be me instead of her, and to hold you so tight and just lift you out of the madness I left you in.'

This was incredible. I was stranded in some sort of time warp of my own making. Some ruthless product of my imagination was mocking me. Or was it? I knew with one rational part of me that this could not be happening, yet at the same time the apparition's words cut through to my heart and ripped out my melancholy. I suddenly realised that not everything can be easily explained away.

'I can't live without you, Mammy,' I said, as I walked to her and put my arms around her neck, and clung to her, because she was my mother and I was her child, no matter what.

'No matter what it says on any file or piece of paper,' she said, finishing my thought. And that was when I knew it *was* her. She really was there, and I wanted to hold onto her forever and never let her leave me again. I held her shoulders, and looked into her face, and every single piece of me pleaded with her not to go away. I noticed that inside her coat she wore a blouse I had never seen before. Underneath the blouse, around her neck, the belt of the dressing-gown remained, like a reminder of every single broken thing in the world, like my heart and her marriage, and the pieces of the picture where ELO's lyrics could never hack their way through.

'What am I going to do, Mammy?' I begged her for an answer. 'What am I going to do?'

'You're a good boy, Hughie,' she said. 'I know you didn't blackmail anyone. It was the other way around.'

'Not that!' I screamed. 'I mean forever. What am I going to do for the rest of my life without you?' She put a hand to the back of her head and pulled up her headscarf. 'Don't go, Mammy, please don't go,' I yelled, knowing that she would, but powerless to stop her.

'I have to go, Hughie,' she said gently. 'I have so much to do and so do you. You will be able to help other people. You will know when they're in harm's way, and you will be able to lead them somewhere else.'

'Take me with you, Mammy,' I pleaded. 'Just tell me what to do to get to where you are. I don't want to be alone anymore. I'm afraid.'

'There's nothing to be afraid of,' she said, and then she was gone.

'Come back,' I shouted. 'Come back.'

'Who are you talking to, Hughie?' my father asked, as he stepped into a church where the glass was still mended but I was all alone.

Chapter 13

As we left Newbridge College, my father had to stop the car momentarily to allow someone to cross our path between Senior House and the church. I'd been looking down at my hands in my lap, but my eye was caught by the movement of something white. The person who was passing in front of the car was Father Flanagan. He looked directly at me for a second. I remembered his threat to wring the neck of the blighter who'd broken the window. I saw that he was carrying a box, from which some coloured pieces of stained glass were protruding. He was going to the church to begin the task of fixing the broken window. He didn't know yet that there was no need. As we exited onto the main road, I saw him in the side mirror. He had come out of the church and was standing at the small roundabout we'd just left, shaking his head in disbelief.

*

'This little piggy went to market. This little piggy stayed at home. This little piggy had roast beef and this little piggy . . .'

The game I was playing in my head became more difficult when it approached the roast beef end of things because I knew that if I took off my shoes and socks, on my right foot at least, there would be nobody to have no roast beef and no one to cry, 'Wee, wee, wee,' all the way home. In my mind, though, I could wiggle all five toes and sometimes still believed that all were fully present and accounted for. I have no idea what prompted me to remember that game from early childhood, but I had begun silently to play it halfway through the car journey home with my father following my expulsion. The first part of the journey had been bathed in absolute silence, from the moment I'd got into the car in the quadrangle.

'Have you nothing to say for yourself, Hughie?' My father opened the silence, like an incision he might make to take out an appendix. The windscreen was suddenly flecked with drops of rain, and he flicked on the wipers as I replied, as if he was switching me on too, twisting the device that made my voice work.

'I was angry about everything, and I didn't believe the stuff the priest said at the funeral about everybody being dead and getting back together again in the sky. That's why.'

'That's why what?' he said crossly, but in a quieter voice than when he'd first spoken.

'That's why I broke the window,' I said.

'I'm not interested in the window, Hughie. I don't care about the fucking window.' I wondered if he would have cared even just a tiny bit if he'd seen it fixing itself. 'I'm talking about the other stuff – blackmail, writing notes and leaving them in people's desks, demanding money, fighting and telling lies.'

'I didn't tell any lies,' I said, 'and I didn't blackmail anyone. *He* was the one who sent the note to *me*, not the other way round, and then when we were in Father Cogan's office, he told lies and ate the envelope.'

'He what?'

'He ate the envelope. You see, it was the only evidence that could have cleared my name, but he chewed it up, showed it to me on his tongue and then swallowed it.' My father slowed the car and turned to look at me and then, with one hand, he began to rub his head frantically, as if trying to rewind a wheel of some sort. His face grew red and he breathed in really deeply, as if he was going to sneeze, and then he *did* sort of explode.

'We didn't send you there to audition for a part in a fucking John le Carré film, Hughie! We sent you there to get an education.' I wondered who he meant when he said 'we', and I could see from his expression that he himself was now reconsidering who, apart from him, had sent me away.

'Who's John le Carré?' I asked, and he nearly crashed the car. The rest of the journey was punctuated by outbursts from him that did not require any input from me.

'What was I thinking, spending all of that money?'

'Jesus Christ, what bloody school will take you in now?'

'How could you have been so stupid?'

Although at first these appeared to be questions, I knew my father probably already knew the answers, and I was not really being asked to help him solve an apparent set of puzzles he couldn't figure out for himself. The only other verbal exchange between us occurred on the outskirts of Galway City, as we drove past Galwegians Rugby Club in Glenina, near Renmore.

'And you didn't even have the decency to say sorry,' he said out of the blue.

'I'm sorry,' I said.

'Sure what good is sorry now?' he said sadly. 'The damage has already been done.'

I remembered an incident, years earlier, when he and I had been outside in the garden at home on Taylor's Hill and he had been fixing something with a hammer. He had hit his thumb or finger, then dissolved into a tirade of shouting and bad language and cursing as he shook his hand, like it was holding a thermometer. Eventually he calmed down and turned to me and said, 'Any decent or normal son would have asked was I all right.' His eyes had been full of hatred.

'Are you all right, Daddy?' I asked.

'Sure what's the good of asking *now*?' he'd fumed. 'Can't you *see* I've hurt myself with the bloody hammer?'

*

We were driving through Galway City now, and I realised that I had not thought about Mammy for the whole journey. Was she alive, or was she dead? Had I seen a ghost, or just made it all up? I recalled the candles going out and that there had been no smoke. If she was real, then why hadn't my father seen her too? I had put my arms around her neck and begged her to stay, and she'd told me she had to go. Why did she have to go? When we'd spoken in the hospital at Halloween, she'd promised to be home for Christmas, and said she'd never leave me again, that we would talk about everything and never have any secrets from each other. The smell of her perfume, and the touch of her hand, and the colour of her hair, and the look in her eyes, and everything else I lost each time she left was more than I could bear. Maybe in a few weeks when I turned thirteen I would be able for it all, but not now, not then and there in a car on Shop Street, going home in the rain with my silent father and my suitcase and my Moons bag full of notes and books I didn't understand.

I wanted her to come back, to be there when we turned into the drive and parked near the monkey puzzle tree. I wanted her to be on the stairs carrying fresh towels for the bathroom, to be matching socks in the utility room, to be planning for next year in the greenhouse, to be outside the door of the bathroom again on Saturday nights saying, '*Both* feet, Hughie, okay?'

I began to cry in the car, and my father said nothing. At least I was glad about that. How could I ever explain to him what I had seen and felt and experienced in the church at the school only three or four hours earlier? What did she mean about me being able to help other people, or knowing when they were in harm's way? What could any of that possibly mean?

I wanted to believe that maybe absolutely everything that had happened was just a mistake, so that I would be able to find my way into the past and live there happily again. But, of course, I wasn't mistaken: this was all too real. I squeezed my eyes shut, but the tears still managed to get out and to stream down my cheeks and fall onto the school shirt I no longer needed. I imagined that I was older, and instead of my father driving the car, *I* was driving, and that I was coming home from somewhere, anywhere, and that the world was different and things were different. I imagined and wished and hoped that *he* was dead instead of Mammy, and that when I stopped the car and creaked up the handbrake, the front door would be open and Mammy would be standing in the hall, and that if an ambulance came and parked on the lawn, it would not be for her but would take *me* away instead, so that she could live forever. But when we arrived home, the house was cold and empty. And so were we.

The first thing I did when I got home was to search for Mammy's dressing-gown, the one my father had brought to her when she was in the hospital. At first I looked in the bathroom upstairs, but it wasn't there. Then I went into my parents' room and opened the green wardrobe, where

I'd sometimes managed to inhale the memory of her from her clothes. I flung open the double doors, not knowing what I would find. The emptiness hit me, like a punch in the face. I hurried to the large dresser on Mammy's side of the bedroom and began to open each of the drawers in turn, although I knew it was very unlikely that I would find her dressing-gown there. Drawer after drawer after drawer, they were all empty. I ran down the corridor to the spare room, hoping to find that the clothes had been moved there to keep the Christmas decorations company. They hadn't. In the main bathroom, the cabinet over the sink, where she had kept her make-up and some of her medicine, was almost completely bare. Instead of those things, I found a pair of earrings I had never seen Mammy wearing. I rushed down the stairs to find my father. He was sitting at his desk in the study with some files piled in front of him. The thin lamp with the adjustable neck, like a giraffe, was on, illuminating the desk like a spotlight.

'Where are Mammy's clothes?' I asked.

He looked up from his work, clearly surprised by the question. 'Why do you want to know?' he asked calmly.

'I just do,' I said inadequately.

'They wouldn't have fitted you, Hughie,' he said, with a sneering grin.

'They mustn't have fitted your friend Breege either,' I said, with as much hatred as I could collect for him in my words. He stood up abruptly, violently, and in putting both hands on the desk to raise himself, he knocked over the lamp. It fell backwards to the floor, and we both watched it happening slowly, as if it were a film in which someone is clinging to a window high up on a building and has eventually let go, and is seen from above as they fall. The glass shattered, and I thought about the stained-glass window. My father stayed on the other side of the desk, his captain's chair now overturned on the carpet behind him, and balancing grotesquely against the window-seat.

'I loved her too, Hughie. You're not the only person who lost her, you know! You're not the only person in this family who lost her!' he roared.

'Is that so?' I shouted back at him, as I began to cry with rage and unhappiness and loss. 'Well, it didn't take you very long to find a replacement, did it?' At this, my father swept all of the contents of the desk onto the floor, where they lay strewn on top of the shattered glass and the plugged-in giraffe lamp, which was no longer giving any light to anyone. He stepped around the other side of the desk and came into the middle of the room, so that he now stood directly opposite me on the wooden parquet floor.

'We gave you a home when nobody else wanted you, Hughie,' he said. 'We went out of our way to put a roof over your head, and food on the table, and clothes on your back. I simply don't know if she'd still be here if you'd *never* been here.' His words flew at me like broken glass, and I instinctively put up my hands in front of me to try to stop them reaching me after they had left his mouth. He was blaming me for her death. I could just not take in the enormity of his accusation.

'You can't stand the fact that she loved me,' I said. 'That's your big problem – Mammy always loved me, and you always hated me, and you never wanted me to spend time alone with her. You always came in and took her away so that we couldn't be together.'

'Stop feeling sorry for yourself, Hughie,' he said, advancing slightly towards me. 'Why don't you just grow up? Of course we both wanted you. All that stuff you're saying is nonsense.'

'You're a liar,' I said.

His face hardened, and he took a step towards me and raised his hand in an implicit threat to me to withdraw my accusation. 'I won't be spoken to like that in my own house,' he said, as an ultimatum.

'"You were the one who insisted on adoption, Deirdre, not me."' I threw the sentence back at him from somewhere inside me where it had been stored. The effect was instantaneous: he turned, went back to the other side of the room and began to pick up the scattered files from the floor. We did not say another word to each other for nearly two weeks. I was glad of the silence.

On the second Saturday after I'd come back to Galway, Nyxi and I managed to meet up. We walked down around by the Spanish Arch and sat on the edge of the Long Walk, outside a mint-green house, and dangled our legs over the edge on the harbour wall. I told her about everything that had happened at school, and then I told her what had occurred in the church on my last day in Newbridge College.

'Come off it, Hughie,' she said. 'People are either real or they're not. Are you saying you saw a ghost?'

'I know what I saw,' I said. 'And it wasn't a ghost. She spoke to me and told me that I would know when people were in danger, and I'd be able to help them somehow.'

Nyxi looked at me, then stared out across the water to Nimmo's Pier. On the lands behind it, known as 'The Swamp', tiny figures were erecting a circus tent. Nyxi turned back to me and spoke again. 'How could you be able to know about people being in danger, and be able to help them? Like Superman or God?'

'I don't know,' I said. 'I'm only telling you what she told me. Do you think I expected to turn around from the glass-filling-in thing and just see her standing there in a headscarf?'

'There *was* no headscarf, Hughie. There *was* no window fixing itself. Things like that don't happen in real life. I know you miss her, but that stuff doesn't sound real to me.' I'd never heard Nyxi speaking like that before, like she was a grown-up and I was a child and we were having the Tooth Fairy talk. I'd always trusted that, whatever else happened, Nyxi Kirwan would always believe in me. Now I wasn't so sure.

'I know what I saw and what I heard. How else could

she know all of the things that happened with my father and his "friend", and you and me in the window seat of Kenny's bookshop, and all of that? How could she possibly know all that?'

'*None* of that is possible,' she said, 'it's just a dream or a makey-up thing, like in a film. Those things don't happen in real life. Or . . .'

'Or what?'

'Or you're just lying to yourself, or to me, or whatever.'

Her words hurt me and I didn't want to fight with her. She had never spoken to me like that before. I stood up and she remained sitting, her legs hanging down over the incoming tide. I turned to walk away.

'You've changed, Hughie,' she said, to my back. 'You're not the same as you were before.'

'How could I be the same, Nyxi? My mother hanged herself.'

As I made my way back towards the Spanish Arch, I had a sudden pain in my head, behind my eyes. I put out one hand, to lean against the wall, or anything, to stop myself falling down. As I steadied myself, I saw a scene in my head in which a man was going up a narrow flight of stairs. I could only see him from behind. He was carrying a blue motorbike helmet in one hand, and it was swinging back and forth as he climbed the stairs. At the top was a door. I watched the man, and suddenly I felt that if he opened the door and went into the room danger was waiting for him there. I was frightened and began to shiver. I wanted the man to turn around, so that I could see who he was. If I knew that, maybe I would be able to warn him against going into the room. I tried to look on either side of the stairway, to see if there might be a picture hanging, or a particular type of patterned wallpaper, which might allow me to identify the house. If I recognised it, surely I would know who the man was. I tried to shout after him so that he would turn around, but I could not speak. Nor could I recognise the house. The pain ceased abruptly, and the picture in my head was wiped clean.

Nyxi came up behind me. I had not heard her footsteps. I thought she might ask me if I was okay, but instead she walked straight past me and said absolutely nothing. I felt around my neck, inside my shirt, and found that I was wearing the chain and cross she'd given me before I'd gone away to boarding school. The thing that had kept me sane while I was in Newbridge was the anticipation of her letters, and the illicit phone calls late at night on the old black telephone on the wall outside the staffroom in Junior House. Now that I was back in Galway, in the same city in which she lived, it seemed we were further apart than we had ever been.

The new school wasn't much different from the old, except that instead of sleeping there I went home every evening after supervised study ended. At break one day I overheard some boys talking about 'going down to the Sancta after school'. Over the course of a week or so, I came to understand that this referred to a burned-out, abandoned building, which had formerly been the Sancta Hotel.

It lay on the corner of Raleigh Row, a narrow street, which led from St Mary's Road just outside the school to an area known as 'The West', which was made up of old red-brick houses, and a square called 'The Small Crane' in the angle between Sea Road and Henry Street. I had passed by the place frequently on my way home from primary school, but for some reason in my last few years there I'd walked home the longer way, round by the Crescent and up to Nile Lodge. I assumed that those older boys went down to the ruins of the hotel to smoke, but one day I realised that much more than that went on there.

It was a Thursday, I remember that. After supervised study had ended, I decided to walk into the city centre instead of going straight home. My curiosity took me left, down Raleigh Row, and as I made the turn I heard the clamour and cry of voices just down the street from where I stood. As I got closer to the hotel, I could see that the entire wall had gone from it at the side, and further on around the front, more was missing. Here and there, parts of the structure were still black from the fire, which had raged inside it the year before I was born. Half-destroyed rooms were open to the air, and the whole surrounding site was full of rocks and rubble, as if the place had been struck by a direct hit in a bombing raid by the German Luftwaffe.

There was some movement on the upper floors, then

warning shouts, as a few boys appeared at the edge of some rooms that had no outer walls, and began to throw stones. They also threw chunks of wood and other debris. I soon saw that their targets were other boys, who were crouching in the grounds. Most of the missiles missed altogether. The ground troops stood up, and began to fire back at the boys occupying the hotel. They did this using catapults, or gabhlógs, not wooden twiggy ones, but proper ones made of metal. The weapons allowed the boys below to return fire with reasonable accuracy. I watched this pitched battle for a few minutes, before continuing down past the Sancta Hotel to get to the sweetshop in Henry Street that sold cheaper cola cubes than anywhere else in the city.

As I walked away I remembered something that had happened years earlier. I thought I'd dreamed it, or seen it in a film, but now I knew that it was a real event, which I'd witnessed and had buried in my mind. I had been standing at a gate looking through it at a scene in which three boys had poured petrol over a dog and set it alight. As I had made my way down Raleigh Row, I'd seen the remains of hinges protruding from concrete in a wall. The gap was now boarded up, but it was part of the grounds of the burned-out hotel. I'd just stood there transfixed, on the exact same spot where I now stood, and I could still hear the spine-chilling and futile howls of pain as the dog burned to death.

I learned later that the boys' wars for possession of the hotel took place almost on a weekly basis. One boy, from the Jes, was reputed to have had a brain haemorrhage, after being struck on the side of the head by a playing marble fired from a gabhlóg. Perhaps that wasn't true. It was difficult to know. I wished the whole place would just crumble to the ground. It was a place where evil flourished – that much I did know.

At home things were very quiet. A lady called Mrs McAdoo came to the house to prepare meals for us on Mondays, Wednesdays and Fridays, and also to do some laundry. She was a tough lady, with a Northern Ireland accent, and she cooked brilliant food. One day, I threw a pair of dirty socks towards the laundry basket on the landing and missed completely. Instead of picking them up, I left them on the carpet where they'd fallen. As I turned to go down the stairs, I was confronted by Mrs McAdoo, who had come noiselessly up from the kitchen. She gave me a look you could have poured on a waffle and that was the last time I ever missed the basket when I threw my dirty clothes into the laundry.

My father and I were like two people who didn't even know each other, but who lived in the same building in a huge city, like Tokyo or Limerick. We passed by each other every day, and even ate at the same table, but since our row in his study, when he'd smashed the lamp, neither of us said a single solitary word to the other. I was no longer afraid of him, I suppose. Something inside my heart made me feel that I *had* grown up a bit, and was now more able to stand my ground than I had been before.

The garage was still a sanctuary for me when I needed it. It held memories, unlocked by toys that had lain there forgotten for years upon years. I came across my cowboy outfit and my pistols, which now felt light and useless, instead of how I'd remembered them. Although the lawnmower was still there, I was less afraid of it now, less wary that it might suddenly burst into life and finish the job on my right foot. I still didn't touch it, of course, but I was much less fearful of it than I had been in earlier years after the accident.

I sat on an old settee, and remembered being bounced up and down on it as a toddler. Or had I been jumping? The hair-dryer unit, which had caught fire with my mother under it, was still there too. But my greatest discovery came just a week before my thirteenth birthday. I was looking for the wigwam, unable to remember where I'd put it at Christmas, and I came across a large black plastic bag full of something soft. When I opened the bag, the wigwam was there, folded away, but underneath it was Mammy's pink and yellow dressing-gown. When I shook it out and held it up, there was no belt in the loops around the waist. I emptied out the rest of the contents of the bag. Mammy's green jumper was there, and the same blouse I'd seen her wearing in the church, the blouse I'd never seen when she was alive. But there was no sign of the belt from the dressing-gown.

*

Two days before I turned thirteen, I opened the *Galway Advertiser* to see on the front page that the Sancta Hotel had inexplicably collapsed in on itself during the night. The photograph showed the place utterly destroyed and unrecognisable, no more than a heap of bricks and glass and splintered wood. The very same day, Granny Daly telephoned the house and Mrs McAdoo had taken the call: Uncle Seán, who lived with her and who drove a motorbike, had died unexpectedly in his sleep.

Chapter 14

There was something frightening about Dublin. I'd only been there a handful of times before, and most of those visits had been to see a pantomime with my parents at Christmastime, or maybe to go to the zoo. I had been to Granny Daly's before and I remembered, or at least I thought I remembered, the house, the garden, and the nearby Esso garage where Uncle Seán had worked. But this trip was different: I felt that as soon as we arrived on the outskirts of the city in my father's car. Snippets of the outside world seeped into the car through the one o'clock news, as we drove through street after street after street, jam-packed with houses and shops and cars and big double-decker buses.

'A part-time RUC reservist has been shot dead in front of his wife and children in the Sandy Row area. Meanwhile, gardaí at Store Street are asking for help tracing an

American tourist who has been missing since Thursday of last week. Sarah Kennet was last seen in O'Connell Street, wearing a pair of light blue jeans and a yellow raincoat. Anyone with information . . .'

Inside the car, my father and I looked out different windows. He concentrated on where we were going, while I was suddenly aware of myself and my relationship with the rest of the world in a whole new way. It was as if the newscaster was talking directly to me, as we sat at traffic lights outside a garage called Deansgrange Motors. Before, when Mammy had been alive, all of our visits to Granny Daly's had been happy and full of life. We would sing songs in the car to make the journey shorter, and sometimes my father had even joined in. A couple of times it had been just Mammy and me who had visited. On those occasions we had travelled by train. Then I'd had Mammy all to myself, the whole way across the country.

But this was a different version of me visiting my grandmother now: this was a version of Hughie Mittman, aged nearly thirteen, who was somehow connected to the bigger outside world and who could see death before it arrived. The news about people dying or going missing now seemed to me something more than just announcements for other people. All of those messages, or any one of them, might have been directed to me or be *about* me in some way. Perhaps I'd been meant to see the man in Sandy Row in my head days earlier, and should have known what was going to happen to him. Was he someone 'in harm's way', someone I could have saved? What about the missing American tourist, Sarah Kennet? Was I part of that? I closed my eyes and thought hard about her, hoping to be told where she was in some clip of film in my brain, but nothing happened. Instead, I found myself thinking that the man I'd seen going up the stairs must have been Uncle Seán. Perhaps I should have known it was dangerous for him to go into the room, that he wouldn't come out alive – but the pain in my head, and the fact that he hadn't turned around, meant I hadn't known who he was until it was too late to save him. And the whole thing about helping people who were in harm's way, was that connected to the collapse of the hotel? Maybe I was supposed to be able to lead people out of harm's way, but I'd gotten the spell mixed up and made bad things happen instead.

Anyway, how were you supposed to save people if they wouldn't at least tell you who they were? I remembered the efforts I'd made to identify the wallpaper, or to solve the puzzle by another means. I should have asked Mammy for more information about the 'harm's way' thing, and about being able to lead people to safety. Now I was travelling into the biggest city in Ireland, and who knows how many more people would be in need of saving here? That was what was frightening about Dublin, I suppose: the scale of everything in it – more people, more worries, more complicated lives full of thousands of different wallpapers I'd never seen before.

*

At the front of Granny Daly's house there was a really steep bit down to the garage door. It was like a ramp, all ridges of grey concrete, and you could feel it as the car went slowly down at such an angle that if the garage door hadn't been there we'd have tipped over completely. Granny Daly looked lost and tired, and seemed to have shrunk since the last time I'd seen her. She'd had only two children, and now they were both gone.

'Hughie, oh, Hughie,' she said, as she hugged me so tightly I thought my ribs would break. Her body seemed to shake then, and when we broke from the hug I saw that the shoulder of my jumper was wet. Granny Daly took me by the hand and led me into the dining room. 'Now you sit down there, Hughie. I'll be back to you in a minute,' she said, leaving me in the armchair at the top of the table, before she disappeared into the kitchen. My father was in the hallway, talking to a man in a suit. I presumed he was the coffin guy, because he looked like one of the men who had been at the graveside for Mammy's funeral.

The table was bare, except for two mats that lay patiently where Granny Daly and Uncle Seán's plates would have rested when mealtimes came around. I looked closely at the one in front of me, and saw that it bore a picture of a steam train. Granny Daly returned with a huge enamel dish of strawberry jelly, and a bowl with a block of HB ice-cream balanced on top of it. She put them all down on the table in front of me. 'It's not your birthday until the end of the week but I know this is your favourite. You've always loved jelly and ice-cream, haven't you, Hughie?'

'Thanks a million, Granny,' I said, hoping she would go back out to the kitchen and allow me to make a token attempt at eating the jelly and ice-cream. Instead, Granny Daly pulled out a chair for herself and sat down to watch me enjoy my favourite dessert. I think I *had* liked jelly and ice-cream once upon a time, but I didn't really like it anymore. In fact the thought of eating the jelly, any of it, gave me a lurchy feeling in my tummy.

In the dining room too, but over against the wall, was a sideboard. It was made of dark brown wood, with very ornate legs, and curvy bits at the corners and round the edges. There were three drawers and two cupboards in it, and the brass bits you pulled to open the drawers and the cupboards were rings, which fell back into place around lions' faces. Mammy had always referred to this piece of furniture as a 'Nelson sideboard'. I thought about Uncle Seán and the last time I'd seen him, when he and Granny Daly stayed with us on Taylor's Hill for a few days after Mammy died.

My father's voice came around the door from the hall as he continued to talk about the arrangements for my uncle's funeral. 'Glasnevin,' he said, and then, 'Send the bill to me in Galway.'

I wondered why he would say that, about the bill for Uncle Seán's funeral being sent to him. And then it hit me. Perhaps he knew I was supposed to save Uncle Seán and hadn't, and that was why he was going to have to pay for the funeral. *I don't know if she'd still be here if you'd never been here.* I saw it all now, the accusation coming back around, like a Ferris wheel at a carnival, with the words on a constant loop, rising into the air and moving until they were level with me again. What if he was right about all of that? I began to re-experience the feelings I'd had just after Mammy had killed herself. Maybe the bits and pieces of the conversations I'd heard between my parents all added up to one horrible fact: if I'd never come along, Mammy might still be alive. After all, that was what my father believed.

I looked at the other placemat through the haze of what I was thinking. It was upside-down from me and I could see it was a large building, but I couldn't make it out from where I was sitting. I looked up into Granny Daly's face and, although she seemed to be staring out the back window into the garden, I knew she was worrying about being all alone.

There was silence in the house now, apart from the tap-tap-tap of my spoon on the enamel dish as I counted out some song in my head I couldn't quite remember. And then, as I looked at my grandmother, as she fixed her stare on the garden, I heard in my head the tapping of my spoon as if it were counting out, not blackbirds baked in a pie, but magpies trapped forever in jelly. I felt certain that, if I looked down, at the bottom of the dish there'd be feathers, blue-black, encased in strawberry jelly.

This was my fault. If I'd been able to get the man on the stairs to turn around, I would have seen who he was and I could have saved him. 'I'm sorry, Granny,' I said.

She looked at me as if she didn't know who I was. 'You don't have to eat it all,' she said kindly.

'No, Granny, not the jelly. I'm sorry about Uncle Seán.'

'I know, Hughie,' she said, lifting one hand and stroking my cheek softly with the back of it, like Mammy used to.

'I should have saved him,' I said. 'It's all my fault.'

'It's nobody's fault, Hughie,' she said. 'It's just that God wanted him. God needed him more than we did.'

I thought about telling Granny Daly about the vision I'd had of Uncle Seán walking up the stairs swinging his blue motorbike helmet. But what was the point of telling her that now? I'd failed in my duty to save people in harm's way, and now she would have to live alone as a result.

'He's with your mammy now,' Granny Daly said, as she stood up and began to clear the bowl and dish away. I stood up to help her carry the things into the kitchen, and I realised I'd eaten very little of the jelly and all of the ice-cream. I began to get one of those ice-cream headaches. As I returned to the dining room, with a wet cloth to wipe the stains from the table, I saw on the other mat an old photograph of the Sancta Maria Hotel in Galway City. I remembered the cries of the boys doing battle in the burned-out shell of that very hotel in the days before it had crumbled into dust. Perhaps I had been responsible for that happening. I felt a little bit frightened of myself.

At the funeral I didn't feel anything at all. It reminded me a bit of Mammy's, but that was pretty much it. As we stood in a small crowd afterwards, people I didn't know shook my grandmother's hand. I remembered for some reason the stone walls and the huge tower in Glasnevin cemetery. Perhaps I'd seen them on television.

'Dev's buried over there,' my father said, as we made our way back to the funeral car. 'And Michael Collins,' he added. These were names from history books. I wondered if that was a sign they would come up in the summer exams.

We drove back to Granny Daly's house in the pouring rain, the windscreen wipers working furiously to clear a space for the driver to see through. I remembered the drive from Galway to Dublin only a couple of days earlier. My father and I were still barely on speaking terms. I wondered if that was how the rest of my life might turn out to be, not really talking to him ever again. I missed Nyxi, but I was angry with her for refusing to believe me. She'd told me I had changed.

All of a sudden, I was seized with a funny feeling, and for no reason at all I saw buildings in my head that I didn't recognise. 'Stop!' I shouted. The driver jammed on the brakes.

'What is it, Hughie?' Granny Daly asked.

'Jesus Christ,' the driver said, as a small child ran across the road in front of the Fanagans Funeral Home Mercedes. A split-second later, the child's mother dashed after him and caught him by the hand. She'd been wheeling a buggy, with another small child in it, and the boy must have been holding her hand and had broken free. 'If you hadn't told me to stop, I'd have killed that child,' the driver said, looking over his shoulder at us.

The rain had cleared and I saw that the buildings on the opposite side of the road were the ones I'd seen in my head. 'What's that place?' I asked, pointing to the large, imposing establishment. I saw a look pass between my father and Granny Daly, but neither of them said anything.

'Some religious gaff,' the driver said, as we moved on through the traffic and away from where the accident had almost been.

At the bottom of Granny Daly's garden there was a huge tree. When I'd been younger, it had seemed to me to be the biggest tree in the world. On either side of the garden a privet hedge separated the space from the next-door neighbours. The end was bounded by a wire fence, and on the other side of the fence was a wood. It was almost as if Granny Daly's tree had escaped from the wood, and had sought and found refuge in her garden.

As we were driving back from the graveyard, I thought about that tree, and, as soon as we got back, I went out the back door and began to climb it. I'd always been too afraid to do it before. I pulled myself up the first few branches, then stood on a fairly stout one and looked back up the garden at my grandmother's house. I couldn't see over the house until I'd climbed quite a bit higher, and then I wondered if I could keep climbing until I reached the clouds.

The view changed dramatically as I ventured further up the old oak tree. I could now see over the house, and across the road. Further down the street, I saw the huge pub on the corner near the traffic lights. When I'd finally climbed as high as I could, I looked down at the ground, expecting maybe to get dizzy, but that was not how I felt. Instead of being muzzy or wobbly, I felt strong and able to do almost anything. I turned to face the other way, into the wood beyond the fence. I felt that if I could just step from that tree to the next perhaps I could travel through the treetops, like Tarzan, until I reached Africa and the jungle.

'Hughie, get down from there!' My father's command cut up through the branches, like the insult it was. I thought about staying up in the tree forever, but I quickly realised I would need lots of food, and probably a raincoat, and I didn't have any of that with me. I thought about Nyxi, and the pink house with the chestnut tree near the quarry, and how the lady had given us lovely milk to drink when we'd stopped in and asked for water. As I made my way back down the tree, I could feel my father's anger underneath me, like a spike waiting for me to impale myself upon it. I ripped my trousers on a broken branch as I jumped down the last few feet to land on the ground beside him. 'For Christ's sake, Hughie,' he roared. 'Look what you've done now.'

'I wanted to stay up in the tree,' I said, really meaning that the only reason I'd come down was because he'd told me to. He glared at me, as if he was about to hit me, but I think we remembered where we were at the same time. We looked up the garden, and Granny Daly was standing in the kitchen, watching us through the window.

As we walked back up the path to the house, my father bent down and touched the longish grass with one hand. 'Not completely dry,' he said, 'but dry enough. Why don't you be a good boy, Hughie, and cut the grass for Granny Daly?'

I froze as soon as he'd spoken the words. He knew I was terrified of lawnmowers, and at home in Galway he'd never let me near the mower since my accident. For years he must have witnessed my horror and fright every summer at the sound of other people cutting the grass. I felt cold and hot at the same time, and maybe it was only one or the other, but I couldn't tell in that moment.

I looked my father in the face, and I saw detachment in his expression. Just then, I hated him more than I'd ever hated anything or anyone, before or since. I saw in his suggestion the sum of all of the anger he'd built up against me, from my relationship with Mammy, my expulsion from the school and the fact that Mammy had insisted on my adoption against his wishes. The disintegration of everything at home and between us, before Mammy's suicide and since, had led him to taunt me to face the thing he knew I feared most in the whole world.

I felt tears beginning behind my eyes, but I turned away and did not give him the satisfaction of seeing me cry. I was almost thirteen, but I was still afraid. He didn't want to be here, in Dublin, on Granny Daly's land, on her terms. As much as he might blame me for Mammy's death, I knew he felt Granny Daly blamed *him* in some way, too, for it. I recalled now that when we'd been getting ready to go to Mammy's funeral, she'd said something about him not telling her what was happening at home, or did she mean to Mammy? Granny Daly hadn't known, until Mammy's death, how sick Mammy had been. I made my way to the garage, shaking, fearful and overflowing with resentment.

The old green lawnmower was housed in a corner dominated by shelves full of paint pots and jars with congealed brushes drowning in white spirits. I placed my hand cautiously on the handle of the mower, and looked at the throttle controls. It was the first time I'd touched a lawnmower since my accident. I got a slight electric static shock, and drew my hand back instantly from the contact.

'Don't you bother about the lawn now, Hughie,' my grandmother's voice said from the doorway. 'I've told him the mower's broken.' She came into the garage, stood beside me and took one of my hands in hers.

'I just miss her so much,' I said. 'I don't want to keep going without her. I know it's been a few months now, and I should be stronger or better, but I can't make myself feel any different than I do.'

'I know, Hughie,' Granny Daly said. 'I know exactly how you feel. I miss her too. And now Seán's gone as well.'

'Do you believe in ghosts?' I asked her.

She gripped my hand tightly and sighed deeply. 'I don't know what I believe in anymore, Hughie. And that's a fact. You go through life thinking one thing, then something happens to shake that belief, or to make you believe something else altogether. There are things we can explain and then, sometimes, things happen that we cannot really understand at all.'

'Like what happened in the car today?' I said, although I hadn't meant to say that. It just came out.

'Like that, yes. Do you know what that building was, where you shouted, "Stop," and the driver braked and didn't hit the child who ran across the road?'

I shook my head. 'I had a picture of it in my mind just before we got there, but I don't know what it was.'

'That's where you lived, Hughie, when you were a tiny baby. That's where your mum and dad went to . . . '

'To adopt me?' I asked.

'To collect you to bring you home, I was going to say, but, yes, that's where you were before you were with them. Somebody must have explained all of this to you, did they?'

'Not really, Granny. I heard bits and pieces, and then Mammy told me she would explain everything to me when she got out of hospital but she . . .' My voice tailed off.

'I know what you mean, Hughie. I know she always

meant to explain everything to you when you were older. She never meant to keep any of that from you. She even said, at one stage, that if you wanted to do anything about it later on, she'd help you.'

'Like what?' I asked

'Like finding out a bit more about where you came from, Hughie,' Grandma Daly said. We stood there like that for ages, saying nothing, and I was as happy as I could be for that short time in my grandmother's garage. I wondered about all of that, and how I'd recognised the building, and why I'd shouted at the driver to stop. Or had I been trying to warn the little boy who was about to run out in front of the car? I didn't understand any of this. At least the child had not been run over. Had I saved him from danger, maybe even death, by shouting at the driver to stop? He was only about a year and a half old. Everything might have been so different for him if I hadn't said something. But I didn't know that child. I couldn't have known that he was in harm's way. Was something more happening to me that I just couldn't understand? Why was it happening, and did it have anything to do with Mammy's appearance to me in the church?

As we turned to leave the garage, I saw through the window that my father was waiting in the back garden with his hands on his hips and a look of growing impatience on his face, much the same pose as he'd struck frequently when he was trying to prise my mother out of my company at home.

'If you ever want to do anything about that, Hughie,' Granny Daly said, 'just let me know and I'll help you if I can.'

'He didn't really want me, did he?' I asked, as we moved across the garage towards the door.

'I'm sure that's not true, Hughie,' Granny Daly said unconvincingly. As we made to leave, I saw Uncle Seán's motorbike, an old Honda 50, up on a stand in the opposite corner of the garage. Hanging from one of the handlebars was a helmet. But it wasn't blue, it was white.

'Did Uncle Seán have another helmet, Granny?' I asked. 'A blue one?'

'No,' she replied. 'He only ever had the white one. I'm almost sure he bought the motorbike and the helmet on the same day. A blue one? No, he never had a blue one.'

I was overcome with a feeling of relief and then, immediately afterwards, by worry. Perhaps it was not too late to save the man on the stairs.

Before we left Granny Daly's, the next day, my father and I encountered each other on the stairs. I was the one who made way while he just looked right through me, as if I wasn't there. I knew he'd be much happier if I just disappeared. That was the moment when I decided that, before we left for Galway, I would ask my grandmother to help me to try and find out where I'd come from. It would be something we could do together to fight back against Simon Mittman – the surgeon who enjoyed inflicting pain on people whose feet he'd saved.

Chapter 15

Somehow I had thought that when I reached thirteen years of age, everything would instantly change. I would be grown-up. I would no longer be afraid of anything. The days would be filled with more important things for me to do. My clothes would no longer fit. I would be able to see over hedges that had, only days before, blocked my view of other people's gardens, other people's lives. None of that happened. The only thing that changed was my age.

On the radio they played a song by George Harrison, 'My Sweet Lord', because it was his birthday too. I had read somewhere that another person who had the same birthday as me was a painter, called Regward or Reindeer, or something like that. Despite this important shared day, I never met either of them, not on 25 February that year or at any other time. I did not know who was the oldest of the three of us, but I reckoned it was probably George Harrison. I'd seen a photograph of him once and he had a beard.

Downstairs in the kitchen, my father and I ate breakfast in near silence, with only the crunch of cornflakes and the ping of the toaster breaking through the stillness. Last year, Mammy had decorated it with balloons and streamers, and when I'd come down the stairs, she had started humming 'Happy Birthday' very loudly. I couldn't see her, but I'd heard her all right, and my heart had been filled with a fizzy kind of happiness. Although she and my father had arguments from time to time, and maybe more often in that last year, that day had been crammed with good things. My father had not been there for breakfast on my twelfth birthday, and maybe that was why Mammy and I had been as happy as a dog with two tails (or maybe as happy as two dogs with four tails between them). This year could not have been more different.

The snap of the letterbox on the front door was followed by something falling onto the mat in the hallway. Neither of us moved to investigate. As I put my bowl in the dishwasher a short time later, Mrs McAdoo came into the kitchen waving a piece of post.

'It's for you, Hughie,' she said, with perhaps the first smile I'd ever seen her give. She handed me the envelope and I tore it open. It was a birthday card from Granny Daly. Inside was a ten-pound note and a smaller envelope. The money fluttered to the floor and I bent down to pick it up. My father stood up and picked up the card from where I'd set it down on the table. As he realised what it was, he began to go slightly red in the face.

'Oh, yes of course it's, eh, your, the, em . . .' he glanced down at the newspaper on his chair '. . . the twenty-fifth. Happy birthday, Hughie,' he said, in a voice which was slightly shaky and quite cold. It was clear that he had had no idea when my birthday was, and now that he knew, it was of little interest to him.

'We'll have to bake you a cake,' Mrs McAdoo said. 'You can have it with your tea this evening when you come home.'

The smaller envelope lay unopened on the kitchen table, and I saw my father glance at it. I wouldn't give him the satisfaction of opening it in front of him. I just gathered everything up and stuffed it into one of the side pockets of my schoolbag. It was ten to nine by the clock on the wall. I'd have to hurry to cycle to school or I'd be late. I saw my father glance at the clock as well.

'Would you like a lift, Hughie?' he asked. 'I'm due at the hospital now.'

'No, thanks,' I replied, not caring whether his motive in offering was genuine concern, embarrassment in front of Mrs McAdoo, or some substitute for a birthday card. I knew that, each time I escaped from the house, the fresh air in my face as I freewheeled down Taylor's Hill was like a tonic for my entire body.

At the bottom of the hill I turned left, behind Scoil

Fhursa, an all-Irish primary school. I had enough momentum to get me all the way down that shortcut street without having to pedal, but I had to stop when I reached St Mary's Road, before exiting into the traffic. As I did, a white butterfly landed on my handlebars. It seemed to look up at me for an instant, and then it flew away, up, up, up into the sky. I watched it until it was too small to see anymore. As I sat there, with both feet touching the road, I knew somehow that the butterfly landing on my bike on my birthday was a sign. I was drawn back to the events of my last morning at Newbridge College, and the fact that so many things had happened to me which I did not know how to explain, not to Nyxi, not to anyone else, not even to myself.

The weather was cold, but I became colder still at that instant. I felt as if I could almost leave my bike behind and float away, up into the morning sky in pursuit of the white butterfly. I was thirteen years old but, beyond that, who was I? From a radio in a passing car a song about taking a chance on someone blared out at me. Everyone knew who Abba were, but who was Hughie Mittman?

Later that day, when I got home from school, I opened the smaller envelope. It contained a photograph of my mother on the day of her graduation from UCD with her B. Comm. in 1956. Mammy was dressed in a long gown, and she wore a funny hat on her head, like the teachers from the St Trinian's films. The picture was a bit strange, because all around her there was a kind of a blurry haze, as if she was emerging from a fog or something. But the most striking thing about the photo was the expression on her face. I had never seen her looking as happy, not even in real life. I wondered if people only reached the top of happiness once, then began slowly to get sadder, and only experienced small bits of happiness from time to time on the way down. A bit like a mountain – as if you reached the summit once in your life, and thereafter you could only climb small hills from time to time. I kissed the photograph, and before I knew it, I was crying in my bedroom. I put the photograph on the shelf beside my bed, and began to talk to it as if it could hear me.

'Why won't you come back again to me, Mammy, like you did in the church? I want you to magic yourself back into my life again. I want you to come downstairs with me and to bake soda bread just one more time. Just please come back, and let me be with you for long enough to remember you, so I'll never forget. That's what I'm afraid of most, Mammy. I'm afraid that I'll forget what you look like, and then, if the photographs fade, you'll be gone altogether. There isn't any place I can go and be sure to find you. Daddy has thrown out most of your clothes, but I don't want him to throw you out too.

'I went to Granny Daly's. Uncle Seán has died, but maybe you already know that. I tried to save him, but then the motorbike helmet turned out not to be his, so I just don't know anymore. I want to be able to touch your face and hold your hand and spend Christmas with you, and decorate the tree even if it isn't Christmas. There's nothing underneath me if I fall now, because you're gone away. I'm thirteen today, but I don't feel grown-up. I just feel so lonely and tired and sad, and filled up with jigsaw pieces I can never fit together, no matter how much I try.

'I wanted to keep climbing that tree in Granny Daly's garden, but there wasn't enough of it. There should have been more branches, so that I could climb up to where you are and stay with you. And then he tried to make me cut the grass, and I knew that he did that because he hates me. He told me that maybe if I had never come to this family you might still be alive. I didn't mean for you to kill yourself. I never wanted that to happen. If you had told me to go away, and told me that if I went, you wouldn't hang yourself, I would have gone back to where I'd come from. And maybe if I try to go back now, it still won't be too late. Tell me it's not too late, Mammy. I'm going to try to fix everything. I'll try to make up for it all.'

And that was why I spent the night of my thirteenth birthday crying myself to sleep over the photograph of Mammy with her graduation hat and gown on, all those years ago when things were different and photographs were blurry and she was happier than she ever would be again. I thought about the conversation I'd had with Granny Daly, a short while before we'd left to return to Galway after Uncle Seán's funeral.

'Are you sure you'd like me to contact them, Hughie?' she'd said.

'I think so, Granny. You're the only person I'd like to write to them for me.'

'I can't promise we'll be able to find anything out, Hughie.'

'I know,' I said, 'but we can try.'

It had begun as an instinctive way to defy my father, but I also knew that if anything happened to Granny Daly, I'd have to wait until I was an adult myself to contact the Adoption Society. That was years away, and by then it might be too late altogether. After we'd got back to Galway I'd had second thoughts about the whole thing: I felt I was being disloyal to Mammy by even thinking of finding anything out about where I'd come from or who I was.

But there, in my bedroom, face to face with Mammy's graduation photograph, I knew that what I wanted to do now had a clear purpose. It was strange in one way but, given everything else that had happened since Mammy's death, it also made some kind of crazy sense: if I could get my birth parents to take me back, maybe that would make me less responsible for Mammy's death. The Resurrection scene came back to me so clearly now, its stained-glass message finally untangled: it was not possible to rewind time and go back to the way things had been, but if a price was paid, people could make up for their guilt.

Maybe my father's role in all of this was two-fold: to continue to make me feel unwelcome at The Moorings in the life we now shared, *and* to offer me the clue to balancing everything, by telling me that, if I'd never arrived into their lives, Mammy would still be here. Maybe if I went back to where I belonged Mammy might appear to Granny Daly instead. Perhaps that was what would happen. If I could reverse the adoption, Mammy wouldn't need to visit me because I'd never have been hers. Granny Daly had lost both of her children in a period of four months and her life was destroyed as a result. If I could fix it so that she would somehow get one of them back, by Mammy appearing to her, I knew that she would be beyond happy. I now had the power to take the faraway look from her eyes. But supposing my original parents didn't want to take me back? Well, I would just have to do my best to convince them that they'd made a mistake in putting me up for adoption in the first place.

I sent Granny Daly the business card, with the address of the Adoption Society on it, and also the letter from Sister Concepta, to help her begin her enquiries. The date on the letter seemed a little strange to me, and I wondered how I hadn't noticed it the first time around. I had been born in February 1965, yet the date on the letter inviting my parents to collect me was September 1966. It dawned on me that instead of being a tiny baby when I'd been adopted I'd been more than one and a half years old. Where had I been for all of that time? Was that why I remembered the building, when we were passing by it on the way back from Glasnevin Cemetery? Maybe there was a misprint on the letter. Who knows what the real answer was.

Another thing I thought about was Purgatory. Our religion teacher in Newbridge, Mr O'Kane, had told us all about Purgatory. It seemed to be like a waiting room at a bus station. A place you went before you got a ticket to go somewhere else forever. If praying for people could help them get to Heaven, then surely doing something even bigger, a really good deed, like finding your birth mother and getting her to take you back, could get God to open the door even sooner. I knew from religion class that people could be stuck in Purgatory forever, if those on earth didn't do enough praying or a sufficient number of good deeds to buy their onward-journey ticket. Maybe Mammy was stuck between two worlds and needed me to do this thing so that she could move on to Heaven. Maybe it was actually Mammy who was in harm's way and I would be able to save her. Perhaps that was why she'd appeared to me – to inspire me to do the right thing and help her escape from Purgatory. It was all so confusing and really hard to know what to do.

Nyxi had been quite cool with me on the last occasion we'd met, down at the Spanish Arch. When next we got together, it was by chance. I saw her wheeling her bike through the market outside St Nicholas's Church on the Saturday morning after my birthday.

'I got you a birthday present, Hughie, but it's at home in Renmore. I wasn't sure when I'd see you.'

'Are you still cross with me?' I asked, as we stopped at a

stand where a man with a craggy face was selling bunches of carrots tied together with orange twine.

She shook her head. 'I'm not cross with anyone, or maybe I'm just cross with everyone. Dad's gone away to Lebanon, and Mum's not feeling well. I think she might be sick.'

A copy of that week's *Galway Advertiser* was flapping up at the edges on the ground beside another stall. The rest of the newspaper was held down by a sack of turnips. I could read the word 'Regatta' but not much else. An old lady on a tricycle was slowly pedalling through the Saturday-morning shoppers. On the back of the tricycle was a cage and inside the cage was a monkey. As I looked at the old woman, as she concentrated all her energy into her feet, I somehow knew that her son was a sailor in the merchant navy, and that he had brought the monkey back to her as a gift from his travels. I wondered if I had ever spoken to her, or had someone else told me that – or was it true at all? It was a different feeling of knowing, a feeling not at all like seeing the man on the stairs, or the picture of the building in my head before I'd shouted, 'Stop.' I suppose that was because it was not accompanied by a premonition that this old lady was in any kind of danger.

When we'd made our way past Lynch's window, we took the shortcut through Bowling Green, and ended up down by the river at Wood Quay. The massive stone pillars, which had once held up the Galway to Clifden railway line, stood in the water of the Corrib, like stranded grey monsters waiting to become useful again. We wheeled our bikes beside us for a bit, then leaned them up against the back of a park bench that we sat down on.

'How did you get on in Dublin?' she asked, after I'd told her where we'd been for a few days the previous week.

I shrugged my shoulders. 'Not too bad,' I said. 'My father tried to make me cut my granny's lawn with a lawnmower after I ripped my trousers on a tree branch.'

Nyxi moved a little closer to me on the bench. 'Did you have to?' she said.

'Naw. In the end my granny told him the mower was broken.' Nyxi said nothing, but I knew she was really saying that she was on my side.

'And your uncle, how did he die?' she asked.

'Dunno. Heart attack, I suppose,' I said. 'I thought I'd seen him in a kind of dream thing, you know that time down at the Spanish Arch when we . . .' I didn't finish the sentence.

'I hope this isn't more of that ghost shite, Hughie,' Nyxi said.

I'd never heard her use that word before. 'It's not, it's not what you said, Nyxi. There *is* something going on about what I've seen, and what she told me, and the stuff that happened in the church, and the stained-glass—'

'The stained-glass window fixing itself?' she said.

'Yes,' I said, delighted that she'd remembered. 'And now I think I've found a way to kind of bring her back for my granny.'

Nyxi stood up in front of me. 'To *what*?'

'To bring her back for my granny,' I said quietly.

'Jesus Christ, Hughie. What are you on about? What planet are you living on?'

'What do you mean?' I asked, but I knew the answer already.

'I mean, when are you going to grow up, Hughie? When are you going to open a few cans of cop-on and realise what the rest of the world already knows? There *are* no ghosts, no windows that you can break and then they fix themselves. What do you mean, "some kind of dream thing down by the Spanish Arch"? Can you just explain that to me?'

'I know it sounds bananas, but in my head I saw a man going upstairs carrying a blue motorbike helmet and I knew he was in danger. I tried to get him to turn around, so I could see his face, but he wouldn't, and I knew that if he went into that room, the one at the top of the stairs—'

'Just listen to yourself, Hughie. You're going mad. You'll wind up in Ballinasloe if you're not careful. Who else have you been telling this rubbish to?'

'It's not rubbish,' I said angrily.

'Then what is it?' she said defiantly. 'What is it you believe in now? Magic, is it? Or are you like the tinker lady at the races in Ballybrit – able to look into the future?' She began to mock me even further now by laughing.

'My mother is alive somewhere,' I said, beginning to choke back tears. 'She spoke to me and I saw her, and I heard her, and she was real and she told me things that nobody else could have known. And then she said that I would be able to know when people were in danger, and there was a child who ran across the road, and I shouted, "Stop"—'

'No, Hughie. *You* stop.' Nyxi took a step backwards and her face became cold and she didn't really look like her anymore. 'None of this stuff you're saying is real. I know you miss her, but you're just going to have to accept the real facts about your mother. She *isn't* floating around somewhere in the clouds and dropping into churches to fix windows. She's in Bushy Park graveyard. That's what happens when people die. And everybody dies.'

'Please don't say those things to me, Nyxi,' I begged. 'You're wrong, you don't know everything. You're not God.'

'I thought you didn't believe in God,' she sneered.

'I don't know what I believe in, but there's something there that nobody can tell me isn't true. Not even you. You're supposed to be my friend.'

'Friends don't tell each other lies,' she said. 'My mam has found a lump on her . . . her . . . Up here,' she said, pointing to her chest. 'If it turns out to be cancer, she might die, and if she dies, I know she won't be able to come back. So I don't need someone to tell me lies, Hughie. I could do that myself.'

With those words, Nyxi Kirwan turned and walked around to where her bike was propped up. She wheeled it a few yards, then hopped on and was gone. I wondered if I would ever see her again.

There was a light on under the door of my father's study after I finished my homework and put my books in my bag for the following day. This was a few days after I'd had the row with Nyxi. My homework had included an essay about summer holidays. I had written about our trip to Portugal, and how sunny it was, and how I didn't like the food. I didn't say anything about Mammy standing up on a chair in the dining room in the hotel, and telling everyone that Elvis Presley had joined the FBI as an undercover agent, and that also their flights had been delayed by fog.

I heard my father's voice as I went back past the study to head up the stairs to bed. He was on the telephone.

'See you Thursday night, then. Leave it fairly late, because he's often up till round eleven.' I presumed he was talking to Breege, organising for her to come and continue their relationship when it was dark and I was in bed. I didn't care anymore about him *or* Breege. What consumed me most was that I might have lost my only friend, and that Granny Daly hadn't telephoned with any news as she had promised she would.

What Nyxi had said hurt me deeply. What hurt me even more was that I then began to wonder if she *was* right about everything. *Was* I just lying to her and myself and refusing to face the truth? Everything that had happened *had* seemed real to me. I'd felt the furnace heat of the window in the church; I'd seen the candles go out and then reignite. And Mammy *had* been there, flesh and blood and hair and headscarf and all. What other possible explanation was there, apart from it all being true? *Was* I going mad, as Nyxi had suggested? Surely I wouldn't wind up in the loony bin in Ballinasloe, with all the poitín alcoholics, and the mad people of the west of Ireland? Would I end up like Mammy did, in a psychiatric unit, unable to be trusted with a portable record-player?

I thought about all this as I went to brush my teeth. The toothpaste was almost all gone, so I rolled up the tube from the very end, hoping that enough of it would emerge from the top to allow me to complete the task. A movement in the mirror caught my eye, and when I looked back and stood in front of it, I was greeted not by my own reflection but by the same scene I'd witnessed in my head at the Spanish Arch a few weeks earlier. Again, a man was mounting a narrow set of stairs, step by step. He still had the helmet, the blue motorbike helmet, in one hand and it was swinging back and forth. I couldn't remember if it was in the same hand. At the top of the stairs there was a door, and I was gripped again by a paralysing and unspeakable knowledge that enormous peril lay ahead of him. I tried to make out the wallpaper on either side of the stairs, but no pattern or even a colour revealed itself to me. I watched the helmet as it swung back and up in the man's hand, and I saw now that it was not a motorbike helmet at all. As the figure reached the top of the stairs, he suddenly stopped, then came down one step with his back still turned to me. I willed him to continue his descent, but he did not. Instead, he slowly turned his head around to look directly at me. I recognised him instantly.

'It was definitely your dad, Nyxi,' I told her, when I telephoned her home the next day. 'I know he's in some kind of danger.'

'Leave me alone, Hughie,' she said. 'I never want to speak to you ever again.' With that she put down the phone.

Chapter 16

St Patrick's Day dawned in dollops of rain over the city. The tourists could easily be distinguished from the locals by their umbrellas. Nobody who is actually from Galway owns an umbrella. They're not much use, because it rains so often, you'd break your arm putting them up and taking them down and, anyway, everyone gets so wet they can't get any wetter.

The parade wound its way through the streets. I stood on the pavement outside the Savoy Cinema on Eglinton Street and watched the dozens of frozen-cold Irish dancers from the rival academies of Peggy Carty and Celine Hession. The floats were the same as the year before, a mix of farm machinery and some thatched cottages on trailers with women dressed in black Claddagh shawls, and the men in overcoats and flat caps, smoking clay 'duideen' pipes beside a fireplace. I missed Nyxi. We hadn't spoken since the night I'd phoned, yet somehow I hoped I might meet her at the parade. I was wrong about that. I couldn't ring her again. She was too angry with me. A marching band of musicians, from Great Falls, Montana, played a tune I thought I recognised from a cowboy film.

A lot had happened over the previous few weeks. I suppose I had begun to feel less of an outsider in the school, yet at the same time I had come to accept that I had single-handedly been responsible for the complete destruction of the Sancta Hotel. This gave me a strange feeling: I could be part of the lives of other people without their knowledge. As I went from the classroom to a science lab, or out around the playground, I felt more part of the school, although I still hadn't made any friends. The other boys seemed to accept me a bit more, or perhaps they just noticed me less and maybe that's the same thing.

There was a boy in my class who was called Iggy Kelehan. 'Iggy' is short for some saint's longer name. He was an expert on absolutely everything you could ever think of to talk about. He had a funny way of talking, really flat Galway, I suppose, but also with a hint that he'd maybe lived in England, too. Anyway, he wore a pair of glasses, but instead of making him look like a swot, they made him look tougher. One side was held together by Sellotape. Every day at break he would be in the playground surrounded by fellas and he would be doing all of the talking. He would ask questions, then answer them himself, so nobody else had to speak at all.

'Do you know what the most powerful handgun in the world is?' Nobody knew or, if they did, they didn't get a chance to answer. 'The Magnum forty-five. If you were sitting in the driving seat of a car [pronounced 'care'], and a fella came up to you with a Magnum forty-five, say the care was a Ford Escort Cosworth, and you were in the driving seat – well, if he put the gun up against the door and pulled the trigger, the bullet would go through the door, through you, across the gearstick, through the person in the passenger seat, and then through the passenger door and, if there was someone walking by the care on the other side, it would kill them too. Sthone dead.'

I wondered why the person wouldn't shoot you through the window, or wait for you to get out of the car, but I didn't ask Iggy Kelehan either of those things. What I did do was listen to his and other people's stories and wonder where we would all be years later, or what we would do when we grew up. I wondered, too, about Vernon Crosby, with his warty hands, and Michael Meagher, people I had known in my first school in Terryglass. What were they doing now? I had almost completely forgotten about Mr and Mrs Cleary, the two teachers there, and the day the magician came to the school and put Joan Davoren into a box, then pushed swords right through her. I remembered they'd been at Mammy's funeral, but they hadn't come up to talk to me afterwards. That seemed a bit strange to me. Perhaps it was hard to know what to say in those situations so some people said nothing at all. I thought about what I would do when I grew up and left school. I wasn't much good at anything, really, except maybe causing people to die or to be saved sometimes, and collapsing the occasional hotel. What did people who did those things grow up to be?

Granny Daly had rung one evening. My father was out, so I answered the phone.

'Are you all right to talk, Hughie?' she asked.

'I am, Granny. There's no one else in the house.' She coughed a little, and I heard the rustle of paper at the other end of the line, then her voice again.

'I got a reply from those people, Hughie,' she said.

'What did they say?' I asked, as I pulled out a chair that was on the other side of the hall table, then sat up on the table with my foot resting on the seat of the chair.

'Well,' she continued, 'they said they couldn't really tell me very much about – about her. It's all very complicated, Hughie. They said that usually only the adopted person could make enquiries and that, even then, you would have to be over eighteen to do that. I told them I was really acting in loco parentis for you now because of Deirdre's death. The letter goes on to say that in most cases they are unable to track the mother down because of the "passage of time".'

'Didn't they tell you anything at all, Granny?' I asked.

'Well,' she said, 'they gave me a few tiny bits of information. They said that the woman was twenty-seven when she had you, and that she was a hairdresser. They also said . . .' I could hear Granny Daly fiddling with the piece of paper again.

'Yes?' I asked, impatiently.

'They also said she was from the Munster area, and that her name might have been Mary, although they weren't sure about that bit.'

'The Munster bit or the Mary bit?' I asked.

'The Mary bit,' Granny Daly said. We didn't speak for a few seconds. I wasn't sure what to say to her about anything she'd told me. It wasn't very much to go on: Mary, the twenty-seven-year-old hairdresser from Munster, who might have had a different name altogether. 'Are you still there, Hughie?' Granny Daly asked.

'Hmm, yes, yes, I am,' I answered.

'So, what do you think?' she asked.

'It's not much to go on, really, is it?' I said.

'It's not. But it's more than you had before,' she said. I could almost hear Mammy's voice instead of hers as she said it.

'Did they say anything else, Granny?'

'Nothing really, just that if they do manage to find her and she wants to be in touch, then they'll contact me.'

So they hadn't said anything about who my father was. At this rate, he could have been Elvis Presley. Anyway, at least it was something. There would be a long way to go to get this lady, Mary – if that *was* her real name – in the hair salon in Munster to take me back, so as to wipe out my debt of having caused Mammy's death. I thought about what would happen if I did go back to my first mother, and if Mammy began to appear to Granny Daly instead. People who killed themselves didn't wait around indefinitely, I imagined, in a place they could appear to people from – so I presumed I'd have to sort it out sooner rather than later.

I didn't want to share my plans with Granny Daly, just in case it took ages, or didn't work. What would the lady in Munster think when she got a letter from the adoption people? Who knew how she might react. One thing that struck me was that, if she'd given me up for adoption, why would she ever want to take me back? Maybe if I explained to her that it was because I'd caused Mammy's death and was just trying to make up for it, she'd agree to take me back. I mean, if clothes shops take things back when they don't fit properly, then why shouldn't you be able to do the same with people?

'We'll just have to wait,' Granny Daly and I said, at exactly the same time. And so we would.

The rest of that evening I continued to think about what Granny Daly had told me. Munster was a big place; I mean, they had mountains and lakes and Limerick and the Cliffs of Moher and the Ring of Kerry and all that. In the geography textbook printed by Folens, there was a map of Ireland with the provinces marked out and the counties in different colours: Clare, Limerick, Kerry, Cork, Waterford, Tipperary . . . And sure how many hairdressers were there altogether? She could be anywhere.

On a couple of occasions over those weeks in March, I had heard a car pull into the drive of The Moorings late at night, and sometimes I'd been woken by headlights racing up the wall of my room, as it turned to park facing out past the monkey puzzle tree. I know that my father had made an effort since my return to ensure that I did not bump into Breege, maybe because of the row we'd had in his study, or perhaps he had some other reason. Anyway, I mostly only *heard* rather than saw her, as she arrived late at night and left early in the morning before I got up for school.

I had not really thought about what was happening between my father and Breege, and although I'd been angry that he had a 'girlfriend' so soon after Mammy had died, I was grateful to him, I suppose, for trying at least to hide it from me. I knew that he and Mammy had been arguing and he had told me she had been unhappy for a long time. I wondered whether Mammy would appear to *him* if I returned to my birth mother. Okay, so people couldn't come back from the dead and be alive again, but maybe they could have a series of conversations in which they settled the differences that had made them unhappy. I knew that my father hadn't been able to see Mammy when she appeared in the church in Newbridge so perhaps my return to my birth mother was what was needed to allow Mammy to appear to him as well. Maybe dead people could only appear to one person. If Simon Mittman hadn't wanted to adopt me in the first place, he would surely be happy to get rid of me now. But I wasn't doing any of this for *him*: it was to try to make things right with Mammy and to help Granny Daly. If everything worked out, I hoped that Mammy would first appear to Granny Daly, then eventually move out of Purgatory, once a space had been cleared for her in Heaven.

A week or so before St Patrick's Day, a Saturday morning – I think it was the day that Ireland were playing Wales in the rugby – I was woken by the sound of Breege's voice on the landing outside my bedroom.

'Come out here now and face me, or I'll break the door down.' She must have worked out that I was trying to help Mammy fix things with my father and realised that she would not be able to continue to see him if that happened. But why was she out on the landing? My door wasn't locked. I didn't know why she hadn't just barged in. 'Come out!' she shouted, and I heard a pummelling of fists on a door, but it wasn't my door that she was hammering on. I got out of bed and put on my dressing-gown over my pyjamas. I opened the door.

Breege was standing outside my father's bedroom, with her hands on her hips. 'Open the door, Simon!' she screamed. 'I know you're in there, and I know she's in there too.'

My father's bedroom door was unlocked from the inside and it opened slowly. My father stood there, wearing a pair of green pyjamas, and in his bare feet. He held the door in one hand and the other he raised to his mouth as if he was yawning, but he really wasn't.

'Breege. What are you doing here? Is everything all right? What time of the day or night is it?'

Breege did not seem to be calmed by his appearance. She didn't answer any of his questions either. 'If there's nothing going on, then let me into your bedroom,' she said slowly, but not in a nice voice. My father looked very uncomfortable and vulnerable, there in the doorway in his yucky-coloured pyjamas. He looked in my direction, then back at Breege.

'Okay, Breege. If you really want to come in and have a look, you're welcome to. But if you don't trust me enough to believe me when I tell you that there *is* nobody else in here, then I don't know where we're going with our relationship, if that trust—'

'Get out of my way,' she said angrily, and she put both of her hands palms-down in the middle of the door and shoved it open out of my father's grip. I had never heard anyone speak to him like that, and I wondered if she would have spoken to him in that way if they'd been at the hospital, and she had been wearing a nurse's uniform and he was dressed in the green overalls he wore for surgery. After she'd gone past him, my father swept his arm out, like a head waiter pointing the way to a table in a restaurant.

'Suit yourself, Breege. There's no one else here.' I heard Breege's heavy footsteps tramping about, then a bit of silence. Finally she spoke, in a different voice, still cross but not as sure of itself.

'Then who owns the other car in the driveway, Simon?' she asked.

'Mrs McAdoo, our housekeeper,' he said. I knew that Mrs McAdoo didn't drive.

There was another pause. And then: 'Does the housekeeper own these silk panties as well?' I heard the sound of the wardrobe being flung open. 'Mrs McAdoo, the housekeeper, I presume? Can you tell me why you look very like that bitch from A & E, Clodagh Hopper?' I heard the scream of a third person, whose voice was new to me. A young lady, who was completely naked, ran out of the room and down the landing to the bathroom, clutching some clothes to her front. Despite that, I saw pretty much everything. The only other time I'd seen a naked woman was on one of the playing cards that Bobby Hester sold behind the bicycle sheds for three pence each.

As the bathroom door was slammed shut and locked by the naked lady, Breege came back out onto the landing, carrying some clothes. She looked over at me, sighed, shrugged her shoulders a little, and gave me a sort of apologetic smile. She began to make her way down the stairs. My father came out of the room, hopping on one foot as he tried to put on a pair of trousers over his pyjama bottoms. I was about to start laughing but I didn't. My father made his way to the top of the stairs.

'Breege! Breege!' he called after her. 'You're wrong about all of this. It's not what you think.'

I expected to hear the front door open and slam shut, but instead Breege spoke again, this time calmly and with almost a laugh in her voice: 'I'm right about one thing,

Simon, one hundred percent right – you're a prick. You're such a prick, that if there was a shortage of them, you'd make two!' The front door opened and slammed shut.

My father never mentioned the incident afterwards, but it hung in the house like a murder we'd both witnessed and couldn't speak about, but couldn't forget. And in a way something *had* been killed off, I suppose: a little bit of his invincibility and my innocence. And somewhere in the middle of all of that there was perhaps a little green shoot of understanding between us that some things were changing.

All of this was going around inside my head while I watched the St Patrick's Day parade. I had the feeling that even though a lot had been happening, much more was still to happen, and I didn't know how it would be when it did. In my imagination, I thought about a lady whose face I couldn't see, the woman who had sold me to the nuns. And now I was setting out on a path to find her and ask her to take me back. She wouldn't have to buy me, of course, because I was thirteen now, but maybe I'd have to pay *her*. I had some money saved in a jar in my room. I'd counted it, and it came to twenty-three pounds and fourteen pence. It was hard to know if that would be enough. Anyway, it was very early days in the search, and Granny Daly and I would need more information than we had so far, if real progress was to be made.

I wondered about Nyxi, and even thought about cycling out to Renmore after the parade to see her, but I knew from what she'd said and how she'd spoken that I wouldn't be welcome there. She was worried because her mam was sick. No wonder she didn't want to hear me talking about dead mothers and apparitions and stained-glass windows. On top of all that, now I'd gone and heaped on more worry about her dad's overseas trip. Who wants to know in advance that they might be about to become an orphan? I knew it was definitely her dad on the stairs, but what could I do to stop whatever might happen to him?

Things stayed pretty much as they were, right past Easter and on into early, mid- and then late April. The weather improved, and the tulips came and went, like they always did. I cycled out to Bushy Park churchyard one day after school, instead of going home. The flowers on Mammy's grave had all withered, and now looked just a sticky mess of stalks and string. I tried to talk to her, but for the first time since she'd died, I couldn't. It was almost as if she was not to be found there, in the one place I actually knew she was. Or maybe she *was* there but she just didn't feel like talking to me or to anyone else. I noticed that there was plenty of room in the main churchyard. Why hadn't she been buried inside the wall instead of outside it? I cycled home over Circular Road.

There had been a martial arts film festival at the Claddagh Palace Cinema shortly after St Patrick's Day and for weeks it fuelled discussion in the playground. 'Do you know why Bruce Lee died?' Iggy Kelehan asked, one day at break. 'He was too fit. You see, there are three levels of fitness. There's unfit, fit and then *too* fit. If you or me went down to the rowing shed and sat into the rowing machine, we'd sthart the thing at wan and then two, and we'd work right up to seven or eight and we'd be exhausted. Bruce Lee would *sthart* at eight, and thin, when he got it up to tin, he'd complain that it didn't go up to twinty. That's why he died. He was too fit so his heart just stopped. Bang. Exit the Dragon.'

At the end of April, there was one day when the sun was so hot through the landing window that I thought it would burn a hole in the carpet. I decided to go out into the garden and put oil on the chain of my bike. I turned the bike upside-down on the patio outside the back door, and I got the 3-in-One oil can from the garage. I allowed the oil to drizzle down over the chain and the wheel cogs, then turned the pedals slowly so that every bit of the chain and the cogs made contact with some oil. When I'd finished, I realised I hadn't brought a cloth with me to wipe my hands. I knew there was a bundle of them in the greenhouse, so I went in there to get one. I saw Mrs McAdoo in the kitchen, carrying a pile of clothes in her arms as I made my way to the greenhouse.

It was like an oven in there, and I saw that some tomato plants were beginning to sprout in the pots on one of the windowsills. I looked out through the window, and could see right down and around the L-turn at the end, to the old orchard and the white brick wall. Between the greenhouse and the turn was the vegetable patch where carrots, cabbage and onions grew every second year. There was a blue J-Cloth, and I picked it up and began to wipe the oil from my hands, wondering if I might someday become a mechanic or maybe even start a summer job with Mr Newell, who ran a bicycle shop called the Café, fixed bikes and sold cigarettes in ones and twos. The door of the greenhouse clicked shut behind me.

I turned around. Mammy was standing on an upturned wooden crate, and she was up on her tippy-toes, untying the dressing-gown belt from the steel pole that ran the length of the roof of the greenhouse. I couldn't move because I was afraid of what might happen if I did. The wooden crate tipped over to one side and for a moment it looked as if she wouldn't be able to undo the knot. Luckily, she managed it, and then the crate righted itself. Mammy breathed a sigh of relief, and stuffed the loose part of the belt down inside her nightdress. It was only then that she seemed to notice me.

'Ah, Hughie,' she said. 'There you are. I was wondering when you'd come to see me. I know you're away at school now in Newbridge.'

'I got thrown out, Mammy,' I said. 'Remember the window and the boy who said I was blackmailing him?' She didn't seem to hear me, because she didn't agree or disagree about remembering. 'I'm working on a plan with Granny Daly,' I continued. 'I think I know how to get you out of Purgatory. It's all about finding people, and asking them to take me in. Like a swap, the way the lads swap football cards.'

'I've missed you so much, Hughie,' she said. 'And I've been trying to fix things from here as well. You're doing really, really well, Hughie. I saw the boy you saved from running out in front of the car. I saw all the stuff about Nyxi's dad and everything.'

'What's going to happen to Nyxi's dad, Mammy? How can I save him? Can you talk to him? Is there any way that I can go with you now and stay with you forever? I promise I'll be good. I'll change everything so you won't be unhappy anymore. I'll get you some new clothes, I have twenty-three pounds and fourteen pence in the jar and you can have it all. Just tell me what to do, Mammy. I don't want you to go away again.'

Mammy stepped down off the box and walked towards me. She held out her hand and I took it in mine. It was different this time because, although when she touched me I felt it, when I tried to touch her face it didn't feel like her at all, not really. It wasn't like it was just thin air or anything, but more like my fingers didn't recognise her in the same way. She opened the door of the greenhouse with her free hand. She led me after her out into the sunshine.

'I'm going to stay with you for a while, Hughie,' she said. 'There's something we need to do together.'

'Are we going to Moons to get you some new clothes, Mammy?' I asked, as the breeze caught the end of her nightdress and blew it flat against her legs.

'No, Hughie,' she said with a smile, 'not Moons. We're not going into town at all. Sure all the shops will nearly be shut. No, we're going to do something here at The Moorings.'

'Are we going to make soda bread, Mammy?' I asked. 'I can't make it without you. I can't do anything without you. I'm so sorry that I was the cause of you taking your own life. Daddy said that if I'd never come along, you'd still be alive. I'm just lost and tired and sad and lonely, and there's nothing I can do.'

'Yes, there is, Hughie. There *is* something you can do. Come on and I'll help you.' Mammy led me across the patio, past the upended bicycle dripping oil onto the stone slabs. She led me into the garage, and across the bare floor to where the now barely red-coloured Iverson petrol-powered Rotary Sickle Mower (manufactured by the Rotary Mower Company of Omaha, Nebraska) lay. Without looking at the tag on the side, I knew by fearful heart the patent number: US 2165551 1938.

'I can't,' I protested, as she began to manoeuvre it out of its corner and started to push it towards the sunlight, which was piling in through the door.

'Of course you can, Hughie,' Mammy said. 'You're thirteen now – you can do anything you want to, absolutely anything.' And so together we pushed and pulled it along the patio, and Mammy filled it with petrol while I stood behind it with the handle in my hand. The last time this lawnmower and I had faced each other, I was seven years old. I was much taller now, but I was still terrified. My absent toes were proof of who the boss was in this struggle. I dropped the handle. I wanted to tell Mammy all about my plans to find my birth mother, and to get her to take me back so that everything would be fine – but what if none of that happened? It would only make things worse. So I said nothing.

'If you don't stand up to your fear, Hughie,' Mammy said, 'you'll always be afraid. That's no way to be.' I closed my eyes, and when I opened them, Mammy was still there. She took my hands and placed them on the handle. 'Don't be afraid, Hughie. Don't ever be afraid again.'

Together we pulled the handle, and the string wheezed its protest, but after two more attempts, the lawnmower roared. I *was* frightened of it, but more afraid that if I ran away now, Mammy would leave. I began, slowly at first, cutting the grass at the back of the house, up and down, then over and across until the smell of freshly mown lawn was all around the back of the house, as welcome a scent as Charlie perfume. Mammy stayed with me all the time, and when I'd got the hang of it, she let me push the lawnmower by myself. She sat on the back step and watched me.

Without really thinking about it, I pushed the still-running mower down the side passageway between the garage and Mr Rennick's garden wall. That was where I'd lost my toes, but now *I* was in charge and my fear began to seep out of me, through some ventilation point in my head, or my good foot, or I don't know where. I mowed around the monkey puzzle tree, and Mammy sat under the tree then, and watched me, and smiled and waved, and encouraged me, as I made deep paths in the grass of the garden, then circumnavigated the front lawn to meet up with them again. I knew that when I finished, Mammy and I would have a lot to talk about. I was going to ask her about the window, and how it had fixed itself. I'd ask her what Purgatory was like. And I knew for certain that she would not have been happy to see a naked woman running across our landing to the bathroom.

It took me more than an hour and a half to cut the grass. Mammy stayed with me all the time, and whenever I looked over at her, she waved and I knew that I was not afraid of this lawnmower now. As I finished the last bit, I eased down the lever, which shut off the engine. I thought it was starting up again itself, when I heard a new noise as I turned away. It wasn't the mower, though: it was the sound of my father's car on the gravel of the drive. I looked to the base of the monkey puzzle tree, but Mammy had disappeared.

Chapter 17

I had never been inside a pub. The noise that greeted my ears when I opened the door into Tigh Neachtain on Quay Street was different from anything I had ever heard before. The pub was made up of a series of little rooms, which all had tables and benches and chairs in them. There was a smell of food in the air, like soup or old rashers, and people chatted away to each other while a man with his back to me sat on a chair, playing the piano. I recognised the song, but couldn't remember very many of the words. But even the fact that I realised I had heard it before was a surprise to me. Something about, 'You know how bad she is up our road,' was all I could recall.

It was the Saturday of the May bank holiday weekend, and nearly all of the chairs and benches were occupied. As I stood there, just listening to the music and the chatter and the noise of a plate being dropped somewhere out of sight, it occurred to me that in a few years I would be going to pubs and drinking black beer with a white top, like they had in the ads on television. There was one ad in which a man was always just finishing his drink and he would put the glass down on the table and say, 'Ah, that's Bass!' I saw a glass with some black beer in it, abandoned on a low shelf, and I picked it up and smelt it. *Ugh*. It smelt horrible. A man came up some steps near to where I was, and he was collecting empty glasses.

'Are you looking for someone?' he asked me.

'Not really,' I said. But I suppose I was.

'Are you with anyone?' he asked then.

'No,' I said. That at least was definitely true.

'You'd be better off somewhere else then,' he said, with a friendly smile, as he turned and bumped the door to the street open with his bottom. I worked out that he did not want me to stay. The notes of the piano followed me into the street. I wandered across the road to a toyshop, and stood looking in at the brightly coloured wooden toys displayed in the window. I was too old for the toy shop and too young for the pub. The person I was looking for was Nyxi but we hadn't spoken in weeks, and hadn't arranged to meet, like we normally did. I knew I probably wouldn't find her by accident.

'Are you on your own today, Hughie?' Mrs Kenny asked me, when I visited the bookshop. I just shrugged my shoulders and gave a little smile. I wandered upstairs and into the top room, which was crammed with millions and millions of books. On a stand was a black stone sculpture of a butterfly; nearby was a frightening green bull made of metal. I didn't know if I would ever see Nyxi again. I thought about Mammy, and Nyxi, and Uncle Seán. I wondered if these people had all disappeared from my life because of me, or perhaps as a result of something I had done.

Sometimes it was the people who you didn't want in your life who invaded it the most. My father had bought me a gift for my birthday.

'I know it's a little late,' he'd said at breakfast, as he'd slid the thin parcel across the table. 'I don't think you have this one.' I opened the plain brown wrapping paper with the Zhivago Records stickers holding down the sides. It was *Moody Blue*, Elvis Presley's last album. I was dumbstruck. 'I hope you like it,' my father said, before getting up to put his cereal bowl in the sink.

'I do. I really do, Daddy. Thanks.' It was the first time in years I'd called him that. I don't know why I did, but it seemed the right thing to do. Maybe I thought that that was what a 'normal' son would say.

I listened to the record over and over in the first few days after I'd got it. The two best songs on it were 'Unchained Melody' and 'Way Down'. Mammy hadn't bought the *Moody Blue* LP, because it was Elvis's last, and she said that if she did, it would mean accepting that he had really died. If she didn't acknowledge that her hero was gone, then in a way he wouldn't be.

I had thought about Mammy a lot after she'd come to help me cut the grass. To be honest, I hadn't been sure after the church thing whether she would ever come back to see me again. I did wonder for a while if, by helping her out of Purgatory with my plan to find my birth mother, I would make it more difficult for her to continue to appear to me if I wasn't taken back into my original family. I then realised that if Mammy got to Heaven, God would be there and He could help her do anything she wanted. Even if she decided not to visit me as often, or not at all, I still had the responsibility to help her as much as I could on her journey. I remembered that I had stopped believing in God for a while. Maybe that was part of the reason that all of this – her appearances, the coincidences, my premonitions – was happening too: to give me a sign so that I would start believing again. Anyway, that part seemed to have worked. There was so much that I simply didn't understand.

Meanwhile, at school, the Gaelic football team won their way through to a final for the first time in about four hundred years (or maybe forty). There was a good feeling in the school and I remembered the cup-song practices in Newbridge College, and the buzz around the refectory as the day of the Senior and Junior cup games approached. Although I was useless at sport, and had no interest in watching it either, I began to understand that feeling of being part of something bigger than myself. It was not clear to me what had caused it to happen, but I recognised the feeling and it was not unwelcome.

One afternoon I was walking along the classroom corridor on the top floor of the school, and I had a sudden sense of something that frightened me. I looked around and expected to see someone behind me, but no one was there. As I walked down the corridor, the feeling began to recede, so I turned and headed back the way I had come. As I approached a radiator on the wall, the feeling of fear came upon me again, and as I got further away in the other direction, it diminished once more and disappeared as I reached the end of the corridor. I learned later that behind the radiator there had been a room, now sealed up, where a suicide had occurred. Iggy Kelehan had all the details, of course.

'Some lads were messing with a Ouija board in the sixties, and they called up this wan who used to do murders around the Claddagh. One of the lads jumped out the window on the other side and was killed sthone dead. He landed head first on the basketball court at the exact same moment that Louis Armstrong landed on the moon.'

I didn't know if any of this was true, but neither could I explain my own feelings, or the bit of me that seemed to tune in, like a radio, whenever I was near that place from then on. But why hadn't it happened to me months ago, on the countless occasions on which I'd walked down that corridor since I'd moved to the school? There was nothing different about me, or what I did, between my start in the school and the first time I had the feeling. I carried the same books. I wore the same clothes. I walked the same way. And then it struck me one night when I was getting ready for bed: the only different thing about me was that I'd stopped wearing the cross and chain Nyxi had given me. Maybe that cross had protected me from tuning in to awful things that had happened. I searched high up and low down for the cross and chain, but couldn't find it. I recalled that I'd taken it off the night Nyxi had put the phone down on me all those months ago. I wondered if somehow I was connected to places where death was. These strange feelings and visions had to mean *something*.

Around the same time, I had started cycling the long way home from school. Instead of simply turning right at the lights at Nile Lodge, and going straight up Taylor's Hill, I now went straight through the junction and headed for Salthill and out along the prom.

The prom is a huge long footpath, which stretches all the way from Whitestrand and Grattan, along past the back of Seapoint, then out beyond Leisureland and the road up to the Hilltop. It continues past Threadneedle Road, and the Ocean Wave Hotel, and finishes at the wall at the end of Blackrock where the diving boards are. If you're a real Galwegian, you kick that wall before you turn back. In two or three spots along the prom there are concrete shelters, with wooden benches inside, and there's also an ice-cream kiosk, which opens during the summer months. All the way along, no matter what time of the day or night or season of the year you go there, you can hear the sea. The prom and the sea are as much a part of Galway as the man with the glass eye who takes the tickets at the Town Hall Cinema, or the blind man who plays the accordion outside Glynn's in Shop Street. I made the most of my bike in those weeks, not knowing how long more I would have it.

'The bike's not in great condition,' Mr Newell at the Café said to me, when I asked him if he'd buy it from me and for how much. 'Maybe six or seven pounds,' he said, holding the back wheel off the ground and turning the pedal with his other hand. Of course I didn't want to sell it, but I was anxious to get a valuation for it, so that I knew how much leeway there was in bargaining with my birth mother, if the money I'd saved in the jar wasn't enough to buy my way back into her family. With the bike as my fall-back position, I could offer *it* as well, or sell it to Mr Newell and increase the money in the jar by whatever he paid me. There was a huge difference between six and seven pounds – I'd have to make sure I wasn't ripped off. I wondered how Granny Daly was getting on with her enquiries, but in my heart I knew that if there was any news she'd ring me.

One Sunday morning my father went out to play golf, and I was left on my own in the house for a few hours. It was sunny outside, and the birds were all chirping in the bushes. After breakfast I went into the garden and walked to the old orchard around the L behind the house. The trees were gnarled and decrepit, and some looked as if they should be in an old folks' home being fed through a tube. I realised that, like people, they would all die someday. I thought about Mammy and the other people buried in Bushy Park. Were their families doing anything to try to help *them* out of Purgatory? They couldn't all have gone straight through to Heaven.

Back inside the house, I put on Elvis's *40 Greatest Hits*, and turned up the volume so that the whole house was filled with music – something that hadn't happened since Mammy had died. She used to put on Elvis when she was vacuuming, so no matter where she was in the house, she could hear him, encouraging her to be 'All Shook Up' or to do the 'Jailhouse Rock' with him, as she cleaned. I was in the downstairs toilet when I heard the song 'Crying In The Chapel'. Suddenly, in my mind, I was back in Terryglass, with Mammy walking me home past the farmyard where the farmer was placing the small record-player on top of the milk churn so that his cows could listen to the music too.

I'd asked her, 'Who is that, Mammy?'

'It's Elvis, love. Elvis Presley.'

I had always thought that she meant the *farmer* was called Elvis Presley. Now, aged thirteen, I saw the joke in that, and realised it had been my mistake.

It's amazing how music can make you feel like you're back where you were when you heard it the first time, instead of where you are now. That was when I began to think about a recipe. Not a recipe for soda bread, or anything you would be cooking or baking, but a recipe for people. If you could write down a recipe for what was needed to make a person appear, then maybe you could always call them back whenever you wanted, just by following the recipe. I was desperate to see Mammy again.

'Crying In The Chapel' had brought Mammy back, but only in my head, and only by way of remembering things that had already happened. That was what memories were, I supposed: moments you thought of that had already been and gone, but that you'd forgotten in between. Like postcards from your holiday or photographs you'd taken, they only helped you remember.

I made a list of the things that both of her appearances had in common. Surely that would be the easiest way to work out the recipe.

The Church	*The Greenhouse*
During the day	Also during the day
Stained glass	Greenhouse glass
Heat in the window	Hot in the greenhouse
Mammy's clothes (strange blouse)	Her nightie
The dressing-gown belt	The dressing-gown belt
Disappeared when my father appeared	Same

I wrote out these lists, and looked at them for a long time. How could I recreate the exact same circumstances in which Mammy had appeared and spoken to me? I racked my brains, and then I remembered that the only items of her clothes I still had were her green jumper, the blouse I'd never seen before and the dressing-gown. They were still in the garage in the plastic bag. I fetched the jumper and the blouse but left the dressing-gown in the bag, in case it might scare her off. After I'd gathered up her clothes, I realised they smelt musty and not at all like Mammy smelt. I took five pounds from my jar, and cycled down to the pharmacy in the shopping centre on the Headford Road. It was the only pharmacy in the whole city that opened on a Sunday. I bought a bottle of Charlie perfume, and cycled back to Taylor's Hill.

It was almost two o'clock when everything was ready. I stood in the greenhouse, with Mammy's blouse in my hand. I had left her jumper on the same wooden crate she'd stood on. I'd sprayed around a fair bit of Charlie perfume so the greenhouse smelt quite sweet; I thought it was probably better to use too much than too little. The sun was overhead now, and I could feel its warmth pouring down into the greenhouse. I held the blouse up to the light, and I felt it growing warm in my hand. Then I waited and waited and waited. But she never came.

That night, as I switched off the lamp on my bedside table, I went over and over the lists in my head, trying to figure out what the missing ingredient was. I knew that nobody else could see Mammy when she'd appeared, and wondered if, that afternoon, someone else had been around and had soured the mix so that she couldn't visit. I really felt that I had done my best to work out the ideal conditions for an apparition. Maybe she had just been too busy. The other, and very worrying, explanation was that maybe it was all up to her, and there was nothing I could do to make it happen more often than it was going to.

As I drifted off to sleep, I remembered another difference between the two visits: in the church I'd been able to hug her, but in the greenhouse, touching her was different. It was like a snowman melting, I thought. I woke up in the middle of the night and remembered my father's belated birthday gift. Maybe by having that record in my possession, Mammy thought I'd accepted that Elvis was really dead. Perhaps if I had the record in the house she would never appear to me here – because she couldn't visit a house where the very thing she had avoided buying now resided. Perhaps she'd seen it on the day she'd appeared in the greenhouse.

To be safe, I threw the record out the following morning on my way to school. There was a big steel bin with a huge lid behind the shop at Nile Lodge, and I broke the vinyl disc and put it back in the sleeve before I dropped it in. Just in case Mammy was watching.

Mr Meehan, our history teacher, told us about it the day we were back after the bank holiday: five UN soldiers had been ambushed in Lebanon. At least one was Irish. Two were dead. None had been named yet, but I knew one had to have been Nyxi's dad. I was afraid to telephone her, but in myself I was certain that her father had been among the group ambushed. I wondered how someone could be ambushed at the top of a flight of stairs.

The many weeks I'd been without Nyxi in my life suddenly all mushed together, and I knew that I loved her very much. She hadn't been right about ghosts and all of that, and people only ever being either alive or dead. Had she? And now maybe her father was dead, and on the evening news read by Don Cockburn. Was it possible that the two of us would only have one parent each now? I didn't want that to be true, not even if it meant that I was completely right about what I'd seen in my head. Nyxi was the only real friend I'd ever had in my whole life, unless you counted Johnny 'Red' Redburn and Lord Peter Flint, but they were from comics I'd read when I was younger so they didn't really count. Mammy had been the only other person who had been my friend, I suppose: there weren't too many people you could share a wigwam with who wouldn't think it was stupid or childish.

Nyxi had a way of always knowing things, like how to cycle past the Rahoon flats and not get killed, or what sweets were called, and which ones you could or couldn't eat after they'd fallen on the floor. I wanted her to be happy because I knew that if she was happy I would be too. I missed the way she laughed, and the way she'd wink at me, if some grown-ups were around and something silly happened – and we both knew exactly what she meant, even though she hadn't said anything.

We had cycled to the quarry so often that it felt like it belonged to just the two of us. I never wanted to have to cycle there on my own, that's what I'm saying. Together, Nyxi and I had found the 'real' Galway, or at least the bits of it that made *us* feel real, whether we were sheltering from the rain in the entrance to the Lion's Tower or cycling in the brightest sunshine along Lower Salthill, trying to see, through the window of Feeney's shop, if the right person was pulling the ice-cream cones. I was afraid for Nyxi and for how she might be feeling now. In my heart I knew her father had been in the ambush, but in another part of my heart I wanted to be wrong about that. I didn't want Nyxi's heart to be broken in the same way that mine was.

Around this time my father was away for a few days at a conference. Mrs McAdoo kept an eye on me while he was away and made sure that I ate properly. The evenings were my own after she'd gone home around seven o'clock. Most times I just watched television and then went to bed, but one night I cycled out to Blackrock. I leaned my bike against the wall of the lifeguards' hut, and began to climb the steps to the diving boards. When I reached the top, I stood at the beginning of the board, which had a green net over it so your feet wouldn't slip. I could see the lights on the other side of Galway Bay, and I knew that out somewhere to my right in the darkness were the Aran

Islands. I stood there, looking up at the sky, and waited until I spotted a star that was in a direct line over where Nyxi's house in Renmore was.

'I don't know if you're awake, God – I'm never really sure about the time zone thing – but if you are and you can hear me, I just want to ask you to save Nyxi's dad. Even if you could get him wounded instead of killed, that would be great. I don't want him to be *too* wounded, though, like still able to drive, because he trains the Galwegians under-tens sometimes and he needs to be able to drive for the away games. I know I haven't believed in you all the time, but this is separate from what happened to Mammy, so I hope you'll be able to deal with this one thing without counting the other stuff against me.' I thought it was well worth giving God one last opportunity to prove Himself.

It was almost the end of May now, and the nights were warmer than the days of spring had been. Granny Daly wrote to my father, and asked if I could come and stay with her for a few days when the summer holidays began. I knew that that had to mean she had made some progress with her search, our search. Two days after I'd stood on the diving boards, the phone rang as I got in the door from school. It was Nyxi.

'I'm so sorry about everything,' she said. 'You were right about the stairs thing and I just wouldn't listen. It *was* my dad. He wasn't wearing his helmet, he'd left it in his room and he was very nearly killed . . . He was in a desert oasis and they were ambushed—'

'Is he okay?' I asked, dreading the answer.

'He's going to be fine,' Nyxi said. 'The bullet hit his shoulder and he has to have a metal plate now with bolts put in that will join up all around the bones. He's going to be home on Sunday, and Mam says that the army can feck off with themselves if they want him back at work, he's her husband.'

I was so glad to hear her voice. I wanted to tell her all about the radiator at school, and the *Moody Blue* record, and how much my bike was worth according to Mr Newell, and how I had stood on the diving boards and thought I could see her house. But I didn't tell her any of those things or any other things, like the list I'd drawn up to try to make Mammy come back, and the tomato plants being nearly choked by the perfume in the greenhouse. Instead I listened to her voice for ages, down the Posts and Telegraphs wire from her house in Renmore, all the way to Taylor's Hill, and I was a little happier than I'd been in a long while. Everything else would just have to wait for the right time.

Chapter 18

The summer weather in 1978 was nowhere near as good as it had been two years earlier. Then, it had been so hot that people still talked about other people being able to fry eggs on the bonnets of their cars. I didn't know if that was true, but Iggy Kelehan, and everyone else who might have known all about it, were on their summer holidays now and school was finished until September. In contrast to the weather, the summer exams had gone quite well for me in St Mary's, and I realised that, without really making a conscious effort, I had settled into my new school and had survived until the end of the school year.

In Salthill, though, the overcast sky and the cool temperatures were no impediment to holiday-makers enjoying themselves all along the seafront. In the amusement arcades the machines gorged on coins and occasionally vomited up small fortunes. Everyone seemed happy.

In another part of the same island, people were still being shot dead: the news on the television showed people throwing stones and petrol bombs at armoured cars and at soldiers, who fired plastic bullets back at them. None of that seemed real to me because I couldn't see or feel it for myself. However, even all of the more recent stuff, which was real, seemed somehow remote, unconnected to the days I was living in, under the cloudy June sky.

I thought again about what my birth mother would be like, if we managed to track her down. Did she have other children? How would I get on with them? Where would I go to school? And then, in the middle of all those questions and thoughts, I realised that leaving Galway would mean leaving Nyxi. A horrible feeling lurched in my stomach and suddenly I didn't want anything to change. I wanted things to remain as they were, just for me to be able to make Mammy appear when I most needed to see her. What was Purgatory like? I hadn't even asked her. I was torn between what I wanted and what I knew I had to do to pay for the tragedy and heartache I'd caused.

But what if none of what I'd seen was real after all? What if I'd imagined, only imagined, that I'd seen and heard Mammy and spoken to her in the church and in the greenhouse? I wasn't sure at all about any of this anymore, yet I had to believe in *something.* No – I did believe that what I had seen in the church and in the greenhouse was real. I hadn't imagined it. I had touched Mammy and held her and spoken to her. Hadn't I? Anyway, the one thing I knew for definite was that I had been the cause of her suicide. That simple fact dictated almost everything else. The sound of lawnmowers was everywhere and I was not afraid. I knew that *some* things inside and around me had changed for the better.

One day, at the end of the prom, out near Blackrock, an old man fell down the steps to the beach opposite the Ocean Wave Hotel. Nyxi and I were in the crowd of people who saw it happen and gathered around. She and I went into the phone box on the other footpath and dialled 999. Within ten minutes an ambulance arrived to take the old man to hospital. His head was bleeding, and some blood remained on the steps where he'd fallen. Somehow I knew that he would be all right. Some sound, between the noise of the sea and my beating heart, had told me he would be fine. I said nothing about it to Nyxi. As the ambulance pulled away from the kerb and put on its siren, I knew that both of us were thinking about our mothers.

'The new tests are very positive,' Nyxi said. 'They say that they've caught it early enough, and that the treatment went well.' As we continued to watch the retreating ambulance, racing towards the city, I remembered the ambulance parked near the monkey puzzle tree almost a year earlier. In one way I felt cloaked in the news of my mother's death by these reminders and signs. I knew that the connections must mean something. Was it something I was supposed to do? Or was it something I was doing wrong? I wanted to believe that some of these signs were Mammy trying to get through to me.

We walked our bikes back along the seafront. As we drew closer to Leisureland, we could hear the sounds of children screaming with excitement as the Ferris wheel in the amusement park took them up into the summer sky. We crossed the road near the Banba Hotel, and the sound of slot machines eating people's savings *ker-ching*ed at us through the open windows of Claude Toft's. 'There are many casinos, but there is only one Claude Toft's!' we said together, as we read the cheesy slogan that ran across the front of the building.

I had to make the most of my time with Nyxi. Who knew what the future held for us. Posters along the front of Seapoint Ballroom promised that the Miami, The Indians and even Gina, Dale Haze and the Champions would be visiting soon, due to 'popular demand'. All the way along the promenade, from Blackrock diving boards to the white sands of Grattan Beach, bathers made splashes of colour and water, making the best of the mixed weather. All the B&Bs had 'No Vacancies' signs up, and it was only early June. I knew that, over the coming months, those guest-houses would empty and refill with relays of people. Some came for holidays, others to attend the races in July. Finally, in late August and early September, just when it began to look like the season was ending, things would explode again for the Oyster Festival – a bit like a novelty candle would reignite just when you thought it had gone out.

In the *Galway Advertiser* they published a poem someone had written. It was called 'Salthill Is A Woman':

Salthill Is A Woman

Salthill is a woman who sleeps with strangers:
ice-cream-mouthed youngsters;
day-tripping elders clutching two-penny cups; metal
orphans leaning against walls and the thought of
February children.

Salthill is a woman, raped by sun-starved maniacs
for two-week holidays which overlap into a season of hurt.
Discarded in August, she recovers in the arms of a
thoughtful city and regains her sanity.
Until next May, when she cringes once again (like
a beaten dog)
at the sight of coach tours.

Further out, beyond the city limits marked by the Corrib Great Southern Hotel in Renmore, the Rahoon flats, Coen's Hardware Electrical on the Headford Road, and the caravan holiday park between Knocknacarra and Barna Woods, it was still summer, but a lot less hectic.

Nyxi's dad was recovering well from his injury: there was a piece about him in the *Connacht Tribune*, and they interviewed him out at his house in Renmore. The two soldiers who had been killed were Dutch peacekeepers with the UN, and it had been a joint patrol with Irish soldiers that had been ambushed at the oasis in southern Lebanon. I looked at the photograph of Nyxi's dad in the newspaper, and wondered about the connection between his ambush and my dream. There was no doubt about this one, among the strange events that had punctuated my life since Mammy's death. If I had never rung Nyxi (the time she'd put the phone down on me) it would be impossible to now convince her about my forewarning image of the man on the stairs. But she had told me since that I had been right about the 'stairs thing'. That confirmed that it had happened. So what was it all about? Was the 'stairs thing' connected to Mammy's appearances? Were the other bits, the kid crossing the road in front of the car, the hotel collapsing, the room behind the radiator on the top floor of the school, all linked?

I thought I should probably be frightened by all of this, but mostly I wasn't. The individual incidents seemed strange as they happened, but they did not scare me. More than anything else, I was puzzled. In my head I was able to separate Mammy's appearances from the other stuff, and I wondered whether I would continue to have such odd experiences for the rest of my life. Maybe these things were all around us, all the time, like flowers we never noticed until we found out what they were called. What was the name for all of this, then? Magic? Hex? Spells? Jinx? If the *Concise Oxford Dictionary* didn't know which name to choose, then neither did I.

I was enjoying the summer, but part of me couldn't wait to find out what Granny Daly had discovered about my birth mother. In the heat of June, it seemed that various parts of my plan were already working out. The date was fixed for my visit to Dublin – 20 June – and that was less than a week away now. I counted out the money from my jar, and put it aside in an envelope marked 'Enough?' The question mark was bigger than any of the letters. What were the chances that Granny Daly had found my birth mother? And, if she had, what were the chances that that lady would want to take me back, thirteen years after she'd sold me to the nuns? I'd just have to wait and see.

One evening Nyxi's mum phoned and spoke with my father. He left the receiver down on the hall table, and came into the front garden where I was reading a Hardy Boys mystery. 'It's Mrs Kirwan,' he said. 'She wants to know if you'd like to go to the Aran Islands tomorrow with Mr Kirwan and Nyxi.'

'Absolutely,' I replied. I saw a smile cross his face, then disappear, almost as if he was happy for me but had then remembered he hated me. I imagined he was feeling what he might have hoped to feel if he'd ever had a child of his own, not one who was shop-soiled. He went back into the house.

The next day I cycled down to the centre of the city and locked my bike to the railings outside the Skeffington Arms Hotel in Eyre Square. I wondered why Nyxi's dad hadn't driven to Taylor's Hill to collect me, but when Nyxi and he got off the Renmore bus, I understood why. Mr Kirwan's right arm was in a sling. He was very tanned, and I thought how different a colour his face had been on the stairs when he'd turned around so that I could finally see who he was: it had been snow white.

'Howya, Hughie,' he said, as he held out his left hand for me to shake. I shook it with *my* right, so that it wasn't like a handshake at all, more of how you'd clutch someone's hand at Mass during the sign of peace, if it was last-minute and both of you were stretching.

'Hello, Mr Kirwan,' I said back. He was a warm person. He smiled a lot and, except for the very rare moment when his arm or shoulder troubled him, he was like a bit of sunshine himself.

I thought about my own father, and of how different my relationship with him was from the one Nyxi and her father had. What brings people together? I know they say you can choose your friends but you can't choose your family. Where did that leave you if you were adopted? I wondered about the building we'd seen on the way back from Uncle Seán's funeral at Glasnevin. How long had I been there? Who had decided that I was the baby who would be placed with the Mittmans in Terryglass? For how much had I been sold to the nuns? How much is that baby in the window? Suddenly I thought again of my absolute very earliest memory, which was of being in a room full of beds or cots, and seeing someone in a blue uniform standing at the end of the cot I was lying in.

*

The *Naomh Éanna* left the docks at exactly eleven o'clock. There were only a few other passengers on board, because mostly it carried cargo for the three Aran Islands. Nyxi and I had the run of the entire ship during the hour-and-a-half-long crossing. The sea was as calm as a sink of tap water, as the ship made its way across the bay and out past Mutton Island and Hare Island. The sun finally came out and shone down as we made our way out into Galway Bay. Bathers on the shoreline were just coloured dots to us, and for all we knew, they might even have been Lego figures instead of people. There were enormous wooden crates on the deck, and we made our way around them and tried to find out what each contained. One was full of roof slates and another had a small red tractor in it. The strangest of all was a crate filled with bales of straw.

'Don't they have straw on the Aran Islands?' Nyxi asked one of the ship's crew.

'They do, but only after we brings it to them,' he said, with a wink. He pronounced the word 'brings' as 'brinks', and I knew that he was a native Irish speaker. They said 'Lesher-land' instead of Leisureland. I'd heard someone else call it 'Lee-gerland' as well once, but I think they were just wrong. Nyxi and I leaned over the rails and looked down into the water, which was being churned up by the ship's propellers. Nyxi's father knew the captain, and had said we'd be able to get into the driving part of the ship when we got near to the islands.

For most of the journey out, we either looked down into the water from the back of the ship, or lay on our backs on the warm deck, just staring up into the clouds and shading our eyes from the sun. Underneath us, the hum and clatter of the engines was comforting and constant. At one point I turned to talk to Nyxi, but she was asleep. I thought back to when we'd first met, that summer when she'd pulled a kettle of boiling water onto herself, and I'd tried to cut the lawn while the gardener was on his holidays. She was my best friend – indeed my only friend – and I hoped that that would never change. As we lay there, I remembered that absolutely everything *would* change if I had to go away. I knew that if I tried to explain all of that to Nyxi, she would be very angry, and wouldn't agree with my decision anyway. So, what was the point of mentioning it to her? But if my plan *did* work, and I had to go away, I knew now that I would probably lose Nyxi too. Even if my birth mother lived in the bit of Munster that was closest to Galway, we'd hardly be able to see each other very often.

Nyxi woke up when I was gazing at her, and I felt that she looked at me just then in a different way, almost as if she'd been thinking the same thing I was.

'I thought you'd gone,' she said, as she blinked.

'I'm still here,' I said. But I wondered for how much longer that might be true.

We watched the Aran Islands get nearer from the bridge (that's what the driving bit was called). The first island we called to was the middle one, Inis Meáin, and four men rowed out to meet us in a currach, towing a cow behind them in the water. It was too shallow in the little harbour for the *Naomh Éanna* to dock so this was how the cattle were sent to market. A large sling had been tied around the beast by the fishermen. The huge hook from the crane on the deck had no trouble hoisting her into the air, then swinging her over the deck of the ship to where she was lowered into a special pen surrounded by metal gates. I had never seen anything so extraordinary.

When we finally arrived on the main island, Inis Mór, there was a line of old-fashioned ponies and traps waiting along the wall of the pier where we disembarked.

'Would you like to see around the island?' their drivers offered. Nyxi's dad bargained one of the drivers down to six pounds, from eight, and the three of us climbed into the trap behind him and set off.

The Aran Islands are extraordinarily beautiful. Everywhere you look, there are stone walls, and tiny fields, and hardly any trees. After the hustle and noise of Galway City, it's like another planet. The other thing I noticed immediately was the calm and quiet. Apart from the clip-clop of the pony's hoofs on the road, the only other noise was of birds. And no matter where you are on the island, you can see the sea. We saw men and women collecting seaweed on one of the beaches.

'They use it on the fields,' our driver told us, 'instead of cowsh—'

'Cow manure?' Nyxi's dad suggested.

The driver looked back at us and nodded. 'Exactly,' he said, letting go of the reins altogether and taking a pipe from one of the pockets of his jacket. He put tobacco into the bowl, and used seven or eight matches before he got it lit. All this time, the pony kept going in a straight line on the correct side of the road. 'Automatic pilot,' the driver said, as he took up the reins once more.

We crossed the island from one end to the other and soon saw our destination in the distance. The fort of Dún Aengus (Dún Aonghasa) is on the top of a cliff, and was built ages ago by ancient Celts. At least that's who I think built it, but history isn't my strongest subject. I'm not exactly sure but, anyway, it's massive and is made up of millions of rocks and stones arranged in a semi-circle on the edge of the cliff. There are three or four rings of walls, which would probably slow up any invaders. We stopped at a small pub and we had lunch. Nyxi's dad had a pint of Guinness, and we drank Fanta, and had Tayto crisps, and egg-salad sandwiches. The man in the pony and trap said he'd come back and collect us in time to make the return trip.

'What's your favourite song at the moment, Hughie?' Nyxi asked, as we left the pub and began to cross the road to start our long climb up to the ancient fort.

'You know the one about "How bad she is up our road"?' I answered. Nyxi and her father both looked at me.

'No,' they said, at the same time.

'Sing a bit of it, Hughie,' her dad said.

I tried without any real success. I suppose, along with my history knowledge, my musical ability is also quite limited.

'"How bad she is up our road?" What does that even mean?' Nyxi asked, as we made our way up the steep hill towards the fortification, which protected the top from attack. As we climbed, I looked back and almost the entire island was visible below me, stretching out like a grey and green blanket on top of the Atlantic, securely anchored below itself to the seabed. This was the last stop before America. When we got to the summit, Nyxi's dad sat down between two of the outer walls to catch his breath. Nyxi and I continued through the layers of the fort until we reached the centre. The semi-circular protection of the last deep stone wall made a cradle for the final boundary, the cliff itself.

'Let's go to the edge and have a look over,' Nyxi suggested. I began to feel as I had when I'd passed by the radiator on the third floor in St Mary's school.

'Don't,' I said, in a voice that sounded slightly strange to me.

'It's okay, I'll be fine, Hughie,' Nyxi said. She began to move towards the edge of the cliff.

I knew in my heart that something awful was going to happen if I didn't do something. 'No, Nyxi, it's not going to be fine,' I said. 'This is how it felt when I saw your dad on the stairs.' I could see in her eyes a mix of mischief and questioning. In that moment, I knew what she wanted. She wanted a reason to disbelieve me, to allow her to go to the edge.

'Don't be silly, Hughie,' she said, taking a step nearer the cliff. I could hear the sea below us.

'Nyxi, please come back,' I said. In my head I heard a sound I didn't recognise.

'Don't be a scaredy-cat,' she said, holding out her hand to me. 'Come on, we'll do it together. We'll just have one look and then we're done.' I shook my head, and began to inch backwards.

Nyxi's hand was still extended towards me, when the sound I'd heard in my head, moments earlier, happened beneath her runners. The rock crumbled, and the chunk of it on which her right foot stood sheared off and dropped three hundred feet into the sea below. Nyxi's foot balanced precariously on thin air and then, almost like a mannequin in a shop display that had been nudged accidentally, she began to topple towards the sea. I grabbed at her hand and missed, but caught her wrist. The weight of the moment was too much, and I found myself being jerked forward after her. The contact between us immediately forced her down rather than out, and I held on as tightly as I could. I ended up flat on my stomach on the cliff top while Nyxi's legs and torso disappeared over the cliff. All that remained above the line of the cliff edge was her right hand. I feared that her arm had been wrenched out of its socket by the force of the fall. I held on to her wrist and screamed at her, 'Don't let go, Nyxi, for God's sake, don't let go!'

But that was meaningless, as *I* was the only one who was hanging on. My face smashed off the rocky surface of the cliffs, as I tried to direct every single piece of my being and my mind, and my heart, and my fear into my right hand. I held my friend in a grip I didn't think I could maintain for very long. I wondered how soon it would be before I myself was pulled over the edge, which would happen if I continued to hold on. I only knew that I simply could not let go. I felt myself slipping on the stones that lay loose underneath me, between my shirt and eternity. I tried to find a hold on the rocky surface with the toes of my runners, but could not get any purchase. I thought about nothing except the girl I loved, and the grip I could not lose. I knew that if we fell, we would not survive. Below us were rocks and outcrops, and deeper water than either of us could dream of. I was now on the precipice, and I was afraid to free my left hand from under me to help grip Nyxi, in case I went sideways in the movement.

I looked down and saw Nyxi's face as she stared back up. In her eyes I didn't see fright or fear, but rather a kind of calmness that told me everything would be all right, even if everything went as wrong as it possibly could. I wanted to tell her that I loved her, but there was no need. Nyxi nodded and silently and soundlessly mouthed, 'I know. I love you too.' I could feel my grip beginning to break free. I closed my eyes. As I screamed, 'No!' I felt someone beside me. Nyxi's dad had crawled over, and although he had only one good arm, he saved us both, gripping Nyxi's hand as I let go, and rescuing me from a nightmare I could never have survived.

*

On the way back on the *Naomh Éanna*, Nyxi turned to me as we entered the mouth of Galway Bay. 'I kept thinking about the song, Hughie.'

'What song?' I asked.

'The one you were trying to sing to us. Go on, sing the words again.'

'"You know how ba-ad she is up our road,"' I sang, in what I hoped was the tune.

She sang back at me. 'It's 'Beg, Steal or Borrow' by the New Seekers.' She sang the right words. I suppose in one way or another that was what I'd been looking for all along.

Chapter 19

Nyxi had to have steel pins put into her shoulder. The painkillers the district nurse on Inis Mór had given her had almost worn off by the time we got back into the harbour in Galway. She was screaming in agony, as her father and I took her in a taxi to the Regional Hospital. I went to visit her on the morning after the surgery. She was sitting up in bed, in a ward with older ladies. She was too old for the children's ward now.

'Hey, Nyxi,' I said, with a smile, as I offered her a Bobby bar I'd bought in the shop on the ground floor of the hospital.

'Hey, yourself,' she replied. She had her right arm in a plaster cast now, and I wanted to write my name on it, like other people did with their friends' casts. But the plaster was still drying, so I didn't write anything. I sat in the plastic chair beside Nyxi's bed and began to eat the grapes from the bowl on the bedside locker. I stopped myself. I hadn't even asked permission.

'Go ahead, Hughie. Eat them all, if you like. I hate them because of the pips. Anyway, you saved my life.'

'I suppose I did,' I said, and turned away. I felt my face going red, as I remembered what I'd thought of saying but hadn't said on Dún Aengus. But Nyxi had known and had replied to me as I'd held on to her wrist and tried to save her from falling.

'So we're even, then?' she said.

I looked at her. 'How do you mean?'

'Well,' she began, and a smile visited her mouth and her eyes at the same time, 'you saved *me* from drowning, or being smashed on the rocks, and *I* got *you* safely past the Rahoon flats on your bike, remember?'

She was joking, but I understood exactly what she meant. Real friends just did whatever had to be done, whenever it was needed, and that was that. I knew I had sort of saved my own life as well by grabbing hold of Nyxi's wrist. I also knew that she would have done exactly the same for me if our positions had been reversed.

'How long are you going to have the cast for?' I asked.

'Till your dad takes it off, I suppose,' she said, with a grin.

'Does he know what happened?' I asked.

'I guess so. My parents probably told him when they came in last night. They met him outside the theatre, I think, when I was being wheeled out. That's what Mam told me anyway, but she didn't say what they'd talked about. They're so proud of you.' I knew she meant her parents were.

Nyxi and I tried to play Monopoly, using the mobile tray to hold the board. We didn't really pay much attention to the game, and from time to time one of us would swap a house for a hotel or take some money from the bank without passing Go. But neither of us minded: we were together, and that was what mattered most.

I thought again about my upcoming trip to visit Granny Daly, and what that might bring. If I ended up going back to live with my birth mother and her family, how would I ever survive without Nyxi? We were both growing up now, and although I'd always known I loved her as a friend, she really did mean everything in the world to me. I had nearly lost her the day before on Inis Mór, and I didn't think I'd be able to live a happy life without her in it. She was the little dog in the game of Monopoly and I was the boot; we were different people but still part of the same bigger thing. I thought about my missing toes, and how Nyxi and I had met in another ward in that same building a few years earlier. Maybe everything went in cycles, and came around again if you just waited long enough.

Nyxi was tired, although she had said she wasn't. I left her to get some sleep and made my way down the stairs to the reception hall at the front of the hospital. A lady in a wheelchair was talking to two nurses, who had accompanied her to the front door where a taxi was waiting. One nurse carried the lady's overnight bag, while the other helped her out of the wheelchair. I thought about growing old, and wondered how long my life would be. It was the first time I'd ever wondered that. If Nyxi and I had fallen off the cliff, both our lives would have been over now.

A man entered the front hall carrying two buckets full of flowers. The smell of them reminded me of something, some other event. As I walked along the footpath, I remembered what it was: the flowers at Mammy's funeral. Lilies. I turned from leaving the hospital grounds and made my way back along the full length of the front of the main hospital building and around the corner at the end. A woman in a white uniform came round the corner in the opposite direction. She stopped and we looked at each other for a moment before she realised who I was. It was Breege.

'Hello, Hughie,' she said. 'How have you been?' It was such a simple question, but the answer did not seem so straightforward. I couldn't really think of what to say in response. I managed a small smile and, as I did, she reached out a hand and touched the tip of my nose with her index finger. 'You'll be fine,' she said, before she walked on past me on her way to look after people who needed minding more than I did.

The exchange between us wasn't really an exchange, I guess, because I didn't say anything at all, but it reminded me of the encounter I'd had ages ago, before Christmas, when I'd stumbled into a laneway in Newbridge, which led to a small collection of cottages. Then, I had been greeted casually by a man with a dog on a lead. His salutation had greatly affected me, as it seemed to puncture the bubble of self-imposed isolation in which I'd existed since returning to boarding school after Mammy's funeral. That simple greeting, by a stranger who said, 'Howya', had led me to collapse in tears on the pavement outside my French teacher's house. Now, I felt a new strength in my heart. The words Breege had spoken were reassuring – a confirmation from beyond myself that things could, and would, get better.

I had decided to visit the psychiatric unit and see if they would allow me to see the room where Mammy had died. In my hurry to figure out a recipe to make her appear, I had overlooked the idea of visiting the room where she had spent the last moments of her life. I didn't know if I'd be able to get into the unit or whether the room would now be occupied by someone else. At the small reception booth, a rather cross-looking nurse was sitting on a high stool doing her nails.

'Name?' she asked disinterestedly.

'Hughie Mittman,' I said. She looked up from her nails and down at me. I was standing on a mat that had the word 'Welcome' on it.

'Who are you visiting?' she asked, in an irritated voice, while at the same time looking down the corridor behind me to where the accompanying adult might be.

'I'd like to visit room twelve, please,' I said.

'Room twelve,' she said, 'room twelve.' She opened her ledger on the desk in front of her, and ran a finger through a list I couldn't read upside-down.

'My mother died in room twelve in November,' I said, to help her out. The nurse's face changed from cross to kind as she looked up.

'Take a seat over there,' she said, pointing to two orange plastic chairs backed up together against the window. I went over and, as I prepared to sit down, I put my hand on the glass. It was roasting hot. I sat down. The nurse left the booth and disappeared out of sight.

There was a wasp in the waiting area, and I thought about trying to kill it with a copy of *Woman's Way*, which was on the floor underneath the other orange chair. The next time the wasp dive-bombed me from a starting point of the light fitting in the centre of the ceiling, something stopped me reaching down and picking up the magazine. Bandits at twelve o'clock, I thought, as it whizzed over my head and swerved sharply before hitting the window behind me. I watched it zoom away. I saw it was a bee, not a wasp.

'Come on, young man,' the nurse at the reception desk said, as she pressed the buzzer that unlocked the door into the psychiatric unit. There was a loud clunking sound as the lock relented.

The nurse walked ahead of me down the corridor, and I remembered another time I'd been there, at Halloween, visiting Mammy and seeing her for the last time before she died. I don't really know why I wanted to visit the room again, but I think I thought it was something I had to face, like the lawnmower, so that I could tell myself I'd done it, had gone back and looked at the place where Mammy's life had ended. As we approached the room, the nurse slowed down and let me go ahead of her. The door was slightly open.

'Stay as long as you like,' she said, as she headed back the way we'd just come. I pushed open the door, half expecting to see someone suspended from the ceiling by the belt of a dressing-gown. A figure standing at the window blocked the sunlight into the room. It was my father.

'Hello, Hughie,' he said, with a look on his face I'd never seen before. 'They told me you wanted to visit this room. I don't have surgery until twelve, so I thought I'd drop over and see you.' His voice was not cross. I had expected it to be, when I'd seen who was in the room. He moved out of the way of the window, and sunlight burst in. The bed was made, and the light made it look like something from an ad on television for Daz detergent.

'I just wanted to see the room,' I said defensively, not sure if I was apologising to him, or to Mammy, or to myself.

'There's nothing wrong with that, Hughie,' he said. 'I sometimes come here myself when it's quiet and there's no patient living here.'

I was stunned by what he'd said. It seemed so far

removed from my expectations of him, that I found it hard to imagine that he was telling the truth. He moved away now, to the side, and sat on the chair at the side of the bed where I'd sat when Mammy had told me she would be home for Christmas.

'Why don't you sit down for a minute, Hughie?' he said. There wasn't another chair and I wasn't going to sit on the bed.

'I'm fine standing,' I said, moving into the centre of the room. It was the first time ever that I'd been higher up than him.

'I spoke to Mrs Kirwan,' he said. 'You did an incredible thing. You saved someone's life.'

'I didn't save Mammy's, though, did I?' I said, looking above his head at the curtain rail, which hadn't snapped under the weight of her. My father rested his elbows on his knees, and looked down at the floor for a time without saying anything. When he finally looked up, I thought his eyes seemed a different, more watery colour.

'I made her unhappy,' he said. 'I said and did some things I shouldn't have. I was never really there when she needed me. I was always somewhere else, doing other things.'

'She said she'd be home for Christmas,' I said. I couldn't think of anything I wanted to express to him that would make things better. I had wanted to be in this room on my own, hoping maybe that Mammy might appear to me there. Or maybe I didn't really hope that would happen: it might have meant being right back at the beginning and failing to save her all over again. He had told me that if I'd never come into their lives, she might still be alive. 'And she didn't keep her promise.'

'None of this was your fault, Hughie,' my father said. 'I'm the one who messed it all up. I always seemed to want something else, never the things I had.' He looked up at me now. In his face I saw a weakness I had never suspected was in him. I thought about the lawnmower in Granny Daly's. I didn't understand. And when he said that none of it was my fault, I knew he was lying: I'd heard their arguments about adoption, about him not being home for breakfast; I remembered the way he hadn't wanted me to be alone with her, bringing her away to the living room with him instead. Even now that Mammy was gone, he was still fighting with people: Breege, Granny Daly, me. Why wasn't he happy either? Mammy had wanted children and he hadn't, and therefore I also knew that, no matter what he said now, what he had said before was true: I *was* the reason she'd killed herself. If I hadn't come along, they wouldn't have fallen out of love with each other. There was no other explanation for the change in them, from the people they were in the wedding album in the cupboard in the sitting-room cabinet, to the people they'd become. Smiling faces didn't become sad faces for no reason at all.

As I looked at my father, sitting on the chair in the room where Mammy had ended her life, I realised that the only thing that had changed in their lives, between the moment of the wedding photographs and her suicide, was the entry into those lives of a child only one of them had wanted. That was why I needed to go back to where I had originally come from: it was the only way I could even begin to make up for the awful harm I'd caused. I couldn't blame my father for her death, and although he was now saying it hadn't been *my* fault, we both knew, in that room of all places, that the truth could not be hidden any longer.

I wondered how my father would cope without me in the house on Taylor's Hill – but, of course, he had always wanted the place to himself. He had sent me to boarding school to get me out of the way, and he had to deal with my presence now only because I'd been expelled. He would survive quite well without me – his parents lived in Lismore, and he'd probably see them more frequently. He had a conveyor belt of other women at his mercy in the hospital, and he loved his work as a surgeon.

My father stood up, walked around the end of the bed and stopped beside me for a moment. 'I'll leave you alone now, Hughie,' he said. 'Take all the time you need.'

I waited for the sound of him shutting the door behind him before I did anything at all. When he'd gone, I walked over to the window and looked out into the small courtyard that was enclosed by the psychiatric wing. A number of patients sat on garden benches in the sun, some reading, some chatting, and some just staring straight ahead of them, like people transfixed by something in the middle distance. I wondered whether Mammy had been facing into the room, or out towards the courtyard, when she'd hanged herself. I went over and sat on the bed. I thought of that occasion all those years ago when Nyxi and I had met, in the same hospital. I thought about the recipe for making Mammy appear: the sunshine, the warm glass, my father's absence. Surely, if ever she was going to reappear it would be now, in that room, the last place where she'd physically been in the world. I closed my eyes and waited and waited and waited, but nothing happened, absolutely nothing at all.

'Where are you, Mammy?' I asked, as I opened my eyes and looked around the tidy hospital room, with its yellow walls, white bed linen, and ghosts who refused to appear. I wondered why I hadn't been able to know that *she* was in harm's way and lead her somewhere else. Was it *because* of her death that sometimes I now had these omens, strange feelings and visions?

A couple of days later, I took the train to Dublin to visit Granny Daly. The train I caught left in the middle of the day, and was not very full. We were delayed in Woodlawn because the stationmaster's wife had given birth to twins in the waiting room of the station, and an ambulance was parked on the level crossing for a while. I remembered the last time I'd been on a train, returning to Newbridge College after Christmas. I remembered my father reaching down to pick up my suitcase, and how my hand had got there before his. That very same day he'd punched me in the face, and I'd also found the information about the adoption society, when I'd been putting the decorations in the wardrobe. I wondered if everything was connected in some way, everything that happened to one person. I fell asleep to the rhythm of the wheels of the train on the railway track that stretched across the country: clickety-clack, clickety-clack.

When I awoke, it was because of an announcement over the Tannoy system on the train. 'Ladies and gentlemen, we will shortly be arriving in Heuston station. Please make sure to take all your belongings with you, because sometimes it's awfully easy to forget them.'

I had a small case with me and took it down from the overhead rack. The train slowed to a crawl, and we were surrounded on all sides by abandoned railway carriages, and water tanks, and everything else that occupies the seemingly endless spread of a city railway depot on the outskirts of the main station. I carried my case to the small hallway where the exit door lay at the end of the carriage. No one else was there, so I put down my case and, using both hands, I pulled down the window in the door. I put my head out, and tried to get a better look at the railway wasteland we were slowly moving through.

I saw, up ahead in the distance, the enormous glass and steel canopies that encased Heuston station. Our train slowed, almost to a halt, and I could see another edging out of the station and coming towards us on the adjoining track. The other train drew level with mine, and then my train stopped completely so that the other one could pass by. The other train was going very gingerly, almost not moving at all. It was a bit like two heavy people trying to get past each other in a narrow shop. As it crept past, it rocked slightly from side to side, almost touching us. I had drawn in my head but had left the window open. The other train stopped for a moment. Almost opposite where I stood there was a door on the other train. I didn't see the other window being opened, but suddenly it *was* open. I expected to be told off by a conductor or ticket seller on the other train. I saw the faintest of figures appear in the window, but it could have been anything or anyone because it was so vague in outline. Then I heard my mother's voice.

'Are you going away for a few days, Hughie?'

'I'm just going to visit Granny Daly, Mammy. She might have some information about my—' I stopped before I said what could only hurt her.

'About your birth mother is it, Hughie?'

'Yes,' I said. 'How did you know?'

'Between us we know nearly everything, Hughie,' she replied.

'I love you more than anything else in the whole world, Mammy, and I miss you so much,' I said. 'I don't want to do anything else to make you sad.'

'Nothing you will ever do can make me sad, Hughie. I'm going away too for a while. I'm going on my holidays,' she said.

'I tried to find the recipe,' I said, 'the recipe to make you come back.'

'You'll find it, Hughie,' she said. 'You need to do whatever you can to make yourself happy again.'

'I'm sorry about everything, Mammy,' I said. 'I'm sorry I made you so sad that you . . .' I couldn't say the words, so I said something else. 'I'm going to try to make up for it. Granny Daly has written to the adoption people and she has some news.'

'That's great,' she said. 'I saw you on the Aran Islands. You were absolutely fantastic. You saved that girl's life. What was her name?'

'Nyxi,' I said. 'Nyxi Kirwan. Don't you remember her? You used to collect the two of us outside the Lion's Tower after we'd been to the Town Hall Cinema, the place where the fella with the glass eye collects the tickets.'

'I don't really remember all that, Hughie. I'm too busy packing, and it's nearly time for me to go.' Her train began to move and so did mine.

'When will I see you again, Mammy?' I asked. Her answer was swallowed in the noise of our trains and my crying.

Chapter 20

Granny Daly was waiting for me on the platform when I disembarked from the train at Heuston station.

'Have you been crying, Hughie?' she asked.

'A little bit, Granny,' I replied.

'That's good,' she said. 'Sometimes our cheeks need a bit of a clean.' She took my suitcase from me and began to walk ahead of me, out through the main entrance to the station. 'Hurry up, Hughie,' she said to me, over her shoulder. 'I've left the engine running. It's a bit dicky.'

Out on the street, a green Morris Minor waited for us, like a bubble chariot. I had never seen this car before. I hadn't even known that Granny Daly could drive. We got in and set off, with Granny Daly doing a U-turn across four lanes of traffic to head back into the city. As she manoeuvred the car from one side of the road to the other, other drivers were beeping angrily at us, or braking suddenly, or making rude gestures with their fingers or their fists. Once we were on our way, down by the river that flows through the centre of the city, Granny Daly addressed me while staring straight ahead at the road. 'These multiple-lane roads are quite awkward to traverse, Hughie.'

I thought about it for a moment and, remembering the near-fatal chaos we had caused by turning the car around, I asked, 'Do you think it would have helped at all, Granny Daly, if you had used the indicator back there?'

'Absolutely not, Hughie,' she retorted. 'You show any sign of weakness to those latchicoes and you're finished.' We made our way through the city, and it was only as we pulled into the slope in front of her house that Granny Daly mentioned the real purpose of her suggestion to my father that I spend some time with her during the holidays.

'The adoption society got back to me and said they couldn't find out any more information about where you'd come from.'

'Oh,' I said, bitterly disappointed. I wondered why Granny Daly couldn't have told me that over the phone.

'I didn't believe them,' Granny Daly said, as she pulled the front door of the house shut behind us and indicated to me to put my suitcase under the table in the hall.

'So that's it?' I asked her.

'Absolutely not, Hughie,' Granny Daly said defiantly. 'Some of those nuns, I wouldn't believe the radio in their car. I wasn't going to take no for an answer, so I telephoned a friend of mine called Lesley Wingfield. She used to be a nun herself and I knew she'd know what to do.'

'And did she?' I couldn't contain myself and just wanted as much information as there was as soon as I could get it. Granny Daly wasn't going to be rushed, however.

'Now, Hughie, let's get you some jelly and ice-cream first and we'll have a sit-down. I'm exhausted after all that driving. I've only had the car about a month. I need to be able to get to the shops now that Seán is gone.'

I sat in the dining room and found myself actually eating the jelly and enjoying it, as I waited for my grandmother to come back in from the kitchen with her cup of tea and a bag of Emerald sweets. She settled herself in the chair at the top of the table. I held my full spoon in mid-air as I waited for her to continue the story.

'Lesley is studying now for a PhD in Education, and as part of that she's doing research into school attendance in the Dublin metropolitan area. Some of her research involves visiting primary schools.'

'But what has that got to do with Mary the hairdresser from Munster?' I asked.

'Well,' she un-wrapped another sweet and popped it into her mouth, 'Lesley decided to expand her research for a little while to include something about the correlation between the education patterns of adopted children and their natural parents. She got a letter from her supervisor which asked adoption societies to help her in any way they could. She asked St Peter's Guild for permission to look at their files and, while she was there, she rooted around until she found yours.'

'And did she find it?' I asked breathlessly.

'Aren't I only after telling you that she did, Hughie? You mustn't be listening to me.'

'I am, Granny. I am.'

'So,' she said, getting up from the chair and going over to the Nelson sideboard, 'she did find some important information. More than they said they had. A good bit more.' Granny Daly opened the top drawer of the sideboard and took out an envelope. She closed the drawer, then came back to sit beside me at the table. The envelope was not sealed and out of it she took a sheet of yellow paper and unfolded it, smoothing it out and placing it on the table where both of us could see it.

The writing on the paper was very scrawly and scribbly, and I had great difficulty reading bits of it. I recognised the names 'Simon and Deirdre Mittman, Raven House, Terryglass, Co. Tipp.'. There were some dates, in 1965 and 1966, and also some other details about my birth weight and maybe some medical notes about blood tests. A lot of it made no sense to me, little pieces about names and places I didn't recognise or couldn't really make out.

'Most of this is administrative nonsense,' Granny Daly said, 'but I think Lesley just copied down as much as she could from the file.' None of it seemed to be of help to me in the task I was about, but I didn't really want to say that to Granny Daly after all the trouble she and her friend had gone to. 'So here,' she continued, 'is the really important stuff.' She turned the page over. In fairly clear writing the few notes on the back of the page read:

> Father: Unknown (possibly university student)
> Mother: Helen Considine (unmarried)
> Considine's Bar & Grocery,
> Inistioge
> Co. Kilkenny

'I thought they told you her name was Mary and she was from Munster,' I said.

'I told you, Hughie, you can't believe anything they say.'

One of the things I thought immediately was how strange it was that the identity of my father was 'unknown'. ('Possibly university student'.) I had imagined that they would be a married couple who'd had to give me up for adoption because they were poor, or simply had too many children to look after. It dawned on me that the reason I had been put up for adoption was *because* my mother was unmarried. She'd had to go away in the first place because of the shame of being pregnant, and had given me up to an adoption society in Dublin run by nuns who mostly told lies. I bet she wasn't even a hairdresser.

Granny Daly handed me the piece of paper and stood up to clear away the teacup and my dessert bowl. 'Have a think about it, Hughie. Have a really good think and then decide what you want to do next, *if* you want to do anything.'

I sat at the dining-room table for ages, just reading through the information: dates, names, and snippets of other stuff I couldn't understand. I saw another word in brackets but didn't realise what it was until I went back down the page line by line to see if I could learn anything more about the child they were talking about in the notes that Granny Daly's friend had copied down as quickly as she could. The word looked like 'Lan', until I realised that the L was an I. It was the name of the baby who weighed six pounds four ounces and who had been adopted by a surgeon and his wife at the end of September 1966. My original name was Ian. I went straight out into the hall to have a look at myself in the mirror on the wall over the table. I didn't look like an Ian. At least, I didn't think so. Nyxi would know whether I looked like an Ian or not. She always knows if people look like their names.

And my father, 'possibly university student', who was he? Could he be one of the teachers I'd had in any of the schools I'd attended? One of the doctors working in the hospital? Or possibly *not* a university student. Who knows? Anyway, it was my birth mother I was really interested in. She was the person who would have to take me back if I had any chance of redeeming myself from having driven Mammy to take her life. I opened my suitcase just to check I'd brought the money I'd saved. I wondered what Mammy had said in answer to my question before the trains parted.

'Jesus Christ, Hughie!' my grandmother screamed from the kitchen.

I ran in to find her looking down the back garden through the window. Out in the garden, the air was black. 'What is it?' I asked.

'Bees,' she said. 'They're swarming. Go upstairs, Hughie, and make sure the bathroom window is shut.'

About an hour later a beekeeper arrived to take the bees away. They had gathered in a huge quivering black cluster at the end of a branch of the tree I had climbed on the day of Uncle Seán's funeral. The beekeeper had his protective suit and hat on, and carried a small smoker device, which he used to 'woof' smoke at the bees to make them drowsy. After a few minutes he took hold of the branch and shook it sharply so that most of them fell down into a cardboard box with 'Jaffa Oranges' written on the side. He covered the box with a large white sheet, then put it into the boot of his car. Before he drove away, he explained to us what would happen next.

'I have an empty hive in my garden, so I just turn the box upside down outside it and they'll all crawl up the sheet and go into their new home. Unless I haven't got the queen bee, of course.'

'What will happen if you don't have her?' I asked.

He grinned. 'Then they'll all fly back here from Killiney Hill. They'll return to the exact same branch, and you can give me a ring and we'll try again.' After he'd left, I thought about the bee in the waiting room of the psychiatric ward in the Regional Hospital back in Galway. I understood that sometimes things seem unconnected but might not be.

*

'I could write to her,' I said to Granny Daly that night, as I came downstairs in my pyjamas to kiss her goodnight. She was watching the wrestling on the BBC. In Galway, we had only one television channel.

'You could,' she replied. 'But maybe she doesn't live there now, thirteen years later. Or maybe someone nosy, who doesn't know she had a baby, will open the letter instead and tell everybody about you. You wouldn't want that to happen, would you?'

I shook my head. I certainly wouldn't. To be honest, I wasn't sure what I wanted.

'We could always take a drive down there and have a look,' Granny Daly said.

'Where?'

'To Inistioge,' she said, picking up a roadmap. It had been hidden from my view on the other side of the settee. 'It's not too far, I think. It looks fairly near on the map anyway.'

When I was in bed, I took out the piece of paper again and stared at it for ages. Helen Considine: who was she? She was my birth mother by all accounts, but what kind of person was she? Was she going to be happy to see me? Did she even still live there? If she did, how much money would she need to be paid to take me back? And even if she did agree to take me back, was that really going to fix the things that had happened which had made me sad? My father said it had been his fault that Mammy had died, but that wasn't true, was it? Surely she had died because she'd been unhappy and she had become unhappy because she wanted to adopt me, and he didn't, so their marriage had begun to break up in bits. I thought about Nyxi and I saw her face before I went to sleep, grinning up at me from just over the cliff. I fell asleep, holding onto the piece of yellow paper, which held the story of the other person I had been for a while – Ian Considine.

Granny Daly was an appalling driver. Even though I couldn't drive, I could see that. She wove her way in and out of traffic with complete contempt for lights or zebra crossings or, indeed, other cars. We were honked at and shouted at and flashed at with angry headlights, even though it was the longest day of the year. But she didn't seem to mind in the slightest. Soon we were away from the city and out among fields full of cows, and hedges with purple and white flowers, which you could smell with the window down.

We drove on narrow roads with little other traffic. In vast meadows, people with hayforks turned hay and built haycocks, which they then secured against the wind with rocks, as they held down an X of baling twine across the tops. There were butterflies everywhere, even inside the car on one occasion, a white one with blue specks on its wings. The wind rushed in through the windows of the Morris Minor. The only sounds for miles were the chirruping of birds we couldn't see and the hum of the engine. Granny Daly stopped the car on a down-slope of a country lane and we got out to have a picnic lunch.

'If it won't start the first few times, we can just let it off down the hill and try again,' she said, with a grin like a schoolgirl. I wondered what she'd been like when she was my age. We had a look at the map and we were well over halfway there. We found a shaded spot under a big tree with reddish-purple leaves. We sat on a huge rug, leaning our backs against the gnarly trunk. We were both full of sandwiches and lemonade.

There was a question I had been asking myself in my head now for a long time, and I wondered if Granny Daly knew the answer. Instead, she had a question for *me*.

'What are you hoping to find, Hughie?'

I didn't know how to tell her the answer to that, about how I felt, about what my father had said, about all the things that had pulled my heart and soul apart since the lady who had helped me paint the wigwam had gone away.

'Do you think Mammy would still be alive if I hadn't come into her life?' There. I had said it. We packed the picnic basket into the car, and Granny Daly didn't answer my question until we were motoring once again.

'When Deirdre was not much older than you, Hughie, just before she started college, she woke up one night with terrible pains in her stomach. We had to get an ambulance and it took ages to come to us but, eventually, they did arrive and they took your mammy to St Vincent's. She needed an operation to save her life, but because of that operation it also meant that she could never have a child. It made her so sad, back then, that I was afraid she would never be happy again. She had to take medicine for depression, and she was going to have to take that medicine for the rest of her life. Then she met Simon Mittman and they got married. A few years later, after a lot of interviews and filling in forms and being sent from Billy to Jack, they adopted you. The day they collected you from the home, they called in to see me on their way back to Galway. For the first time since the awful night when she got the pains and nearly died, I saw that your mammy was happy again. She loved you more than anything else in the whole world, Hughie. Don't you ever forget that.'

'Then why did she kill herself?' This seemed to me the most obvious response to all that Granny Daly had said. She continued to look straight ahead and moved the indicator to alert any other traffic that we were about to turn off the main road – or maybe not.

'Sometimes there's something inside people that makes them believe they're not good enough. Not a good enough mother, not a good enough wife, not a good enough person even. There isn't always a cure for that, no matter how we try to help. Sometimes medicine or hospital or even the people you love most, and who love you most, aren't enough. Sometimes, Hughie, too, there isn't just one answer, and sometimes there isn't one at all. Your mother stopped taking her medication a few years ago because she thought she didn't need it anymore. And maybe she didn't. If you hadn't come into her life, Hughie, she might have ended it all years ago. Anyway, I don't think we'll ever know, but I do know that she didn't decide to leave this world because of you, Hughie. In fact, you were probably the only reason she stayed in it for so long.'

I was crying now and hoping Granny Daly hadn't noticed. But she had. She handed me a tissue from her sleeve as we turned left at a crossroads to follow a sign for Inistioge. We entered a tunnel of trees, which met in the air above the road, and when we emerged at the other end of the canopy of leaves and branches we were on a road that was high up over a golden valley of hay meadows. Down in the centre of the scene was a stone bridge with ten arches spanning the River Nore and linking a small village with the rest of the universe.

The village was a gorgeous nest of small streets and terraces of beautifully painted colourful houses. The place seemed to sparkle in the sunshine, and it was like something out of a storybook or a film, instead of being real. A couple of swans lounged on the grass beside an old mill, while the millwheel barely turned under a fairly weak trickle of water. Down under the bridge, I could see stones jutting out of the water, in the slow drift of what remained of the river in the heat. Granny Daly slowed the car to a halt outside a church: St Mary's Church of Ireland. A notice board said that Sunday Service was at 10 a.m., and that the rector was the Reverend Colin Maybin. We got out and walked. We turned a corner to find ourselves in the centre of the village: a cluster of houses and shops around a green. In the shade of a monument, three children were sitting on the grass making paper planes.

Considine's Bar & Grocery lay across the square from us, its sign painted in maroon on a white background – like the Galway county colours, I thought. I was afraid now, afraid of what I might find, or of what might not be there to find. It had seemed like a great idea, turning myself in like a fugitive to the woman who had given me life. I was doing all of this in order to . . . To what? To say sorry somehow to the woman who had taken her own life? I began to turn away.

'Come on, Hughie,' Granny Daly said, taking my arm. 'Nobody knows us here. We're just out for a drive and we've stopped to buy a few things. We can't turn back now.'

So we didn't turn back. We walked around the village square until we reached the shop. The door was shut but we pushed it and it opened easily. Somewhere in the distance a bell jangled. There was a noise of shuffling and then an old man came out through a door behind the shop counter.

'Can I help ye?' he asked. I didn't know what to say.

'We're just looking for a few things,' Granny Daly said, 'some plain white flour and a bottle of buttermilk.'

'We have flour all right,' the old man said, turning to reach above his head to where a small sack sat beside a box of Jacob's biscuits on a shelf. As he took down the flour, he asked how much we wanted and Granny Daly asked for two pounds' weight. He was a slight man with a grey moustache. His face was slightly grazed on one side, as if he'd cut himself while shaving. I noticed, as he placed the sack on the shop counter, that the tips of two fingers on his right hand were all yellow. He took some weights from a drawer and put them on one end of an ancient scale. I wondered if he was my grandfather.

The door behind him opened and a woman stuck her head around the corner. 'Is everything all right, Daddy? Can you manage?'

'Yes, yes. I'm well able to manage,' he said. 'Do we have any buttermilk, Helen?'

Helen! Was this my mother, my birth mother? I could barely bring myself to look in her direction. I waited until I heard her voice again before I did.

'No, no, we don't. We have some fresh milk and you could sour it with a lemon, I suppose.'

As I glanced up towards her she seemed startled by something for the tiniest of moments. Maybe I looked like someone she had been in love with a long time ago, possibly a university student. Maybe she had never stopped regretting having to give me up. She was younger than Mammy, and she had a kind face. Her eyes were the shade of brown you'd see in a swirly marble. She wore earrings, which dangled, and I noticed that one was a little dog and the other was a boot, just like the Monopoly playing pieces Nyxi and I had each chosen. She glanced at me again with a quizzical look on her face. It was as if she was trying to remember something or someone she'd forgotten. The bell sounded again, as the door of the shop opened. The three children we'd seen on the green burst in, shouting and screaming and throwing paper planes that wouldn't fly.

'Would you like some fresh milk?' the lady asked my grandmother.

'Mammy, Mammy, Colette doesn't want to go to Liam's party because their dad has fleas,' the young boy said, to the lady behind the counter.

'Ian Hartigan, go in right now and wash your hands. They're filthy. And *you*, Miss Snooty Boots, go up and tidy your room. Alice, your mam phoned about an hour ago and you said you were going home then. So go on now, scoot.' I felt a cold rush sweep over me: was the little boy with dirty hands my replacement?

Granny Daly told them she'd try to get buttermilk when we got home so all we bought from Considine's Bar & Grocery was plain flour.

'Do you want anything, Hughie?' Granny Daly asked, as she began to open her purse.

'No, no. I'm fine,' I said. 'Please let me.' I pulled an envelope out of my pocket and took out enough money to pay for the flour. I was more than glad to be able to do that. I suddenly knew that I didn't belong there. We left the shop.

We sat in the car for a few minutes, in the shade of that old Protestant church, thinking about what we'd seen. As I looked over the ivy-topped wall at the church tower, with its elegant clock, I realised that those people had their own lives, lives they'd grown into and made for themselves. Was that lady my birth mother? Were the little lad and girl my half-brother and sister? Maybe they were, and then again, maybe they weren't. Either way, who was I to come blundering into their lives? What could ever be achieved by that? None of them could ever take Mammy's or Nyxi's place in my life or in my heart. I had been crazy to think they'd take me back and that all would be well again. All I'd been doing, I thought now, was running away from my own life.

As well as that, I *had* a mother, the lady who shouted through the bathroom door, '*Both* feet, Hughie, okay?', the woman who understood who I was because she had made me into that person, the mother who had painted the wigwam with me, who had picked me up after the cinema when it was raining and read me stories and stood up for me against my father, and who had let me cut the cross on the top of the soda bread before she put it into the oven. She was gone now, but she was my *real* mother, the lady who'd loved me when nobody else had wanted to. It was as simple as that. Maybe I had never known it, or maybe I had always known it but had just never said it out loud.

'You only get one mother,' I said to Granny Daly.

'And that's more than enough for anyone,' she said, as the Morris Minor started first time and we left the village that belonged to other people – people I did not know.

Epilogue

I'm way older now. I turned fifteen last February. Things have moved on and I've got a bit taller, although Nyxi says I've stopped growing, and that she hasn't, and that when she passes me, I won't ever be able to catch up.

Julie Andrews said to start at the very beginning so I did, and I've told you everything I can remember, from seeing the farmer with the record-player on the milk churn, right through to Granny Daly's bad driving and our trip together, all that time ago, to look in at another life that perhaps had been mine until I was eighteen months old. Why had I been adopted so long after my birth? Had my birth mother hoped that the student might make an honest woman of her, but had been let down? Or was I in the window for a long time in the mother and baby home but no one had come shopping for me? I will never know now, and it doesn't much matter anymore. What was done was done.

Galway has changed a little bit. There are new factories, like Digital and Thermo King, and a lot more people. The hurlers are in the All-Ireland final next month. But the heart of the city is still the same. The intimate narrow streets and the higgledy-piggledy shops and the pubs are all well. The sea remains the comforting presence it has always been, and 'real' Galwegians still kick the wall at the end of the prom before turning back at the Blackrock diving boards to head for Seapoint Ballroom and the places beyond. The lady who gave out the large ice-cream cones in Feeney's shop no longer works there. The man with the glass eye who collects the tickets at the Town Hall Cinema is going strong. They've started an arts festival, and although there was talk of Kenny's bookshop closing, I don't think that will ever happen, not soon or even in a million years. Galway is saturated with students in the winter and is still jammers every July for race week. Of course the people who come and go change every year, every month even, but down in the middle of it all, the place is still the same as it always was.

The monkey puzzle tree in the front garden of our house on Taylor's Hill hasn't stopped growing. It still tries, year after year, to inch up further into the sky until it reaches the clouds, safe in the knowledge that it is far too difficult for anyone to climb. My father remains equally prickly and difficult, but it is a softer brand of bitterness that drives him on now, less abrasive and more human. He continues to cut people open in his professional and his private life, but I think he is a little more careful now when he's taking out the stitches, and maybe that's no bad thing. We're never going to close the space that exists between us, but perhaps we need all of that space anyway.

The smell of the sea is still everywhere, like a blanket of salty mist over this entire world in which I loved and lost my mother. That universe of mine is marked out at its extremities as a lopsided triangular kingdom, contained between three points: Nyxi's house in Renmore, the diving boards at Blackrock and the stone quarry where they blast away with dynamite below the grass verge on which we parked our bikes and lay on our backs looking up at the clouds.

I did not know back then that people and places really only live and die in our hearts. The 'real' Galway is not dependent on stone or glass or the scent of coffee from Lydon House café, or the touch of rain on the wind, or the broken-nosed statue of Pádraic Ó Conaire in Eyre Square. It needs neither the accuracy of an Ordnance Survey map to continue to exist nor the thin approval of the tourist board to render it valid. It is not nullified by the absence of native Irish speakers from Connemara on New Year's Eve in the Imperial Hotel. No, the 'real' Galway exists inside the people who believe in it, and who keep it alive in their own veins. It's a little like knowing that the people you love continue to live on inside you, even after they have gone.

*

Everything I've seen or experienced is still inside me, like the stained-glass window fixing itself and the night I spent in Bushy Park graveyard wrapped in the wigwam. I know that some things lead to others and that somehow, everyone and everything in the world is in some way connected. When stars fall, maybe it's because an angel is crying, or perhaps it's a science thing, like gases and light years and Darwin, all getting mixed up together; the important thing is that I'm trying to understand a little more about how it all works. I don't know if every coincidence is just that, or if someone or something, like God or Mammy or the universe, is trying to attract my attention. Maybe I'm supposed to be doing other stuff. All I can really do is try to keep watching and listening.

In at least one way I'm different now, because of all of this, from the person I was before Mammy died. I now have some weird or special ability to be aware sometimes when danger or death is approaching. Occasionally I see someone, a complete stranger, and I know they're near the end of their life, even if they don't realise it. Last year at the parent–teacher meeting I saw Iggy Kelehan's father talking to our maths teacher, Mr Tighe. I got 'the feeling', and knew that one of them was very sick, but I couldn't figure out which it was. To try to help, the following day I grabbed a pile of leaflets from my father's office about the medical card scheme and put half of them in Iggy's Army and Navy satchel and left the others in Mr Tighe's post-box outside the staff room. Mr Tighe was out sick for three months this year and we had a substitute teacher.

But there are other things too, smaller things, which happen all the time to me, like knowing who it is when the phone rings, or hearing a phrase or seeing an action in my head moments before someone says or does exactly that. Spectacles feature a lot, so I often know when someone's glasses need cleaning, and within seconds they'll take them off, breathe on the lenses and dry them with a hanky. Mostly it's not life and death, it's more everyday, mundane things, but still, I suppose knowing in advance that they're going to happen is quite out of the ordinary.

I don't know what this thing is, or why it happens, or even if I'll always have the gift – or curse. The important thing is that it doesn't frighten me. Sometimes I even find it a bit funny. Nyxi knows about it, although we never discuss it. We don't have to. She says I need to concentrate really hard on what's likely to come up in the Inter Cert in June and just make a note of it – then tell her, of course. 'Start your concentrating in May at the latest,' she keeps saying.

We're closer than ever, and I know that if she wasn't in my life I wouldn't be able to cope. In lots of different ways we've saved each other and continue to do so whenever saving is required. We have bigger bikes now but we still cycle out past the Rahoon flats once in a while and lie in the grass overlooking the quarry, just past the pink house with the chestnut tree. We've never spoken about the moment on the Aran Islands when, silently yet aloud, we said we loved each other. We don't need to say anything about that because we both know it's still true.

The future doesn't scare me like it used to. After Mammy died, I thought I'd never be able to go on, that nothing would ever have meaning for me again, or that maybe I'd just wither away from the inside out and, I don't know, become an accountant or something equally horrific. I don't feel like that anymore. I know that one day I'll be all grown-up and have to do grown-up things, like booking flights and having the phone bill in my name. I want to go to university and study English or something.

I can't talk to Mammy anymore. I mean, I can talk *to* her but she can't answer back, and I can't really see her at all. But she *is* still here, in small ways, like when I'm taking a bath and I imagine her voice outside the door saying, '*Both* feet, Hughie, okay?' Or when I'm cutting the grass with the cranky old Iverson Rotary Sickle Mower (manufactured by the Rotary Mower Company of Omaha, Nebraska), and I sense her watching over me, as it splutters its bronchial way around the garden on a summer's evening.

Or like now, when I'm baking soda bread and using the recipe Granny Daly handed down to her daughter – the same recipe Deirdre Mittman left behind for her only child to remember her by, each time he cuts a deep cross in the dough when it is ready to be baked.

Acknowledgements

Many people have helped me to get this book to a point where it is finally ready. I would like to take this opportunity to thank them.

Mary Honan, Anne Griffin, Lisa Harding and Hayley Lawrence all read early drafts and were hugely helpful in the suggestions they made and in the encouragement they gave me.

My warmest thanks to Breda, Jim, Ciara, Ruth, Joanna, Siobhan and everyone else at Hachette Ireland. I have been overwhelmed by your kindness, your patience and your professionalism in getting my writing from the handwritten page to the shelves in the bookshops, both here in Ireland and elsewhere.

I have been lucky enough to spend time in the Tyrone Guthrie Centre. Most of this novel was written there.

Thanks is due to all of the staff there, who make it easy to be creative by providing time, space and sensational food.

In January 2018 I spent a wonderful few days writing in Roundwood House, Co. Laois. My thanks to Hannah and Paddy for their hospitality. The work I achieved in those few wintry days would not have been possible but for the generosity of Hannah's father, Frank, in allowing me access to his wonderful library of the evolution of civilisation.

Because I handwrite all of my first drafts, I am indebted to the kindness of the people who typed the manuscript for me: Lilian Bell, Hannah Bowman, Sylvia Draper and Elaine Doyle.

Thanks to Vanessa O'Loughlin for all your help. Thanks also to the Bray Literary Festival organisers.

To Antonia, Helen and Barbara of Antonia's Book Store (Navan Gate, Trim, Co. Meath) I offer my gratitude and admiration for your organisation of book sales for my launches and for your unending enthusiasm in always managing to find the book I want, no matter how obscure the author is.

To Liosa Beechinor for the provision of scarce, but vital, desk space. To John Minihan for taking the photograph on the back of the book. To Monique Rigney for all your local knowledge research in Galway. To Mia Gallagher for saving my soul.

Thanks to my agent, Claire Anderson-Wheeler, for continuing to support and believe in my writing. Every time I hit a brick wall, you're there with a sledgehammer to find a way through! You are truly inspirational.

Horace Winter doesn't have friends. Ever since the long-ago day when the Very Bad Thing happened, he prefers to spend his time studying butterflies – less intimidating, less likely to disappoint.

The last thing he wants is to retire from his job at the bank, but he has no choice – and now faces an endless number of empty days where he has nowhere to go and no one to need him.

Then he receives some surprising news. And he meets Amanda, and Max, and discovers a mysterious letter his father never posted. Suddenly he finds his previously unexceptional life filled with important things to do. Before he'd thought he had too much time. Now he may be looking at not enough.

But can he find the courage he's sought for so long to finally start living?

Also available as an ebook